ALSO BY JESSICA SIMS

Beauty Dates the Beast

Desperately Seeking Shapeshifter

Must Love Fangs

Are *you* curious what else Midnight Liaisons has to offer? Read these glowing testimonials from satisfied customers!

MUST LOVE FANGS

"This offbeat and humorous tale is layered with a touch of pathos, proving Sims is on a roll with this series."

—*RT Book Reviews*

"A great read filled with an abundance of lusty desire and captivating predicaments. . . . Sims has not lost her magical touch."

—*Single Titles*

"I continue to fall in love with the Midnight Liaisons books with each new installment. Sims has the perfect blend of humor and romance, both sexy and sweet. The cast of characters are always a hoot and the situations they find themselves in never disappoint."

—*The Book Pushers*

"I loved this story. It had quite a few laugh-out-loud moments, a super sweet alpha hero, and plenty of chemistry and sexy times."

—*Fiction Vixen*

"Fun, relatable, and complex characters. . . . Hard to resist."

—*All Things Urban Fantasy*

"A fun, sexy romp. . . . You won't be able to stop until you've turned the last page."

—*Vampire Book Club*

"This series is a hit for me. . . . It's sexy and fun and makes for a quick, enjoyable read. You really can't go wrong here, folks."

—*The Demon Librarian*

"Funny and snarky with unexpected twists. . . . I really enjoyed this fun, intriguing, fast-paced story."

—*Fresh Fiction*

"Simply riveting. *Must Love Fangs* is a page-turner, sexy and fun. Can't get enough of this series. Definitely a must read."

—*Anna's Book Blog*

DESPERATELY SEEKING SHAPESHIFTER

"Sims unites two terrific characters. . . . Though the romance remains paramount, keeping the wolves at bay provides suspense, and Sara's strong relationship with her sister is a sweet undercurrent."

—*Publishers Weekly*

"This skillful blend of humor, emotional turmoil, and enticing chemistry adds up to a terrific and fun-filled read!"

—*RT Book Reviews*

"Super flirty, super sexy, and super fun."

—*All Things Urban Fantasy*

"One of the best shapeshifter romances I've read in some time! . . . I have been singing the praises of this book to anyone who will listen."

—*Parajunkee*

"A fun and flirty read. . . . I had tons of fun with this book."

—*Wicked Little Pixie*

"A sweet and sexy love story that will curl any reader's toes, a story that will delight you, characters that will charm you, and a read you don't want to miss out on! An unforgettable romance!"

—*Addicted to Romance*

BEAUTY DATES THE BEAST

"A world that is both dangerous and humorous. Add a heroine who is plucky and brave and a hero who is sexy and powerful, and you get a story filled with sizzle and spark!"

—*RT Book Reviews*

"The adorable relationship between Bathsheba and Beau drives the story and will leave readers eager for more."

—*Publishers Weekly*

"This page-turning debut . . . possesses humor and a protective male character similar to those of Katie MacAlister. This will likely be a popular series."

—*Booklist*

"Will leave you feeling wickedly satisfied!"

—*Coffee Time Romance*

"A fast-paced story that's got both humor and heat. Beau is a meltingly sexy hero."

—*Romance Junkies*

"What an awesome debut book! . . . If you enjoy shifter books, then this is a must-add to your reading list."

—*Bitten by Books*

JESSICA SIMS

WANTED: WILD THING

Pocket Books
New York London Toronto Sydney New Delhi

Pocket Books
A Division of Simon & Schuster, Inc.
1230 Avenue of the Americas
New York, NY 10020

This book is a work of fiction. Any references to historical events, real people, or real places are used fictitiously. Other names, characters, places, and events are products of the author's imagination, and any resemblance to actual events or places or persons, living or dead, is entirely coincidental.

First Pocket Books paperback edition September 2014

Cover art by Aleta Rafton

Manufactured in the United States of America

10 9 8 7 6 5 4 3 2 1

ISBN 978-1-4767-5397-3
ISBN 978-1-4767-5401-7 (ebook)

WANTED:
WILD THING

Chapter One

As we pulled up in front of my house, my date, Jordan, parked the car and glanced over at me. "I had a nice time tonight, Ryder."

I gave him my cheeriest smile. "It was a lot of fun. Thanks for asking me out."

He grinned back, handsome in a cocky, confident sort of way that I found appealing. After a moment, he reached out to touch my blond hair. "You're really sexy, you know."

I shied away, narrowly avoiding his touch with a laugh. "I'm a lot of things, Jordan, but sexy isn't one of them." And I batted his hand away with my pink Hello Kitty purse, which acted as both shield and proof that I wasn't anyone's idea of sexy. I was cute.

Cute like puppies and kittens and pink lipstick with glitter in it (which I was currently wearing). My hair was in two tight blond pigtails high on my head, and I was wearing a bright pink A-line dress with a Peter Pan collar, yellow stockings, and matching pink Mary Janes that looked like something Baby Spice would wear. When my date had seen me tonight, he'd commented that I looked like I was dressed up for Easter. I wasn't. I was dressed up for Tuesday. I just liked bright, happy things and loved to wear them.

You know the saying "Fake it until you make it"? I lived that every day of my life. On my date I was nervous as heck, but you'd never know it from the way I giggled and flirted and chattered nonstop. I was in Ryder On mode. When Ryder was on, I was an endlessly effervescent personality. When I was Ryder Off? Well, I didn't show the world Ryder Off.

No one got to see Ryder Off but me. It was best for everyone involved.

Jordan stroked a finger down my arm in a flirty move and I shuddered, thankful that I'd worn long sleeves. I held my breath, waiting for something bad to happen, but nothing did. The nervous knot in my stomach eased a little.

"I haven't been able to take my eyes off you all night," he said in a seductive voice, sliding a bit closer to me.

I giggled inanely again, inching away. I knew where this was going, and I was terrified. My palms were sweating profusely, and my forehead broke out in an anxious sweat.

It wasn't that I didn't want to kiss Jordan; he was handsome and funny and attentive. I wanted to kiss him more than anything. Heck, I wanted to drag him inside and introduce him to my bed.

But that wasn't going to happen. I knew that deep in my bones.

Still, I was on this date because I was an eternal optimist. I had to hope—or I had nothing.

"Ryder," he said softly, sliding even closer to me.

I pressed up against the car window to put as much distance between us as possible. "Jordan, I really like you, but I don't know that we can take this further than friendship."

He gave me a surprised look. "If you like me, why do you say that?"

"It's . . . complicated." Extremely complicated, in ways he couldn't possibly imagine.

"I like you enough to work with complicated," he said in a smooth voice, reaching out to touch my hair again.

I squeezed my eyes shut, waiting . . . but nothing happened, and I relaxed. Maybe . . . maybe this time it'd be different?

Hope rising, I didn't flinch away when he scooted so close that I felt his warm breath on my skin and smelled his scent. Fresh. Clean. Human. A quiver of pleasure shot through me at being so very near an attractive man.

Jordan gently brushed the backs of his fingers over my cheek. I felt a tingle, but it was muted, and I smiled at that. He took my smile for encouragement, and the next thing I knew, his lips were pressing on mine.

Shock flickered through me, quickly followed by a burst of pleasure when his tongue darted into my open mouth. A man was *kissing* me. Oh, wow! It was even better than I'd expected. I made a small noise of pleasure, closing my eyes and sinking into the feeling.

Then my cheek rippled. Not in a pleasant, shivery way; more like the sensation of something coming alive and trying to escape. Of skin trying to pull away from bone.

My eyes flew open and I pushed at Jordan's chest. "No." My good luck had just run out. Jordan wasn't The One.

His eyes remained closed, his mouth seeking mine as if my protests would be swallowed by another kiss. If I'd been any other woman, they might have been.

But I wasn't any other woman. One could argue I wasn't even human.

An awful prickling sensation crept through my skin, like a thousand needles. My feet cramped painfully and I felt the press of claws inside my shoes. I groaned, pain flickering all over my body, and I felt my skin shift and creep again. Now my bones ached; I had only seconds before they'd pop and crack with the onset of my transformation.

And Jordan was going to see it all if I didn't do something fast.

I pushed frantically at his chest again, breaking away just as fangs cut through my gums and I tasted blood. I fumbled for the car door, tumbling out backward and falling onto the driveway.

"Ryder!" I heard his car door open and his gasp when he saw me sprawled on the concrete. "Oh, my God, are you okay?"

I jumped to my feet and ran for my condo. Thank God I was on the first floor. I ran down the hall, heading for my door and safety. My forehead throbbed, hard and bony protrusions growing under my skin as I fumbled for my key with claw-tipped fingers. My legs were cramping hard, and the bulges protruding from my back would soon rip through my cute pink dress.

With shaking hands, I managed to unlock the door. I slipped inside and locked it, then leaned back against the thick, heavy wood, relieved.

Safe.

Leathery wings suddenly burst from my back with a wet snapping noise, and I groaned in pain as my loose, swingy dress became chokingly tight. I clawed at the zipper in the back, then gave up and shredded the fabric with my thick, curved talons until it pooled at my feet. My shoes were the next to go, wrecked by the transformation, and I pressed my hands to my awful face and slid down the door until my tail and ass hit the floor.

Damn it. For a brief, shining moment, I'd really thought that Jordan was The One. But he wasn't. He wasn't even close.

I was unsurprised when he knocked at my front door a moment later. "Ryder," he bellowed, his concern evident. "Are you okay? What happened?"

"No means no," I yelled back, hoping he wouldn't notice the growly rasp in my voice now. "Don't call me again."

"Open up so we can talk about this."

"Go away." I meant it, too. Jordan was nice, handsome—and completely and totally useless to me. Just like every other human man out there, his touch triggered my curse.

The monster under my skin had something to do with sexuality. I could flirt harmlessly all day or hug a female friend. Shake hands. No problem. But the moment a man's hand caressed me with sexual intention? Out came the scaly fanged beast. I ran a finger over the thick fangs now protruding from my gums over my canines. Those always hurt the worst and were the last to disappear.

"Please, Ryder," Jordan said, his voice softer. "Can't we talk through this? I really like you."

"You're not who I thought you were," I yelled back. Oh, the irony of those words. "Go away before I call the cops."

There was a long moment of silence, then he slammed a fist on the door. "Fuck you, cock tease." I heard him stomp down my sidewalk back to his car. A moment later, it screeched out of my driveway and down the street.

Well, now. It was a good thing Jordan *wasn't* my True Love, because it seemed like he was hiding a douchey side. Not a surprise. We all had our hidden sides.

Mine just happened to be scarier than most: I was a changeling.

At least that's what the old fortune-teller had told me. I'd had my first experience with my monster shortly after getting my first period. I was fourteen, and I'd made out with a guy on the docks at summer camp. He'd blushed and gotten a boner; I'd grown scales and a tail. My date had chalked up his horrific monster visions to some bad mushrooms. Me? I'd been terrified, so I'd done what any logical fourteen-year-old would have done—I'd stolen my mother's wallet and taken a bus across town to consult a fortune-teller and get some answers.

It turned out that was the best thing for me. The moment I'd met the tall, willowy fortune-teller, I'd known she was different from other humans. She'd had a soft radiance that I hadn't been able to identify then. I now knew what it meant—she'd had fae blood.

The fortune-teller told me as much a few minutes into our conversation. She wasn't entirely human, her fae ancestry coming from her great-grandmother. Her great-grandmother had schooled her in the occult arts, teaching her everything she'd needed to know about the supernatural. Great-grandma had married a satyr, she'd told me, and I'd scoffed. The woman was clearly nuts.

Now, ten years later, I worked at a dating agency for the supernatural and had set up more than one lonely satyr on a date. Life was funny that way.

Anyway, the fortune-teller had had all the answers. She'd told me I was a changeling. That back in the days when the fae folk mingled more openly with humans, the fae would steal a human child and leave a changeling in its place for the parents to raise.

I'd heard the fairy tales, but I'd always thought

that changelings were scary, legendary things. I'd been a cute blond teenager who'd happened to look thoroughly human until someone touched me.

The fortune-teller had explained that, too: my natural guard was down in those moments, and the "glamour" that had been cast on me faded. By the time I hit twenty-five, if I remained a virgin, the glamour that made me look human would be unable to overcome my beast side, and I'd be a monster forever.

At fourteen years old, I'd been shattered. Not only were my parents not my real parents but I was also a monster of some kind and would be cursed forever if I didn't beat the deadline?

The fortune-teller had patted my hand and given me a ray of hope. According to her great-grandmother, every changeling had a perfect match in the world. He'd be The One for me, my True Love. If I found that man, I'd be able to touch him without triggering my monsterlike changeling side. Then I could break the curse, securing the glamour so I remained human, not scaly-clawed-bony-gargoyle-ish. I couldn't even say what my monster form was; it just seemed like a mix of everything hideous.

So I had to find my perfect mate. And like the fairy tale where the girl kissed a lot of frogs? I had to touch a lot of men. I flirted freely, just a happy, cheerful, young woman. When I got the nerve up, I'd touch a guy. Just to see.

It triggered my monster every time. I'd become a master at escaping before people noticed. I'd feign food poisoning and hide in a bathroom until my creature side faded. I'd bail on a date through the back door—I did that a lot—and transform in the dark parking lot, where no one could see me. My changeling side never lasted long. Already, I could feel my fangs throbbing, a sign that they were about to slide back into my gums. I extended a hand, watching the hint of scales on my skin disappear, my curved, clawed fingers returning to their regular length, my pink-tipped manicure still flawless.

This guy hadn't been The One, but that didn't mean the right guy wasn't out there. I'd keep looking for the answer to my problem, and I'd find it. I wasn't about to let a little monster side slow me down.

The fact that my twenty-fifth birthday was less than a month away? I didn't dwell on that.

I worked at a dating agency for the supernatural, after all. Midnight Liaisons catered to vampires, shifters, monsters, and everything else that went bump in the night and wanted a mate. If there was a perfect, magical man who would break my curse, and if he was out there for me, I'd be able to find him through connections at work.

I just had to keep on kissing my frogs until then.

Chapter Two

Not everyone was cut out for the night shift at a supernatural dating agency. You had to be aware of things like full moons, species-specific allergies, late-night vampiric booty calls, and the ability to sound alert while answering the phone at two in the morning. It was a strange job, but I loved it. Our clients were weird, and I embraced weird. Weird was fun. Weird was interesting.

Weird, however, was not for everyone.

I eyed the empty desk across from me as I prepped my third cup of coffee, readying to start a long evening at work. And I sighed with loneliness. "I sure do miss Marie."

Sara made a face. Her mate, Ramsey, was waiting for her, and she slipped her hand into his huge mitt. As they headed for the door, she said, "Don't let Savannah hear you say that. It'll hurt her feelings, and you know how easily pregnant women cry."

"I know. I just . . . miss Marie."

Marie Bellavance was my bestie. We'd been thick as thieves ever since we'd started working at Midnight Liaisons. If either of us thought it was strange that two humans were running the late-night shift at a company catering to an exclusive, secret clientele that hid the fact that they were supernatural, we didn't comment on it. We liked getting paid, after all. And Marie was a hoot. She was acerbic, witty, wry, and always had interesting observations.

She'd been fired last month for dating vampires, but she'd had serious reasons for wanting to date the fanged persuasion. She'd been dying from an extremely rare, fatal disease, and the only way Marie could see to get around it was to be turned undead. Luckily, those issues had been solved by Josh Russell, a big, hunky were-cougar who'd saved her from her disease and had turned her into a nice, healthy were-cougar. Now Marie was working for Beau Russell, the leader of the Paranormal Alliance.

Savannah Russell, Beau's cousin, had taken Marie's place on the night shift. She was sweet and quiet, nothing like my witty, outspoken Marie. I gestured at Marie's former desk. "Speaking of, is Savannah okay?"

"She's got the barfs again," Sara told me. "Called and said she'd be in late."

I nodded and tossed another spoonful of sugar into my coffee. "I'll hold down the fort."

"You sure? I can stay awhile if things are too busy."

I made a shooing motion, then picked up my coffee. "I'll be fine. You two lovebirds go have fun. Don't do anything I wouldn't do." I gave them an outrageous wink.

Sara giggled, and her mate—a big, burly were-bear—flushed bright red. So adorable. With a wave, they headed out.

I was alone.

Alone was boring, and it made for a long night, especially when the phones were quiet. And it wasn't a full moon, or a Friday night, or anything else that would cause the agency to be busy, which meant I was alone with my thoughts.

I hated being alone with my thoughts.

I decided to text Marie. *What's up, chica?*

It took a moment for her to respond.

Just left work. Beau and the wolf packs are still meeting all the time. Such a mess! Josh is taking me out to dinner tonight to make up for it, though.

Maybe you'll get lucky, I teased.

I'll be mad if I don't! She punctuated it with a smiley face, then added, *Gotta run. TTYL.*

I sighed, trying not to feel jealous of my friend, and stared around the empty office. I fired up the coffeemaker again. If I wasn't going to have anyone to talk to, I was going to need some major caffeine. I loved caffeine—it made me jittery and awake. And I adored jittery, because when I relaxed, it was easier to lose control of the monster side if a male client touched me. If I was cranked up on caffeine, it was harder to relax and get aroused.

So, coffee? My friend. I used caffeine pills, NoDoz, Red Bull, energy drinks, and anything else that could keep me hopped up, but coffee was my favorite vice.

While the pot gurgled, I sipped the sugary concoction I'd made before and headed back to my desk to tackle my to-do pile. At the top of my list was upcoming activities for our singles. We'd had a wine tasting last week, but no one had shown up except vampires. Big strikeout; no one wanted to date vampires. Well, except Marie.

Things were usually complicated around here. I still had bad memories about the time I'd set up a nice werewolf guy with an anxious were-bobcat lady. First rule of a supernatural dating agency—don't mix cats and dogs.

I sighed, thinking of Josh and Marie. I wanted a big hunky were-cougar boyfriend, too. I'd take were-anything, actually. I'd even take human. Nothing wrong with a little normal in a guy. Unfortunately, none of my dates went past the first one, thanks to my monster.

No sense in dwelling on it; I'd only end up in a bad mood. I turned on some upbeat music and was soon singing along and dancing around the office, my blond pigtails whipping about my head as I boogied between my desk and the copier in the back room, creating flyers and printing them for an upcoming mixer.

The cowbell on the front door clanged, and I called, "Be right there!"

Probably Savannah. Several months pregnant, the poor girl still had morning sickness, afternoon sickness, night sickness, and anytime-she-smelled-anything-at-all-sickness.

But when I entered the main part of the office, I stopped in my tracks, surprised to see two men. One was a nearly seven-foot-tall, muscle-bound guy with weird hair and weirder clothing that looked like something out of a historical movie.

And the other was . . . well, he looked like Ryan Gosling in a leisure suit, but the odds of a movie star showing up here were slim to none. Which meant he was a fae prince. The fae occasionally used our service; my guess was that they got bored with finding their own dates. They were weird customers, though. They liked to use their glamours to take on the appearance of famous actors, and they always had a bit of a chip on their shoulders when it came to humans. Like we should bow down and kiss their feet in gratitude for being able to serve them.

I usually let the others deal with fae, since I found their attitude boorish, but tonight it fell to me to be the welcoming committee. "Hi, there," I said in a chipper voice, beaming a smile at the two men as I turned the radio down. "Welcome to Midnight Liaisons."

The blond, smaller man—the prince—studied me and gave me a slow, pleased smile. "Well, aren't you the cutest thing?"

Ugh. "Thank you! How can I help you gentlemen? Do you have profiles set up in the system? One of you is clearly fae and the other . . ." I stared at the big bruiser. You usually couldn't tell just by looking at someone, and a fair number of Alliance guys were big and scary. But this guy . . . this guy exuded danger and wildness. I couldn't help but draw back a little at the sight of him.

"I'm here to meet someone," the prince said.

"Oh?" I pulled up my datebook and didn't see anything marked. "Did you arrange something with one of the other dating specialists?"

"Actually, you're the person I came here to see."

The hairs on the back of my neck prickled, but I kept it cool. "Oh?"

He moved closer, that delighted smile still on his face, and circled around me. "Perfect. Just perfect."

"Thank you," I said, "but I'm afraid I don't recognize you as one of my clients."

His lip curled. "As if I'd use your cute little service."

"I don't understand why you're here, then?" I glanced at the big bruiser behind him, but the man said nothing. The more I looked at him, the scarier he seemed. I decided to avoid looking at him after that.

"Why, I'm here to see you, precious." The fae's tone became sweet and soothing. "I wanted to see how my little prize was coming along, and it looks like you're almost ripe for the picking."

"Ripe . . . for the picking?" Who *was* this guy? "Excuse me?"

"Come now, my little changeling. Don't act so surprised." He reached out and stroked my arm.

Scales prickled to the surface, and I jerked away from him, wide-eyed with shock. "How . . . how did you know?" I'd never told anyone I was a changeling. Marie knew that I transformed into something yucky (she'd caught me mid-act once), but she never asked questions and I never volunteered answers.

Yet this man knew instantly what I was.

He gave me a gorgeous smile. "Why, how do you think you got here? Into the earth realm?"

Earth . . . realm? Huh?

Just then, the door banged open and Savannah rushed in. "I am so sorry, Ryder," she began, her cheeks flushed. "I'm late, but I'm here now."

"No problem," I said, gesturing to my two "clients" to wait for me as I stepped over to Savannah's desk. I was a master of fakery, so I pulled her chair out for her, acting as if nothing was wrong. "You take a seat. I'm with a couple of clients, but once I'm done, we'll review tonight's dating logs, okay?"

She gave me a grateful look and dropped into her seat. "Okay." It was only eight at night, and she already looked exhausted. Rough pregnancy and a new job to boot, but she never complained.

"Sara left the mail for you; why don't you handle that for now?" I said as I picked up the rubber-banded bundle on the corner of her desk and held it out to her. "And drink some water."

"I will," she said meekly, taking the mail from me.

"Now," I said brightly as I turned to the fae prince and his scary friend. "Why don't we go to a conference room and continue our conversation?"

"But of course," the prince said in that silky-smooth manner.

I ushered them into a conference room and shut the door, then turned on a CD of classical music.

The big lug stared straight ahead, but the prince raised an eyebrow at me. "Mood music?"

"It ensures privacy for our clients," I told him. "Several of our species have very keen hearing."

"Of course."

"Who are you?" I asked as he sat at the round table. The guard—I'd come to think of him that way—thumped into the chair next to him. I sat across from both, not trusting them. This man knew who and what I was. Surely he'd have more answers for me.

"Yes, I suppose you would ask that, wouldn't you?" He leaned back lazily in his chair, looking for all the world as if he'd been invited to the most boring party on earth and was only deigning to be here because he had to. "My name is Finian." He studied his long fingers and perfect nails. "No last name. That's a human affectation, and I most certainly am *not* human." He smiled at me, and his eyes gleamed iridescent for a brief moment, shining all colors of the rainbow, like a soap bubble.

I was fascinated despite myself, unable to look away. "Who's your friend?"

Finian's gaze flicked to the hulking man at his side. "He is unimportant."

Unimportant said nothing, which was no surprise.

"How did you know what I was?" I asked. "How could you tell?" I'd been around shifters for a year and had seen fae on several occasions, and no one had ever figured out my secret. My guess was that I smelled just as human as everyone else.

"Why, I could tell because you are mine."

I stilled. "Yours?"

"Yes. I was there at your birth. I saw you bred, saw you born, and brought you here so you could grow up."

Saw me . . . bred. My jaw dropped a little. "Bred?"

"Yes. Your father was put out to stud, and we brought in your mother—a sweet little filly if ever there was one—and voila, magic happened. You were created."

A sweet little filly, huh? That was creepy. Maybe it was a fae thing. "So where are my parents now?"

"They're not parents, my darling changeling. Parents imply child rearing. They were simply the vessels in which you were created." He looked at me fondly. "They bred an excellent specimen, if I'm any judge. And I am."

Suddenly feeling cold, I pulled my baby pink cardigan closer. "You're talking about me like I'm some sort of prize poodle."

Finian's smile grew broader. "That's exactly what you are, my dear. Think of yourself as a prize poodle for the Otherworld."

"Otherworld?" I echoed.

"The fae realm."

I shook my head, trying to absorb all of this. "I don't understand. If I'm fae, why bring me here?"

"You're not fae." He looked offended at the thought. "You're a changeling. And your kind has a very high mortality rate in the fae realm, I'm afraid. Lots of creatures prey on your kind. You're very showy and beautiful in your natural form, but with very few defenses. Hence, you're here for your protection." Finian gestured at me munificently. "You're welcome."

I was still staring at him, trying to absorb all of this. I was this man's . . . poodle? I was born in the fae realm? My parents were . . . stud dogs? Or horses? Of a sort? "I still don't understand."

"Well, your kind wasn't bred for its intelligence." Finian gave me a dismissive look. "Exactly what part is so hard?"

I spread my hands, trying to think of where to start. I glanced around nervously to make sure no one was listening in to our conversation. Then, I leaned in and spoke. "I'm not even sure that I *am* your changeling. My other form isn't beautiful at all. Quite the opposite."

He tilted his head. "Beauty is in the eye of the beholder, my pet. And my changeling has a mark on her upper thigh in the shape of a sun with a Celtic eternity knot in the center."

I stilled, my eyes going wide. I had that mark on the inside of my thigh. No one had ever been able to give me a straight answer as to why a baby girl had been branded right after birth, and my adoptive parents had given me the option to have it removed when I hit adulthood. I'd elected to keep it because I liked its uniqueness.

I'd never told anyone about it, either.

"Shall I get you to show me?" Finian asked. "My friend here can hold you down while I check to ensure that you're the one I seek."

I gave a wide-eyed look at the giant at his side. "No, I'm good, thanks. I know the mark."

"I thought so. Your twenty-fifth birthday is in a month, correct?"

"If you know about the birthmark, you should know when my birthday is," I told him, not wanting to volunteer any more details. Part of me wanted to run away from this bizarre conversation, but I needed information. This man seemed to have lots of it.

"Don't be prickly, my pet. It's not becoming."

I gritted my teeth behind my smile. I really, *really* wasn't a fan of the way he kept calling me "my pet" after referring to me as a poodle. "I don't understand why you're here, after so long."

"It's very simple. Changelings take time to ripen," Finian said, steepling his fingers. "At twenty-five, you'll be ideal for breeding, which means it's safe to take you back to the fae realm. I have the perfect stud lined up."

My eyes widened with horror. "You're going to *breed* me?"

"Of course, precious." He gave me a pleasant look. "Changelings go for quite a sum on the Goblin Market these days, and my family's had a bit of financial difficulty in the past millennia. Your offspring will take care of that problem."

I swallowed, feeling sick. This . . . wasn't happening. It *wasn't*. This guy couldn't just *own* me and treat me like a prize dog. There had to be a way out of this.

"What if I say no? What if I don't want to go with you?"

"Don't make this difficult," Finian told me in a condescending voice. "Hugh here has plenty of friends that are ready to ensure that you come with me. I'd hate to have to collar you."

Hugh's expression didn't change. I shuddered.

"Besides," Finian said in a cheerful voice, "once you hit your twenty-fifth birthday unbesmirched, it's going to become impossible for you to hold your beast side at bay. Your mating frenzy is going to take over, and then you'll be begging me to take you away."

My hand went to my throat. It sounded horrifying. "What if I pay you? Can I pay you for my freedom?"

He gave me a pitying look. "Oh, pet. Fae don't deal in human currency. Trust me when I say that what we want, you can't afford. I'm afraid that's just the way it is. And even if you could buy your freedom, it wouldn't help you contain your beast. Only breeding you will fix that."

I felt like vomiting. "But . . . but I have a month. I'm not twenty-five yet."

"Yes. This is a tricky period, which is why I'm here today. Since you're coming up on your fertile time, you're going to start throwing out pheromones everywhere. It's going to be impossible for you to hide your identity."

"Like when the shifters go into heat?" God, this just got worse and worse.

"No. Right now you stink of human." He gave me a polite smile and lifted a tiny flower from his lapel, pressing it under his nose as if to ward off my stench. "But that smell will change rapidly over the next few weeks, and it'll be obvious to any fae what you are. You're going to need protection so someone doesn't steal you out from under my nose." He reached over and patted his companion's burly arm. "Which is why Hugh is here."

Aghast, I looked over at Hugh and stared up fully into his face for the first time.

He was one scary fucker.

Hard all over, he reminded me of Sara's mate in his size and strength. But where Ramsey had handsome features and kind eyes when he looked at Sara, this man had not an ounce of softness in him. He had a thick body, with muscle bulging up around his neck like a bodybuilder's. His longish hair had messy braids at the crown to keep it out of his face, and the reddish-brown color had a rippling pattern, a bit like tiger stripes. He had long sideburns that ended in thick tufts at the base of his jaw. He wore a plain brown tunic belted at his waist, and his arms were as big as my thighs, corded with muscle and veins. His forearms were lightly dusted with reddish hair, which also seemed striped. He was like a cross between Thundercats and Braveheart.

The worst thing about him was his eyes. Not because they had slitted pupils like a cat—that was actually kind of neat. It was the emotion in them that bothered me, or rather, the lack of. They were cold and empty as he gazed at me. There wasn't an ounce of softness there.

I didn't like the look of him at all. "Nice to meet you, Hugh," I said nervously. "But I'm sure protection isn't necessary."

After all, who was going to protect me from *Hugh*?

Finian smiled. "It's not your decision, my pet. It's mine, and I intend to keep an eye on my investment. Hugh is the best mercenary magic can buy, which is why he's going to be your shadow until delivery day."

My gaze flicked from Finian back to Hugh. "Oh, but I don't need a shadow. I'll just be very careful."

Finian got to his feet. "Hugh, she's all yours. I expect her unharmed and in perfect condition on delivery date. Understand me?"

"Understood," Hugh said in a low, growly voice, and my eyes widened again.

As he'd spoken, I'd caught a glimpse of two long, pointy teeth. Hugh had . . . fangs.

Oh, God, this wasn't good at all.

Chapter Three

I'm not sure this is a smart idea," I began, unable to stop staring at Hugh's mouth. Had I really just seen fangs?

"Silly me, I forgot to give you a vote." Finian got to his feet, straightened his jacket, and smoothed his lapels, as if going out for a stroll. "I'll be by to check in every now and then. Not too often, you see, lest others start to suspect something. Wouldn't want my prize snatched up before I get my money's worth out of her, now, would we?"

"Heaven forbid," I murmured, my mind whirling. I was surprisingly calm after being told that I was someone's breeding animal and he was coming to take over my life. I guess I'd always been waiting for the other shoe to drop. Now that I finally had answers, the fear of the unknown was gone. There were a million things to consider, and I had to think about a way free of this, but I wasn't panicking.

Maybe once Finian was gone, I could reason with Hugh. Pay him off. Something. Then I could . . . what? Escape? How? I'd turn into a monster permanently in a month unless I found my Prince Charming.

And unfortunately, the prince who knew the most about me intended to breed me like a prize show dog.

It was not looking good for the home team.

I got to my feet, and Hugh did as well. I pretended not to notice and headed for the door. From the way Finian was glancing at his Rolex, it was clear that he was done with me. "When will you be back?" I asked, opening the door.

He reached out and patted my cheek, and I felt that ugly ripple under my skin once more, no doubt to remind me exactly what I was. "I'll be back when I feel like it, precious. Don't worry. Hugh will be standing by to ensure your safety."

Finian turned and strolled back through the office, giving Savannah a polite smile as he headed to the door.

I wanted to scream for him to stay longer and answer more questions, but the fae did what they wanted, when they wanted. Finian had dropped his bomb, and now he was leaving.

As the door shut, I gave an unhappy sigh and turned around.

And nearly walked into Hugh's chest.

I staggered backward. "Oh, excuse me."

He reached for my arm to steady me, then hesitated, dropping his hand as if he remembered what I was.

"I'll get out of your way so you can go," I said, gesturing at the front door.

"I'm not leaving. You know this." His voice was cool and brutal with efficiency.

How embarrassing. I gave him a sunny smile to mask my reaction and headed back to my desk.

"Everything okay?" Savannah asked in a mild voice.

"Just fine," I said as I sat down, my smile starting to feel pinned to my mouth. "I forgot that I was going to fix up a profile for Mr. Hugh here. Isn't that right?"

"No," he said bluntly. But he moved to sit across from me in one of the chairs.

My eyes narrowed. Didn't he realize that to keep my secret, we were going to have to spread a little white lie or two? "If you want to remain here at the agency with me," I said in a low, pleasant voice, "you'll have to have a profile set up."

"Do what you like," he said, rising from the chair and frowning at it. It was too small for him, the wooden arms making it impossible for him to sit comfortably. It would have been funny except for the fact that he looked as if he'd rather destroy the chair than tolerate its presence a moment longer. He turned and affected a very soldierly stance, feet spread, arms crossed over his chest.

I noticed with shock that his fingers were tipped with massive claws. Where the heck was this guy from? Were they in the Dark Ages in the fae realm? If so, they were feeding them Wheaties, because

Hugh was so immensely broad and muscular that he looked as if he could crush a small car with his hands.

Savannah didn't seem alarmed, though—just confused. She eyed him, and then me.

It was clear that if I was going to get anywhere with Hugh, I'd have to try charm. That was fine. I was good at charming people. "Hugh, sweetie, why don't you sit down and I'll make you a nice cup of coffee?"

He glanced around the room, then at me. "I prefer to stand."

"Yes, well, that's impolite. You're making me nervous," I said with a wink at Savannah, as if to say, *Oh, these crazy customers.* "If the chair's uncomfortable, I'll get you a stool from the back room."

I headed back into the storage room, where we had a stair step stool that doubled as a ladder. I didn't move more than a few steps before I realized that Hugh was still following me, though. I sighed and gritted my teeth. Was this what I had to look forward to for the next month?

I was an optimist, though; I'd just have to figure out a way to get Hugh off my tail, or make the best of him being here.

I snagged the stool and turned around, doing my best to keep the pleasant expression on my face. "Since you followed me, why don't you carry this?" I shoved it in his hands.

He stared down at the wooden stepladder. "What is this for?"

"It's for you to sit on, since the chairs are uncomfortable."

He snorted. "I do not need this. I will stand."

"I prefer for you to sit."

"A soldier does not sit on the job."

"Yeah, well, you're not a soldier right now," I snapped, then inwardly berated myself for losing my temper. I needed to be nice. The Ryder everyone knew was sweet and pleasant. I smiled. "Humor me, okay?"

I swept past him without waiting for an answer.

In the main office, I could tell from Savannah's curious look that my hulking "shadow" was right behind me. I pushed aside the two chairs and indicated that he should put the stool down. He did so, but he didn't sit.

All right, it was a start—if a crappy one. Irritated, I headed to the coffeepot. I scooped grounds and poured water, then clicked the On button. "You want coffee, Savannah?"

No answer.

I glanced over just in time to see her face pale. She pressed a hand to her mouth and bolted for the bathroom again. "I'm going to guess that's a no," I said and turned to Hugh. "Do you like coffee?"

He simply watched me with those cat-eyes. "What I like does not matter."

"Oookay, then." It was getting harder to keep the smile on my face. "Well, I like coffee." I sat back down at my desk and tried to concentrate. If Hugh was going to lurk around me constantly, I needed a cover story. I cast about for an idea . . .

Maybe I could tell everyone that Hugh was a shifter. That would work, since he had fangs and, um, stripes. So maybe he was some exotic-tiger shifter who was awkward around humans and needed to be taken under my wing. Except . . . 99.9 percent of the world was human, so he had to have run into people before now.

Hmmm . . . Maybe he had trouble dating, and I was acting as his life coach?

I picked up my glittery ruler and began to tap it against my palm. There had to be a good cover story somewhere. I couldn't tell anyone, *Oh, yes, I'm apparently a prize poodle, and when I hit my prime I'll be worth a fortune, so he's guarding me.*

Because I didn't intend to be anyone's poodle. I was going to figure a way out of this. I was going to find my True Love, and he was going to save me from my curse, and there *would* be a Happily Ever After.

The coffeepot hissed steam, a signal that it was about to brew. Before I could blink an eye, Hugh lashed out at the machine.

Claws flashed and I heard a growl, then there was a gigantic spark and a shatter of glass.

The lights flickered.

Everything went silent.

I stood up, staring at the remains of the coffeepot, which had been neatly sliced in half by Hugh's claws. He was standing over the broken pieces, big shoulders heaving, fangs bared, looking as if he was about to attack.

As I watched, another spark flew from the coffeepot, and Hugh raised an enormous, clawed hand.

"Wait," I yelped, charging forward. "Don't touch anything else. You'll get electrocuted. Just stay right there." I raced for the back room, flipping the circuit breakers to turn off the power in the office. Once that was done, I sprinted back into the main room . . .

And stopped. Hugh's eyes were glowing an eerily bright green, brighter than anything I'd ever seen. Creepy. I had to ignore that, though. I pushed past him and yanked the plug from the now very dead coffeepot, then returned to the back room and flipped the breakers on again, hoping that we hadn't scared the life out of Savannah.

I returned to the office as she emerged from the bathroom, a paper towel pressed to her mouth, her eyes wide with alarm. "Everything okay?"

"Just fine," I assured her. "Hugh here has an itchy trigger finger, and the coffeepot startled him." I went to a closet for the broom and dustpan, then held them out to Hugh. "And now that he broke it, he's going to clean it up."

Hugh bared his teeth at me in a snarl. Dear God, they were big; his canines practically looked like tusks.

I refused to be intimidated, though. He wasn't going to hurt me; he had to protect me. According to his boss, I was worth more alive than dead, so I gave him a sweet smile and pushed the broom and dustpan into his hands.

As he glared at me, I patted his arm. "Now, please clean up your mess while I see to Savannah." I stepped past him and turned to Savannah. "You okay, sweetie?"

She blinked slowly, leaning against the door frame of the bathroom. Her gaze went to Hugh, then me. "What happened?"

"Just an accident," I said in a sunny voice. I moved to Savannah's desk chair and pulled it out for her. "Come sit down. You don't look so good."

She dropped heavily into her chair, pulled out a bottle of water, and sipped delicately.

"You need some crackers or toast or something?"

"I had that earlier," she said in a whisper-soft voice and took another sip of water. "It didn't help."

I brushed her sweaty brown hair off her forehead. "How about some nice hot tea?"

"That might help. Maybe with some lemon. Except . . . our coffeepot is dead." She looked over my shoulder, her brows drawing together.

I glanced over, too, and saw Hugh standing there, still holding the broom and dustpan and giving them a ferocious frown, the mess of the broken coffeepot still at his feet.

His bare feet, I just now noticed. They were clawed, as well. Oh, dear.

Savannah looked over at me, then picked up a pencil and a notepad. She wrote something down, then nudged the pad toward me.

What is he?

Savannah was a were-cougar and a member of

the Russell family, who spearheaded the Alliance. She was familiar with weres of all kinds—even the more unusual supernaturals, like harpies and satyrs and sirens. There was no doubt that Hugh was supernatural—anyone could tell that with one look at him—but the question was . . . what?

I didn't know either, but I intended to get some answers.

Deliberately misunderstanding her question, I quickly wrote down *Customer?* "Well, since our coffeepot is dead, I'll head to the coffee shop for your tea. Hugh, why don't you come with me? You can finish cleaning that up once we get back."

"Oh, no, you don't have to go," Savannah protested. It was clear from her alarmed look that she didn't want me going out with Hugh alone. "I'm fine." She gave a hard little swallow midsentence, but she kept her brave face.

"Nonsense," I told her. "We'll be back shortly. Leave that mess for us, and if you need to go be sick, just put on the answering machine." I bounded over to my desk to get my Hello Kitty purse. "Come on, Hugh."

I held the door open, staring pointedly at his scowling face. After a moment, he headed out.

One hurdle down. I followed, telling Hugh, "That's my car." I pointed at the baby blue hatchback that I'd put kitty ears and whiskers on, and gestured for him to take the passenger side.

He simply stared at me, then at the car. Then back at me.

Sure, everyone mocked the cat-mobile, but it made me smile to see it, so I didn't care. "Just get in, already." I pulled open my door and slid into the driver's seat.

It was only after I got into the car that Hugh opened his door very slowly and examined it, then folded his immense body into the passenger seat. His knees pressed hard against the dashboard, and his shoulders hunched as he tried to squeeze himself in, the door hanging open on his side. He looked so comical that I giggled despite myself.

"I do not fit," he said sourly, shifting in his seat.

"Just extend the seat backward," I told him. "You'll have room."

He gave me an uncomprehending look.

I reached between his legs to grab the seat release, and Hugh jerked in response, his hand gripping my arm.

Immediately, that hot, snakey coil of excitement thrummed through my body, and I felt my monster jerk awake. I sucked in a breath and shook his hand off, recoiling backward. "Don't touch me," I whispered.

He looked just as scandalized as I was, his hand clenching into a fist. "I . . . apologize. I thought . . ."

I could guess what he thought I was reaching for. "It's okay," I said, flicking my hand rapidly to try and shake myself back to normal. "Just . . . get the seat release yourself."

The look on his too-savage face was puzzled.

"And you can shut your door, too," I pointed out helpfully. "And put on your seat belt."

Hugh's cat-eyes narrowed at me. "I do not know these things you speak of."

It was my turn to frown as I shoved the keys into the ignition. The car chimed helpfully, reminding me that the door was open and not all passengers were buckled in.

Hugh startled again, eyes going wide as he tried to decipher the sounds.

Okay, this . . . was odd. "Haven't you ever been in a car before?"

He shook his head slowly, then leaned forward, as if puzzled by the sound of the chiming. Then he leaned back and grunted, shifting in his seat, knees still pressed to the dashboard, big body squeezed like an accordion.

"They must not have cars in the fae realm," I grumbled. Well, that would explain Hugh's odd choice of clothing, I supposed. Maybe they were all medieval there or something. I glanced back into the office and saw Savannah watching us through the windows. "Okay. We need to get going. For starters, pull the lever under your seat to release it. That will move it backward and give you more room."

He did so, and when the seat slid backward a foot, he immediately looked relieved. His knees were still pressed to the dash, but he no longer looked as if he was in pain.

"Now shut the door," I instructed him, then proceeded to show him the seat belts. Then, once everything was buckled and inside the car, I turned it on.

Eyes going wild, he immediately clenched the dashboard, and a low growl began in his throat.

"It's fine," I reassured him. "It's mechanical. We turn it on and it goes." And to show him, I reversed out of the parking space and pulled forward through the parking lot. "You okay?"

"I am well," he gritted between his teeth.

"All righty. Heads up, then, because we're going to go faster. Don't jump out or anything. You could seriously hurt yourself."

He gave me a scathing look that seemed to indicate he knew better than that, so I turned onto the road and began to head for the nearest drive-thru coffee shop. My awkward, enormous passenger seemed to be handling things okay. Hissing and growling, but okay.

Why had Finian thought this man could protect me? He was out of his element in a major way. "So, where you're from . . . they don't have cars?"

"No," he said flatly.

"Ah. Horses? Do you ride everywhere?"

"We walk or run. We do not require assistance." He practically spat the word. "We are not weak like humans."

Well, this was a fun conversation. "Which brings me to another point," I said, determined not to lose my temper at his sour attitude. "What *are* you, exactly?"

"The fae call my kind 'long-tooth.' "

I had no idea what that was. "Is that fae for 'big wild man'? I meant, what is your animal? Some sort of cat? It's clear you're a shifter."

"I am a primordial," he told me bluntly, then leaned forward to peer out the windshield as we pulled into the all-night coffee shop that I liked to frequent.

"I don't know what a primordial is," I told him. "Some kind of cat?"

"Long-tooth," he repeated, as if that explained everything.

Okay, we were getting nowhere with this. I pulled into the drive-thru line. "I'm about to order. You want something to eat?"

"I should like a meal," he admitted, his tone grudging, as if he hated to ask.

"This is good. This is a start," I told him encouragingly. "What's your favorite meal? Maybe we can order something similar."

"Haunch of unicorn."

I stared at him. Just stared. Was he . . . messing with me? But his face was deadly earnest. "Um, I don't think they have that here. Just sandwiches and cookies and coffee stuff. How about I order you something?"

He shrugged.

I clicked the button to roll down my window and heard Hugh's sharp inhalation of surprise. A second later I heard his claws scrape against the door, and he began to play with the window on his side. I ignored it and placed my order. "Large hot lemon tea, heavy on the lemon, a large triple espresso, heavy on the espresso, and a large soda. And a dry bagel," I added, thinking of poor Savannah. I looked over at my companion, then added to the drive-thru window, "And I need some sandwiches. How many do you have?"

"What kind?" came the voice over the speaker. "We're running low, since it's the end of the day, but we might have what you need."

"Actually, just give me all of them. Doesn't matter what kind they are." I winced at the total that was read back to me, then pulled forward. "Sorry, Hugh, they're fresh out of haunch of unicorn."

He peered out the window. "Who is there?"

"Who is where?"

"You are yelling at someone."

Oh, boy. How to explain drive-thru logistics. "Never mind. You wouldn't understand."

He grunted and went back to rolling up the window, then rolling it down again.

I paid, then took the drinks and bags of sandwiches they handed over. Once we pulled out, I thought for a moment, then parked in the lot and looked at Hugh. "Before we go back, I think we need to talk."

Hugh's nostrils flared and he sniffed the air.

"Hungry?" I asked him, offering him the bag of sandwiches. "There's bound to be something in here that you will like. Help yourself." I put Savannah's drink in the cup holder, along with Hugh's, and took a sip of my own heavily caffeinated beverage. Mmm. Pure heaven. I closed my eyes in bliss.

The crinkle of sandwich wrappers caught my attention, along with the rip of paper.

I opened my eyes and stared as Hugh took another enormous bite out of the unwrapped sandwich in his hand. A piece of paper disappeared between his lips and he grimaced, clearly not enjoying the taste.

I stifled my giggle and reached over to help him out. "You take the paper off before you eat."

He blinked at it, took another bite, and grunted, clearly more pleased.

If this situation hadn't been so absurd, I would have been having a great time watching Hugh try to figure out everything. As it was, I kept circling back to my own problems. Hugh wasn't here to entertain me—he was here to make sure another fae didn't snatch me away before Finian claimed me. The espresso I was sipping suddenly didn't taste so great, and I sighed and turned to Hugh. "You and I need to come to a bit of an understanding before we go any further."

He gave me a displeased look. "I do not take orders from you, female."

"Okay—first of all," I snapped, losing my temper, "if you call me 'female' again, I'm going to punch you in the face. I have a name. It's Ryder. Ryder Sinclair. Got it?"

"Ryder Sinclair," he repeated.

"You can just call me Ryder," I told him. "But if you call me 'female' again . . ."

"You will attempt to attack me with your small fists," he said, clearly amused. "I understand."

He was infuriating. "Look, you're going to have to blend in, or you're going back with Finian."

"I do not take orders from you, Ryder," he said, stressing my name. "Only Finian may order me. My vow is with him."

I blinked. "What vow?"

"I will be his soldier for this task, in exchange for a reward. The vow is made with magic, and I cannot break it."

All this woo-woo fae stuff was giving me a headache. "So what did he promise you? Maybe I can pay the difference."

Hugh ignored me and just took another big bite from a sandwich.

"Is it money?"

"It is not money. It is something you cannot offer."

Back to square one. "That brings me to my original point—you and I have to come to an understanding."

"And I will repeat, female, that I do not take orders from you. I take orders from your owner."

I sputtered, raising my fist. Female. Owner. He was *so* asking for a smack in the face.

And judging by the way his cat-eyes glittered with amusement, he was daring me to do so.

I scowled, lowering my fist. "God, you're annoying."

He chuckled, unwrapping another sandwich and taking an enormous bite.

"I'm serious, though. You're going to have to blend in if you don't want me approaching the Alliance for protection from all this."

He snorted. "Who is this Alliance?"

"The Paranormal Alliance? It's shifters and such. Your kind of people."

"Whoever they are, they are not my people." He gave me a flat look. "Explain this Alliance."

"Okay." I thought for a moment. "The Alliance was started because wolves run in packs, right? And they're led by an alpha. But that's not the case for most shifters. Things like were-coyotes and cougars and harpies don't have packs. They don't have that family association or protection that's associated with a pack. They were all out on their own. So for a long time, the wolf packs kind of ran the place. They were bullies, I guess, for lack of a better word." I shrugged, then continued with my explanation. "The Russells—that's the ruling were-cougar clan—started the idea for the Alliance. All the non-pack shifters came together and formed an even bigger group, so now everyone's protected. It's like a big, friendly, furry mafia. Does that make sense?"

His lip curled. "And you think I need protection from wolves?"

"Well, no. You don't look like you need protection from anyone or anything. I just meant that the Alliance is your people. Shifters. That sort of thing."

"I told you. I am a primordial. Not Alliance." Hugh looked affronted at the very suggestion. "I am not one of these puny, scared weaklings, and I need no help against wolf packs."

"I just meant—"

"And these shifters cannot protect you."

"Why not? They protect all supernaturals."

"Because I will destroy all of them to ensure that my vow is not broken."

A chill ran down my spine and I stared at him, noticing again the length of his sharp teeth, the claws tipping each finger, the absolute slabs of muscle covering his frame.

Hugh was dangerous. He was here to "protect" me from anyone and everyone that might get in the way of Finian's wants. Because Finian was holding something over his head. Something he wouldn't tell me about.

This had me stymied. How could I fix this?

Could I go to Beau and Bathsheba for protection? As the head of the Alliance, Beau Russell ran everything paranormal-related and had a really long reach. He could solve almost any problem. His wife, Bathsheba, "Bath" for short, was my boss at the dating agency, and I could go to her, too. Explain what I was and ask the Alliance to help protect me from Hugh and Finian. They'd do it. They'd be miffed that I'd been hiding my real nature from them, but they'd help me out. That was what they did.

But . . . then what?

I'd still be turning fully into my changeling self on my birthday, unable to help it.

It wouldn't help me find my True Love, the one who could break my curse.

And . . . Hugh would apparently destroy all of them to ensure the vow was not broken.

Like it or not, I had to throw my lot in with Hugh and Finian for now to keep everyone safe. I looked over at Hugh as he ate. He was watching our surroundings with keen-eyed fascination, clearly trying to absorb everything he could.

I needed Hugh on my side. Maybe if I could get him to work with me, he could share more information with me about what I was, and how I could break my curse before I became a full-blown changeling.

That seemed like the best plan available. So I smiled at Hugh, turning on the charm. "Enjoying your meal?"

He grunted, unwrapping yet another sandwich and eating half of it in one bite.

Undeterred, I said, "Since you and I will be working closely together for the next month, you need to understand more of what's going on."

Hugh looked over at me, eyes narrowing. "Do tell."

"Well, for starters, no one but you and Finian knows that I am a changeling."

He grunted again and gave a quick nod. "That is for the best."

"It is," I agreed. "But everyone is going to wonder why you are constantly around me and guarding me. They will ask questions. You need to tell them that you're with me because you're signing up for the agency and you're shy, and I've offered to help you ease into the dating waters."

He chewed slowly and looked over at me. "Female, I understand naught of what you just said."

This man was making it awfully hard to be cheerful. My smile became tight with strain. "First off, I'm not going to answer you if you continue to call me 'female.'"

"Ah, yes. You shall put your wee fist in my face." He chuckled.

Now I was pissed. "Actually, I will push *this,*" I said, pointing at the hazard lights button on the dashboard and bluffing, "and your seat will move forward so hard and fast that your balls will end up in your throat." I let my finger hover over the button. "So go on—call me 'female' again."

He stopped chewing, and the amusement vanished off his face, replaced by speculation and a hint of admiration. "Ryder," he said gruffly.

"That's better." I let my voice become sweet, and I dropped my hand away from the hazard button. "All I'm trying to say is that you have to blend in. It'll be easier for you to guard me if no one suspects your real motivation."

"This is true," he admitted. "But I cannot lie. It is against the nature of a primordial to portray themselves falsely."

"It's not a real lie," I cajoled. "Just a teeny-tiny one. We'll sign you up for the agency, and you can pretend to be shy. It's not such a stretch that I'd take you under my wing and help you out. I'm known to be a bit flirty with men," I said, and fluttered my eyelashes at him.

Hugh stared at me. Swallowed his bite of sandwich. Shook his head, ever stubborn. "I will not lie."

I gave him an exasperated look, resisting the urge to dump my coffee over his tangled braids and scowly face. "What do you do when someone asks you something incriminating? That would be bad to answer?"

"I simply do not answer."

"Good," I said, seizing on that. "Perfect. If someone asks you something that will contradict the story that I make up about why you're here, just don't answer. It'll go well with the whole 'shy' cover story."

He glared at me. "I do not like this."

"Well, welcome to my world, Hugh. I don't like *any* of this."

Another noncommittal grunt.

"All I ask is that you let me do the talking, and if you don't agree with something, you just say nothing. That helps me keep my secret, which helps you keep me safer."

A long pause. Then a grudging "Very well."

"Good." I turned the car on again. "Let's go back to the office and see how poor Savannah is doing. Hopefully she hasn't puked her guts out."

"She is dying?"

I raised an eyebrow at his question. "No, she's pregnant. Don't tell me they don't have women in the fae realm, either?"

"They might," he said. "But I am a primordial."

Like I was supposed to have some idea what that meant? The man was like a skipped record.

By the time we returned to the office, Hugh had

demolished all of the sandwiches and my car was filled with wrapper after empty wrapper. I spent a few minutes picking them up and grumbling about men before heading inside, Hugh trailing after me.

Savannah was at her desk, a bit drawn but typing, a step in the right direction. She gave me a relieved smile when I presented her with the hot tea. "Thank you, Ryder. You're so sweet."

"No problem," I told her. "Marie and I used to do coffee runs all the time." I couldn't help the wistful note that rose in my voice.

"You miss Marie?" she guessed.

I nodded. "Now that she's working days and I still work nights, we don't see each other much." We had lunches together and chatted by phone and email, but it wasn't the same as sitting across from each other eight hours a night.

I shrugged and turned to Hugh, who was looming over my shoulder. "Go have a seat." I pointed at the stool.

He opened his mouth, clearly to contradict me, then snapped it shut. Scowling, he moved to the stool and sat with a thump, glaring at my back. Whatever. I turned to Savannah. "Any clients on the books tonight?"

She opened her day planner. "A vampire. Frederick. Comes in at ten."

"Oh, I know him," I said. "He was one of Marie's. Just flirt with him and you'll be fine."

She gave me a repulsed look. "Flirt? With a vampire?"

"Yeah, he's difficult unless you know how to work him." I leaned over the desk and gave her a saucy wink, tossing my hair over my shoulder. "Why, look at you, Fred," I cooed. "You here to visit me? I was just telling myself that I needed a tall drink of vampire tonight." And I licked my lips in an exaggerated fashion.

There was a sound of crushing Styrofoam and the clatter of ice cubes hitting the floor.

I turned . . . and blinked. The remains of Hugh's destroyed cup were in his hand, and soda and ice lay splattered on the floor around him. His cat-eyes were gleaming, but the look on his face was impossible to read.

Geez, the man was tough on our floors. "You made the mess, you clean it up."

Chapter Four

The hours crawled by. It was a slow night, and I filled the evening with backlog projects and training Savannah on Marie's old tasks. We were repeatedly interrupted by her trips to the bathroom and Hugh's occasional ridiculous question. He was worse than a bored toddler.

I put him at my desk and turned on a local news feed to keep him occupied. Savannah gave us a few curious looks, but she seemed distracted.

While I worked, Marie sent me a text. *Hey! We having lunch this week?*

I sent back immediately. *Okay! Sounds awesome!*

I peeked over at Hugh, thought for a moment, and texted, *Hey, Marie, do you know of any cat shifters with furry forearms, big claws, and stripey hair? Oh, and fangs?*

Uh, not off the top of my head. Want me to ask Josh?

No, I sent quickly. *I was just curious. New client and all. See you at lunch!*

I clicked off my phone before Marie could ask

more questions. I didn't want her getting suspicious, not when I wasn't sure what to do with Hugh myself.

I started to yawn around 2:00 a.m., an hour before we normally closed. Savannah looked as if she wouldn't make it another five minutes, much less another hour. I felt sorry for her. "Why don't you go ahead and call it an evening? I'll be fine here."

"You're sure?" She looked uneasily at Hugh.

"I'm sure." I waved a pink manicured hand in the air. "It's not at all busy."

"All right, then." Savannah picked up her purse and pulled out her car keys. "I'll see you tomorrow night."

"I'll be here," I said cheerfully and returned to hanging the newest calendar of events on the bulletin board.

The moment the door shut and it was just myself and Hugh, I glanced over at him. "Speaking of calling it a night, where are you sleeping?"

He looked up from the news feed, and I was again struck by how catlike his eyes were. They weren't remotely human, not like a regular shifter's. His pupils were thin and elongated like a cat's, and his eyes reflected light when he turned his head. "Mmm?"

"I'm going home after work. Where do you plan on going for the night?"

Those catlike eyes grew heavy-lidded in a way that would have made him look sexy if it hadn't been for the fact that he'd irritated me all evening. "I am going with you."

Wha-? I should have expected it, considering he'd even tried following me to the bathroom at one point, not realizing where I'd been heading. Yet hearing it stated out loud? It was still mind-boggling. "You can't go home with me. I didn't invite you."

"I know this. Yet I cannot be assured of your safety if I leave you unattended. I will remain at your side."

"Not while I'm sleeping," I said in a harder voice. I was never going to get any sleep if he was standing over my bed and staring at me all night. No way.

"Then I will guard your doorway."

"You're kidding me, right?" Then I shook my head. "Never mind, I know you're not kidding. Fine. It's clear I'm not going to win this argument."

"It is not an argument if we both agree, Ryder," he said, amusement in his voice.

My fingers itched to go around his neck. This man was driving me insane. Why was it that I could flirt the pants off every other man I was around, yet the moment Hugh opened his mouth, I just wanted to stuff a sock into it? I grimaced. "Just let me finish up here and we'll go. I guess."

The bulletin board was my last project for the evening. It was a simple update—just pin the calendar and be done. But my desk was occupied by a big, weird guy, and I wasn't about to go and hover around him. So I took my time straightening the calendar and moving some of the other items on the bulletin board around. Profile of the month. Helpful dating tips. Local restaurant suggestions. Wedding photos of fruitful matches. Even though we had a very particular clientele, Midnight Liaisons was very successful with its pairings. I looked at the married couples wistfully, running a finger along the edge of one picture. The couple looked so very delighted and carefree—no one would know from their photo that one was a were-badger and one was a were-mongoose, and their families hadn't been pleased with the union until the wedding day had arrived and everything had been forgotten. Once the couple's devotion had been vowed before all, it hadn't mattered what their animal side was. All that mattered was love. And that was what I wanted—complete and utter devotion. Happiness with my chosen partner.

I'd never get it, though. Not with the path I was on. I was heading straight for poodle territory.

I sighed and turned away from the board. "Come on. Let's lock up."

Hugh was wildly out of place in my condo.

To better disguise my inner ugly, I kept up my cheerful theme. My sofa was pink with lemon-wedge-shaped cushions and a lacy dust ruffle. My curtains were white eyelet, and knickknacks of unicorns and baby animals cluttered my shelves. One of my dates had once complained that it looked like the living room of a ten-year-old.

Hugh took in my living room soundlessly as I locked the front door behind us. "I guess you can sleep on the couch," I told him. "As long as you promise no funny business."

"Funny . . . business?" he echoed, clearly not understanding the sentiment.

"You know. No trying to touch me. No hanky-panky."

He stared at me, then snorted. "You are quite safe in that regard."

Ouch! "You sure do know how to sweet-talk a lady. A *lot* of guys happen to think I'm quite cute."

Hugh regarded me for a moment, and I could have sworn there was color in his cheeks. Embarrassed? He crossed his arms over his chest. "It would not matter if you were the most beautiful creature on earth. I am forbidden to touch you, as outlined in my vow."

"Oh. So what exactly does your vow entail?"

He was silent.

Ah—clearly one of those questions that would give away too much information. "Gotcha. Well, it doesn't involve sleeping with ugly changelings, so it doesn't matter, I suppose."

"I did not say you were ugly."

I suspected this was as close to a compliment as I'd get from him. Mollified, I shrugged and headed to my linen closet. "I'll get you a blanket."

I didn't often entertain visitors, so I didn't have much in the way of extra linens. I ended up using an old throw quilt from the rocking chair. By the time

I returned to my living room, Hugh was checking things out. I watched as he picked up one of my strawberry-vanilla scented candles, sniffed it, and gave it a tentative lick.

"Um, you don't eat that," I told him, trying not to laugh at his revolted expression. "You don't have candles in the fae world? Really?"

"I am primordial," he said simply, as if that answered everything. But he put the candle back down.

"And I *still* don't know what that is," I said, patting the blanket. "So do you care to share? Or are you just going to keep tossing it around like it means something that I should understand?"

His mouth twitched with amusement. "The latter, perhaps."

I rolled my eyes. "More of your vow?"

"No. Just . . . difficult to explain." He rubbed his jaw, and I noticed that there was stripey fur at the edges of his jaw, almost like sideburns. Why was that so oddly attractive? "We are like your shifters, but different. Very different. Much where I come from is nothing like . . . all this." He gestured at my bright, colorful living room.

"I'm told this isn't like most people's stuff anyhow," I said, heading to the couch and beginning to toss stuffed animals and cushions off of it. "Marie laughs at my fondness for pink."

"It is quite . . . interesting in here." He gazed around and then looked back at me. "Very colorful."

"Blinding. You can say it. I like the color. It makes me happy."

"Yes, outwardly you seem easily pleased."

I wanted to ask him what he meant by that, but Hugh knew all my secrets. It made me feel vulnerable to realize that he knew everything I was, yet I knew nothing about him.

It was starting to bother me.

"We weren't talking about me," I said. "Don't change the subject. We were talking about you and your people."

"Mmm."

"Brothers? Sisters? Big family? Get along with your parents?"

"None."

"None what?"

"I have none. No brothers, no sisters. No parents."

"Everybody has parents."

"If I do, I do not recall them."

"How can you forget if you have family?"

He simply stared at me.

Okay, our agreement that he would be silent when he didn't want to answer was getting a little annoying. "How old are you?"

"That is a question I have no answer for. Time passes differently in the fae realms."

"Well, you are just a fountain of information, aren't you?" I was getting testy. "So I'm supposed to know nothing about you but trust you with my life for the next month? Is that right?"

"It is."

How was it that a guy who couldn't lie managed to be so incredibly unhelpful? "And then I'm supposed to just go along with the fact that someone thinks he can own me?"

He shrugged.

"So what happens if I say no? What if I want to live out here in the human world, and just embrace my changeling half or something?"

He looked intrigued. "Is that possible?"

I had no idea. But I wasn't going to go down without a fight. "I don't see why not. There are people other than the fae who have information on changelings."

"Is that so?" He seemed nonplussed.

"It is," I told him in a lofty voice. "I can break the curse if I find a man to give my virginity to before my twenty-fifth birthday arrives."

He said nothing.

That infuriated me all over again. "And furthermore, if I find my True Love, I won't turn when he touches me. I just have to find him before I hit my birthday."

Hugh remained silent. Was he irritated that I knew so much already? Had he and Finian conspired to withhold this information from me?

"Well?" I said.

"So this is your plan? To find a human man and have relations with him?"

"It beats the alternative, don't you think?"

"You do realize that your changeling body is much stronger than a normal human body?"

"So?"

"So you might overcome a human male. You could damage him or even kill him."

I swallowed hard. Hugh said he never lied. "Then I'll have to find a nonhuman man, won't I? I can get a nice shifter guy to hook up with." I'd just have to explain my little "problem" and hope for the best. Surely someone that changed into another shape himself wouldn't mind that I changed into . . . something.

"I'll have to prevent it." Hugh's look was stony.

"You will not!"

His smile was cruel. "Why do you think Finian sent me to your side now? You are getting desperate to escape your curse. You'll try anything . . . and I'm going to be at your side to make sure it doesn't happen."

"I hate you," I spat at him, throwing the quilt down on the couch. "You're an awful, awful man."

He gave me a grim look. "I know. But that is how it must be."

I stomped to my room, slamming the door.

Despite my fury and the bizarre events of the day, I slept soundly and woke up around noon. My condo was quiet and I sat up, cocking my head and listening for Hugh. I could hear nothing. Even putting my ear to my bedroom door, I could hear nothing. I tossed a robe over my frilly pink pajamas and went to check things out.

Immediately, there were signs of Hugh. I picked up an empty Pop-Tart wrapper in the hallway and, a few steps later, a demolished chip bag. Half-eaten cookies were crumbled on the wooden floors, and it looked like the contents of my pantry had been strewn about and taste-tested, including boxes of uncooked spaghetti noodles. I could hear water running somewhere in the house and headed toward that.

The tap was running in the kitchen sink, and I turned it off, frowning. The room was an unmitigated disaster area. My electric stove had been turned on; the burners were bright red, and I quickly clicked them off. The refrigerator door hung open, and plastic wrapping covered the floor, including an empty package of steak and some tubing that had held ground beef for the spaghetti I'd planned on making for dinner.

Irritated, I swiped the wrapping up and tossed it in the trash. "Hugh?"

No answer.

He'd left? That made no sense. He'd declared he was going to be my shadow for the next month; why would he leave me here by myself? I could almost think I'd imagined the whole thing if it hadn't been for the fact that every bit of food I owned had at least one bite taken out of it.

I walked down the hall of my small condo again. "Hugh? You here?"

Still no answer. I checked all the doors—even the closet—but nothing. I went to the front door to check outside . . . and it wouldn't open. I tugged at the handle. Nothing. Alarmed, I ran my hand along the door frame, looking for something jamming it, but there was nothing. It just didn't respond. I could turn the handle, but the door was stuck fast.

Perplexed, I took a step back. What to do now?

There was nothing *to* do but wait. I went back to my room and showered and dressed. Wearing my favorite pink-and-white tracksuit with a pair of sneaker pumps, I blow-dried my hair, fixed it into two topknots with puffy pink bands, and curled my bangs. Then, as I waited for Hugh to return, I set about cleaning the mess that he had left.

I'd just finished sweeping the last of the crumbs off my hardwood floors when I heard a sound at the front door. I tossed aside the broom and rushed to it, just in time to run into Hugh's enormous chest entering the room.

"Eep!" I staggered backward, automatically putting a hand up to push him away before he could get too close. "Hugh! Where have you been? What's going on? Why couldn't I open the door?"

Hugh stepped inside and shut the front door behind him, blocking me from the outside. He was holding a large fast-food bag and a coffee, and he looked down at me with one raised eyebrow. "Which of your questions do you wish for me to answer?"

"All of them!"

He brushed past me, his strange tunic sliding against my skin as he moved by, and the smell of burgers wafted into the condo. "I hunted for food. Finian was clear that I am to provide for you if possible, to ensure that you receive the best care until he is to retrieve you."

Perplexed at this answer, I glanced at the front

door, then watched as Hugh strode to the couch with his food. "How come the door's working now?" I went to it and tested the doorknob. Sure enough, it opened easily. "I don't understand."

"I sealed it," Hugh said. "Come and eat what I have provided. You are a small female and need to fatten up."

Well, that was something a girl didn't hear every day. "I am a perfect size four, thank you. And I wish to stay that way." I sat on the couch next to him and blinked at the mountain of wrapped sandwiches he pulled out of the bag. There had to be at least twenty burgers of all kinds on my table. "Goodness. Did you get enough food?"

He considered the burger mountain and then eyed me, quite serious. "Do you eat much? Shall I get more?"

"I was joking," I told him and picked up the closest sandwich. "Thank you, I suppose. How did you get these? Did Finian give you money?" Hugh didn't seem like the type to carry a wallet.

"I took them."

I stopped unwrapping my burger and looked over at Hugh. "You . . . took them?"

"Yes. I walked up to the window like you showed me last night and demanded their food." He shook his head, began to unwrap the first burger, and took an enormous bite out of it. "They were most disagreeable until I snarled at them."

My eyes widened. I stared down at the burger in horror. "Hugh, you have to *pay* for sandwiches.

You can't just go to a drive-thru and growl at people until they give you things. You pay for them!"

"I do not understand this word *pay,*" he said between bites. "Your land is strange." To my surprise, he reached over the mountain of burgers and handed me the cup of coffee. "I acquired the beverage you like."

"Oh. Thank you." I took it from him and gave him a smile. "I'm surprised you remembered."

"I did not forget it. The smell is most foul."

I giggled at the way his nostrils flared. "Not to me." I gave it a deep sniff. "Mmmmm, coffee."

"I prefer the smell of these," he said and lifted a burger to his nose. "Mmmm, animal flesh."

And just like that, I lost my appetite for my burger. "We call it meat here," I said, wrinkling my nose.

He shrugged and took another bite. "I like it better cold."

I remembered the packages he'd pulled out of my fridge and shuddered. "You mean raw? That's unsanitary."

Hugh simply grinned at me, flashing those big canines as he took another bite.

I sipped the coffee—lukewarm, but it was the thought that counted—and glanced back at the front door. "So how did you seal the door shut?"

"Portal magic." He devoured the burger in his hand in two quick, enormous bites.

"And that is . . . ?"

This time, he gave me a brows-furrowed expression. "Do you not have portal magic here?"

"Um, we don't have magic anything."

"You have changelings," he pointed out. "And shifters."

Good point. "We don't have magic that I am aware of," I amended. "How does this portal magic work? Can anyone do it?" I was incredibly curious. More than that, I wanted to know how I could use it to my advantage. "Can I do it, as a changeling?"

He shook his head and reached inside the neck of his tunic, pulling out a necklace with two small stones hanging from it. "Because I am sworn to serve Finian, he gave me these. This one calls Finian." He held up a blue stone. Then he lifted a pebble-sized garnet with some sort of rune carved into it. "This one is a portal stone. I can lock or open any portal using it. I have to give it back once my vow is completed."

"So why did he give you that one? Where do you need to open a portal to?"

"Home, if I so wish." He shrugged. "Or need assistance. I won't, but it's available to me. Also to ensure that you remain where I want you at all times."

That sent a chill down my spine. "Like you did this morning?"

"Aye." He picked up another sandwich.

"So basically, you can imprison me whenever you want to?"

Hugh ignored my question.

"That's not a no," I pointed out tartly. "I don't like this little situation one bit."

"It's not for you to like or dislike, little changeling. It simply is. There is no sense in fighting it."

That bleak desperation curled in my stomach again. "Please help me, Hugh. You know what he has intended for me."

"I do." His voice was flat with dislike. He didn't look me in the eye.

"Then don't deliver me to him," I begged. "Let me go. Or better yet, help me figure out how to break my curse. Please. You know about changelings. You can help me. I'll pay you."

He shook his head. "You know I cannot break my vow with Finian. No matter how many times you ask."

My shoulders drooped. "This vow must be pretty compelling for you to callously sell me out."

Hugh hesitated, then tossed his burger down on the table as if his appetite was gone, too. "If you must know, it is the thing my people desire most."

It was clear from Hugh's attitude that he didn't like the fae prince. So Finian had clearly offered something pretty dang amazing.

And that made me curious. It was time to try a different tactic.

I wiped my hands off and stood up, determined to change topics. "So tell me how this portal magic works. You said you can go home?"

Hugh gave me a skeptical look. "I am not leaving you, female. Get that thought out of your mind."

"I didn't say you should," I told him in my sweetest voice, the one I used on our most irascible clients. "I'll go with you. I want to see these primordials for myself."

"No," Hugh said flatly.

That wasn't a good enough answer for me. "Why not?" I fluttered my lashes at him, then sat down a bit closer, leaning in because men always seemed to appreciate that sort of thing. And I gave him my most fascinated, intense expression. "I want to learn all about you, Hugh. Is that so wrong?"

He blinked at me a few times, and I watched his nostrils flare out—a sure sign that he was taking in my scent. He looked a bit . . . dazed at the turn in my mood.

I'd been handling Hugh all wrong.

He'd driven me so crazy with his high-handed ways and bossiness that he'd made me forget my best weapon—flirting.

I put my hand on his sleeve. "Please?" I made my voice soft, sweet, and girlish.

"It is forbidden to show outsiders the primordial lands," he said, but his gaze went to my hand—small, pink, manicured. Dainty on his big arm. I had to resist the urge to feel his bulging muscles, because he definitely was bulging.

"What's it going to harm?" I asked him softly. "I'm going to be at your side for the next month, and then I'm leaving with Finian. When will I have a chance to tell an outsider anything?" I leaned even closer. "I just . . . want to understand. That's all."

Hugh's gaze went to my mouth. He said nothing, just stared at my mouth.

I licked my lips deliberately. It was weird how I was getting all flushed and bothered by this as well.

It was just the power trip, I told myself. I loved the ego-stroke of bringing a man to his knees.

"I . . ." he began.

"Yes?" My voice was breathy and soft.

"I . . . you must vow to secrecy." His catlike eyes focused on my eyes, finally tearing away from my mouth. "Vow that you won't speak of it to others."

Yes! "I vow it," I said, slowly and deliberately, so he wouldn't see my eagerness.

"Then come with me." He jerked to his feet.

Chapter Five

"We need a portal," Hugh told me. "Something we can step through to the other side." He examined my small living room. "Your dwelling is strange and full of angles. You pick what we use."

"What about the front door?" I suggested.

He shook his head. "You can only use a portal spell on an object once every day. It won't hold otherwise."

Odd. Okay. I considered my small condo. The kitchen and dining room were open to the living room, so that was out. My back door was sliding glass that led out to the balcony, so I wasn't sure if that would do. "Maybe the bedroom? Or my closet?" The bathroom seemed too weird.

Hugh shrugged and looked at me, waiting.

"Closet," I said firmly. I led him there, feeling a blush come to my cheeks. This was the first time I'd ever brought a man to my bedroom, and we were about to take a trip to a fairy realm. Not exactly what I'd imagined.

Still, learning about Hugh's people would help

me understand him more. And if I knew what made him tick, maybe I could figure out what he wanted so badly that he'd agree to work for a man he clearly disliked.

And then maybe I could make a counteroffer.

It didn't fix all my problems—I still had to find my True Love, or at least a man to take my virginity while I was in my scaly form—but it was a start.

I had to admit, though, I was pretty curious about Hugh.

I gestured at my closet door and Hugh moved in front of me. There was something wild about Hugh . . . and it wasn't just his very obvious cat-shifter side. Maybe it was the way he moved, or the fact that his clawed feet were still bare, or those tufts at the square of his jaw and the wild braids in the tangle of his striped hair. There was something about him that screamed feral and predator, and it appealed to me despite my love for pink and fluffy things. He was neither, but . . . I liked that about him.

As I watched, Hugh took off his necklace. He lifted one arm (which was thick with muscle and deeply tanned) and traced the garnet around the edges of the door, including the carpeted floor. Once he'd made a perfect rectangle, he stepped back and put the necklace on again.

I crossed my arms over my chest, looking at my closet door skeptically. "Nothing happened."

"Patience, little changeling," he said with amusement. He looked down at me. "And remember—"

"I know; we can't talk about this." I held my pinky out. "You can trust me. Pinky swear."

"I was going to caution you to stay close to me." He eyed my outstretched finger. "What is a pinky swear?"

"Oh. Um." I lowered my hand. "You lock your little finger with another person's and it's an agreement."

"A binding agreement?"

"Yeah, sure," I agreed. "Totally binding."

He held his claw-tipped pinky out to me. "Then I shall do this pinky swear with you."

Touching Hugh could trigger my changeling side . . . unless he was my True Love, like the fortune-teller had told me. I hesitated, then extended my pinky. *Just another frog to kiss*. As his finger linked with mine, I immediately felt my monster ripple under my skin. I ripped my hand away, shaking it as if it had been burned.

So Hugh wasn't The One. I ignored the disappointment in my gut. I still had a month to kiss frogs. I was going to be okay. I was.

"Are you well?"

"Touching someone does bad things to me," I reminded him.

"Changeling," he agreed. "I thought it only affected you if you were attracted?"

My face grew hot. That was how it was supposed to work, yeah. "Maybe mine's just really sensitive right now," I muttered.

"Perhaps," Hugh said.

How embarrassing. I crossed my arms over my chest again, staring at my closet door and waiting.

Sure enough, as moments ticked past, it began to change. It was subtle at first. I heard the sound of crickets and smelled damp moss. Fog began to spill out of my closet, and stars began to twinkle as the sound of rustling leaves drew my attention. I stepped forward in wonder, staring at the space where my closet door hinged.

It was like watching a slowly developing photograph. It darkened into shadow and slowly changed, and I began to pick out scenery. Wet, swampy marshlands in the distance. Large, leafy trees rustling in a breeze that now ruffled my hair. It was nighttime in that other realm, and the mist was full of fireflies.

"Holy cow," I breathed. "That is so cool."

"Fae magic is quite impressive," Hugh said in a flat voice that implied that he found it anything but. "Follow. Stay close to me."

"Yes, sir," I replied. I wanted to put my hand in his, but I couldn't touch him. So I grabbed one of his bell-shaped, heavily embroidered sleeves and clasped it as he moved forward.

We stepped through the portal, and I was hit by a wall of humidity. Immediately, I blanched. I was accustomed to air-conditioning in the summer. This . . . felt disgusting. It was so starkly humid that I could practically feel the dampness in the air sliding over my skin. It was at least ninety degrees, too. "Ugh. Is it summer here?"

"We do not have seasons like your realm does. It

is always like this," Hugh said, his voice sounding hollow as we stepped through. "Stay close."

I glanced behind us. The portal was fading as we stepped away, my comforting, cheery bedroom disappearing as I stared at it. That made me nervous. "How do we get back?"

"We find another place to make a portal." Hugh strode forward, jerking his sleeve out of my grasp before I could protest. "Come. Follow."

I followed as best I could, though it didn't take long before I was lagging behind. For one, it was clear that changelings didn't have the night vision that primordials did. I couldn't see a thing beyond a few feet ahead, and I had to focus to keep Hugh in my sights. My sneaker pumps, not made for this kind of terrain, squished on the muddy ground and sank a bit with each step. This was some sort of disgusting swamp, I decided, judging by the immense number of bugs that flew through the air and started to land on my skin. An enormous dragonfly buzzed past, startling the hell out of me. A fly as big as a canary landed on my arm and I yelped, slapping it away.

"Hssst," Hugh said, turning to glare at me. His eyes gleamed like saucers in the low light.

"I'm not used to bugs that size," I told him, raking a hand down my arm again. My skin was tingling and damp, and I didn't know if I was sweating or if it was just the humidity. Either way, it was gross.

Then my back suddenly ached, my tracksuit

jacket growing tight over my shoulder blades. My skin rippled and I dropped to my knees, a low moan of fear escaping my throat.

Hugh was at my side immediately, his hands going to my waist as he tried to bring me back to my feet. "Ryder?"

I slapped his hands away and collapsed again. "Don't touch me!"

My beast was coming. Oh, God, oh, God. In front of Hugh, too. Shame wracked me, mixed with pain and fear. My hands crept over my face to shield it from his gaze. Not now. Not in front of someone else.

"Are you changing forms?" Hugh asked, his voice low. One big hand touched my back.

I shied away from his grasp, hunching low and folding my body tight. Maybe if I concentrated hard, I could get this under control. Even as I told myself this, my mouth filled with hot, metallic blood, and fangs tore through my gums. "Don't look at me," I whimpered. "I—I'll be fine in a minute."

To my surprise, a big, heavy hand stroked my damp hair. "I worried that this might happen," he murmured. "I didn't want to concern you, but . . . the fae realms have a strong effect on most. Your other side is emerging because this place calls to it."

"Take me back," I moaned. I didn't want to be this thing. "*Please*."

"We have to find another gate," he told me. That big hand stroked my hair again, trying to soothe me. "Are you afraid I will think you are hideous?"

Was he kidding? I *knew* I was hideous. The creature I turned into had hard, scaly skin, horns on its forehead, and bony protrusions on its cheekbones. Ugly, membranous wings shuddered and pushed through my skin, my shoulders on fire, my clothing tight. My tail bulged and snaked along one leg of my pants, trying to emerge. And all over, my skin ached as it scaled over and turned hard.

A sob escaped my throat, humiliation burning through me. My body hurt, my soul hurt, and to make matters worse, I was going to have to rip off my clothing. "Hugh," I moaned, my clawed hands flexing. My voice had gotten raspy and deep, my vocal cords shifting to something more feral. "You should get away."

"I am not afraid of your tiny claws, little changeling," Hugh said with amusement. "Mine are much bigger."

"I . . . need to take my clothes off," I rasped. My wings ached, desperate to escape, and it took everything I had not to rip through my top like the Hulk. "Please . . . don't look."

"I will have to look at some point," Hugh told me, and that big hand stroked my hair again. His thumb brushed against my cheek—my hard, ridged cheek. "Will it make you feel better if I confess that this tunic is not mine? Finian insisted I wear it. My people do not normally wear clothing. Trust me when I say your natural form will not offend me."

A giggle escaped me, the sound a deep gurgle in my throat. The thought of a big, scary Hugh stalking naked behind prissy Finian was utterly amusing.

"Good," he said in response to my chuckle. "Then you will not mind if I change as well."

And before I could look up, his tunic landed on the ground.

I raised my head to look at his naked body, but the transformation split through me and my vision blurred as pain flashed. I tore at my clothing, ripping it with my claws and not caring that I was destroying it. Then I was naked and panting, crouched on the ground, but at least I was no longer in pain. I lifted a hand, studying my transformation.

That had been the most painful, most difficult one yet. It wasn't hard to see why. Normally my skin transformed gradually, in patches, scales mixing with my pale skin until it was all changed. In the fae realm, I was completely morphed in seconds. My arms gleamed with scales, and the leathery wings on my back felt larger than ever. Here I had a full-length tail lashing behind me instead of a half-formed stump. I touched my face; it felt foreign, gargoyle-ish. Hideous. I looked down at my body. Wet, gleaming scales covered my chest. Even my nipples were hard little scaly points.

I shuddered, my hands going to my hair—only to meet up with twisted horns that jutted from my forehead. I choked back a sob. I was revolting.

Big, clawed toes appeared in the corner of my vision. "Can you walk now? We should get moving."

"Give me just a minute," I said, and my voice was rough, not my own. A ripple of loathing moved through me, and I forced myself to get to my feet—my scaly, unnatural feet—and stand. I'd have to show him my hideous form at some point. Might as well do it now. I lifted my head . . .

And found that, despite his proximity, he didn't look over at me. His face was carefully turned away.

God, I was worse than I'd thought. I bit my lip, only to wince at the pain it caused. Was I so hideous even to him that he wouldn't look at me? My pride, already battered, hurt worse than my newly transformed body.

To make matters even worse, Hugh wasn't hideous in the least. Since his gaze was averted, I openly stared. His chest was broadly massive, and lightly furred with that same stripey coloration his hair had. I'd missed the chance to stare at his privates, I realized too late, so I ogled his legs instead. They were thick and strong, and surprisingly long, given the barrel-like massiveness of the rest of his body. His powerful thighs flexed as he turned to reveal a tight, delicious ass that made me feel all kinds of wild longings. I wanted to touch him for some reason, and my hand lifted involuntarily. He was sinfully gorgeous naked.

And I . . . was a scaly beast. I lowered my hand.

"Can you walk now?" Hugh asked. "We've much ground to cover."

"I can walk," I said, my words slurred around my fangs. "Where are we going?"

"To my tribemates."

"Lead on, then."

He nodded and tilted his head, his messy hair rippling in the breeze as he sniffed. His eyes gleamed, reflecting the low light, and I wished that changelings had shifters' gifts. My hearing wasn't extra keen, I couldn't smell anything on the air but moss, and I still couldn't see more than a foot in front of myself.

I loathed every bit of being a changeling. There were no advantages. None. I might be stronger, like Hugh had said, but it just meant that I could harm a human man if I tried to have sex with him and he wasn't my True Love.

And really, who would want to touch me in this form? Hugh was barely human himself, and he couldn't even look at me. I choked back my bitterness and followed behind him.

We moved through the swampy growth of trees, and the farther we moved inward, the more confused I became. This was the fae realm? I'd pictured something far more civilized. Delicate buildings and cultured gardens. The terrain we were slogging through was wild and a bit disgusting, quite frankly.

Was Hugh lying to me? Was he leading me somewhere to trap me? No, that didn't make sense.

Hugh said he never lied, and whatever Finian had promised him, he wanted it badly enough to sell me out.

I said nothing as we trekked through the underbrush, my clawed feet sinking into the murk with every step. I focused on Hugh's flexing buttocks ahead of me, the occasional glimpse of his cock and balls between his legs. It made me blush even as it fascinated me, and I wanted to stare at them. Was that weird? Did it even matter?

All of a sudden Hugh halted, his hand extending out to stop me.

I was so focused on his tight ass that I didn't notice and ran smack into that big hand. I gave a yelp of surprise, even as he flinched away.

And seeing that flinch? Just made my heart sink a little more. A hard knot formed in my throat.

"Silence," Hugh whispered.

I waited anxiously, staring at him, since I couldn't see a thing in the fog.

After a long moment he lifted his head, testing the breeze, and looked over at me. "We are being followed. Something is downwind."

"Finian?"

His mouth curled into a sneer, huge fangs on display. "He would never come here of his own accord." He gestured for me to follow him as he launched forward.

I trotted behind him as best I could, unable to stop peeking behind me out of anxiety. Was something hunting us? Was it one of Hugh's people?

Hugh halted again.

I jerked to a stop behind him, glancing around. I saw nothing. I looked over at Hugh again. "What is it?"

He stared at the thick bushes ahead of us, not moving a muscle. I followed his gaze, curious.

An enormous shape moved forward and I gasped, staggering backward. "Oh . . . shit."

A rhinoceros on steroids headed toward us. It was like nothing I'd ever seen before. Even in the low light, I could make out a huge, bulky body, the head lowered. It was as big as an elephant, maybe bigger. Shaggy fur covered it. On the nose was a horn three times the size of what I assumed a rhinoceros would have. The horn was larger than I was.

And it was pointing right at us.

Involuntarily, I took a step behind Hugh's broad shoulders, seeking protection. "What do we do now?" I whispered. Somehow the creature that had been following us was now in front of us. How had we not heard this monster tromping around behind us?

But Hugh only snorted and said, "Change, Artur. You're frightening my guest."

My eyes widened. I looked at the massive creature, then at Hugh. "That's . . . one of your people?"

"He is a primordial," Hugh said, his eyes narrowing as the rhino moved forward. "And he treads on thin ground."

My eyes widened as the enormous head—and horn—moved forward, heading straight for me.

The creature seemed to be ignoring Hugh, determined to check me out.

Which frightened the heck out of me. I gave a distressed squeak when it nosed forward, and I moved around Hugh, determined to keep him between me and the monster rhino.

"Artur!" Hugh snapped, a feline growl in his voice.

The rhino only made a noise in its throat and continued to move toward me, disregarding Hugh's warnings.

The low growl in Hugh's voice deepened, and he dropped to a crouch, alarming me. I took a step backward. "Hugh?"

As I watched, fur sprouted along his spine, rippling down his back. The transformation ripped through him, stronger and faster than I'd ever seen with any shifter. Within seconds, Hugh was in complete cat form.

And I was stunned.

More than eight feet long and weighing several hundred pounds, his enormous body was knotted with muscle, his chest thick and barrel-like. He had no mane but was covered with more of those strange, bizarre stripes that were evident in human form. Hugh's animal form looked like a tiger on steroids. Most startling of all were his jaws: his massive head swung, and I caught sight of two foot-long, protruding fangs as he snarled at the rhino and swiped at him with a giant paw.

I stepped backward, shocked, as things clicked

into place. When Hugh had told me he was a primordial, I hadn't realized what that meant. But looking at his animal form now, I realized . . . he was a saber-toothed tiger. I stared at him, then back at the strange rhino he was herding away from me with irritated swipes of his paw.

Holy cow.

Were all the primordials Ice Age shifters? Was that what this place was? Some pocket dimension, where the fae kept supposedly extinct shifters?

Chapter Six

The saber-tooth growled low as I stood there in shock, and when the rhino swung that massive horn, Hugh pushed it away with a gigantic paw. I expected the rhino to react badly, but it only gave a humanlike snort and squatted. A moment later, its form morphed—again, so quickly that I could scarcely blink—and a man crouched in its place. He straightened and glared at me from behind craggy, thick brows, a heavy forehead, and an enormous nose that dominated his ugly face.

If it was possible, he was even bigger than Hugh.

I crossed my arms over my scaly chest and took another step backward, my tail flicking with anxiety. "Hugh?"

The saber-tooth crossed in front of me, growling low.

"I smelled a female," the rhino-man boomed, his voice incredibly deep and incredibly loud. "You bring one here? Is this—"

He was interrupted by a ferocious cat-growl from Hugh.

"I see," the man said. "Very well."

"See what?" I asked.

Hugh growled at me.

I frowned at him. "Don't you growl at me. I'm asking a question. I don't know what's going on."

"You are changeling," the rhino boomed.

"And you're a freaking rhino."

"I am a primordial—" he began.

I rolled my eyes. "Yes, I know. Hugh, can you please change back so we can have a conversation about this?"

The saber-tooth's eyes gleamed, and he hunched his shoulders. Moments later, Hugh was crouching on the ground, naked, then he rose to his feet. I felt a hot blush cover my cheeks when he stretched to his full height in front of me.

I blushed. I mean, I couldn't help but notice that he was a shower and not a grower. Hugh was definitely big everywhere.

"Artur heard us coming and decided to meet us," Hugh said, striding past me to clap a hand on Artur's big shoulder. "And now he is going to quit staring at you."

I glanced over at Artur curiously and noticed him suddenly averting his eyes, looking over at Hugh. "Forgive me," he said. "I did not mean to be impolite."

"It's okay," I told him. "I *am* standing here naked, and it sounds like you don't get a lot of changelings."

"We do not—" Artur began.

Hugh clapped him on the shoulder and forcibly turned him away from me. "Lead us back, friend," he said, interrupting Artur's thoughts.

The rhino-man gave Hugh a curious look. "Come."

I trailed behind them, frowning. Now no one was looking at me. God, was I that disgusting? I pinched my scaly skin, hoping it would respond and I'd change back to human form. Transformations normally didn't last this long, but this one didn't seem like it was going away anytime soon.

I followed the two men as they moved ahead a short distance. They mumbled things to each other, but their voices were so low and my hearing so bad that I couldn't pick it up, which was frustrating. I felt like a freak, an outcast, and my feelings were hurt. I knew my form was hideous, but they weren't supposed to be shocked by it, were they?

I mean, I'd just met a woolly rhino and a prehistoric saber-tooth, and I wasn't flipping out, was I? No, I was not.

The thick underbrush gave way after a time and led to a crude set of caves set into the side of a sheer cliff. It looked like a rat warren, almost, with the hillside riddled with cave entrances. A curving, twisty path led between the entrances, and several of the caves were covered with crude animal hides as makeshift doors.

Hugh glanced over his shoulder at me. "These are my people, Ryder."

This . . . was not what I'd been expecting. As I stared, my arms crossed over my chest, more and more people emerged, until soon enough, two dozen men had emerged from the caves. The center of the area was churned with muddy footprints, and the trappings of a crude civilization were here—an animal hide stretched over a low-hanging limb, strips of meat drying.

All the men, though, were naked. All had equally wild hair and enormous bodies. And they were all staring at me like I was a freak.

Hugh snarled at them and stepped in front of me, shielding my hideous naked form from them. "This one is my vow," he explained to them. "Do not touch her. Do not stare at her."

But some of them stared anyhow, trying to look at me from around Hugh's big shoulders. Artur moved to Hugh's side, effectively shielding me from the others' view.

"How many of you are there?" I asked.

"There are two dozen males of my people."

Two dozen? Out here living in the wild? "I don't understand," I whispered to Hugh. "I thought you guys dealt with the fae a lot? Why are you here living in caves?"

"We have always lived here," Hugh told me. "The fae only enter our realm when they want something."

"And we *normally* turn them away," Artur sneered.

Hugh glared at him, his eyes gleaming with

anger. "Say no more, Artur, lest you compromise our friendship."

Artur's mouth snapped shut, but I could see the anger burning in his craggy face. "You torture us all with your decisions," he said. "It is only my friendship with you that allows me to remain at your side."

Torture? Decisions? I leaned down and peered at the others from under Hugh's arm. The men here were naked, huge, and just as savage as Hugh, from the looks of them.

All men.

And they all stared at me.

I gasped as things clicked. "Oh, my God. There aren't any women here, are there? That's what Finian offered you. A bride."

"Silence," Hugh snapped at me.

That pissed me off. I kicked his calf from behind. "Don't you tell me to be quiet! I'm not some meek little creature that you can boss around. You're protecting me for the next month, remember? Nothing about that says I can't talk." I stepped from around Hugh and glared at him with irritation. Just as quickly, he moved to step in front of me. "I'm right, aren't I? There aren't any women here."

The men looked at Hugh, frowning, but I noticed a few kept gazing at me. Even though I was hideous, they still wanted to look at me. Yeah. I strode to the tree and grabbed the animal hide, shrugging it over my warped wings to cover my body in a semblance of modesty. "Okay, can I just say that this is fucked-up? Pardon the French and all, but seriously."

"You were the one that wished to see my people." Hugh gestured at the surrounding men. "Here we are. Does this make you happy?"

He sounded offended. Angry.

It was too much for me to process. I just shook my head. I'd wanted to see them because I'd wanted to understand Hugh. I'd hoped that understanding Hugh would help me come up with a counteroffer to entice him away from Finian's deal.

But if Hugh wanted a mate . . . I was screwed. "This female that you're doing the vow for. Is she a primordial?"

"She is," Hugh told me in a low, serious voice.

I couldn't compete. "What's her name?" I asked softly.

"I do not know it." His eyes gleamed. "The fae keep our females separate from us. We do not know how many there are, or who they are. The fae created this realm for us." He gestured. "They hold us here. We cannot leave except by their means. No one comes. No one goes."

I hugged the pelt closer to me, staring at my surroundings. At the naked, enormous men and their crude cave dwellings. "I don't understand. You have the portal necklace that Finian gave you. Why not take that and just get everyone out of here?"

"And leave our females?" Artur's deep voice was clearly disapproving. "Abandon them with no hope of reunion?"

I shivered at the bleak looks on the men's faces. "Do they always offer you this reward? A mate?"

Hugh shook his head. "This is the first time."

And judging by the avid looks on the men's faces? It was the thing they all craved most.

Well, hell. I was screwed. "I . . . think I've seen enough," I said faintly. "Can we go back now?"

I felt sick. Finian had promised a mate to Hugh for selling me out. How could I possibly compete?

We used one of the caves to draw the door. The others hovered nearby, and it was clear they had questions about me. They kept staring, even after Hugh snarled and tried to drive them away, and even after Artur pitched in to assist him. Eventually, though, they backed away, and we created the portal.

I looked behind us as the portal slowly developed. The men watched me from afar, eyes gleaming. "What's stopping them from coming after us?" I asked Hugh. "Why not follow us through? There's only a mate for you, not them."

"Finian said there were mates for all of us," Hugh told me. "No one will risk his female's life."

"Wait . . . so if you do this, he promised *all* of you mates?" At Hugh's nod, I felt even more miserable. It was bad enough when I thought I was just competing with Hugh's future mate. To learn I was competing with the future mates of twenty-four lonely males? I was doomed. Finian had played the ultimate trump card. "I must be worth a lot of money to him."

Hugh's grunt of reassurance didn't make me feel better.

Silence fell, and with it, a weird tension. No one spoke as the air shimmered, the square outline of the portal slowly coming into view like a developing photograph. Once it appeared, Hugh gave the others a meaningful look. "Patience, brothers." He took the fur throw from my shoulders and tossed it to one of the nearby waiting men, then took my hand and pulled me back through.

And then, a brief second later, we were in the bright, comforting light of my bedroom.

I blinked in surprise. My stomach growled, as if I'd been starving, even though we'd eaten not too long ago. I clutched a hand to it. Immediately, my body shuddered and I felt my wings tighten, aching. Oh, no. "Reverting," I moaned, crouching low on the carpet in my bedroom. I panted, trying to get breath into lungs that suddenly ached too much.

Hugh squatted next to me and stroked my hair again. "It is the fae realms that affect you. Here, you are able to control things much better. Just relax and let it happen."

Easy for him to say. His body didn't feel as if it was twisting inside out. I scrubbed at my scales, waiting for them to disappear under my skin again, and was relieved when they began to recede. I felt my tail and wings shift, and knew they were folding inward. As I changed, Hugh continued to stroke my hair, trying to ease me in the only way he knew how. It was weirdly . . . comforting. I knew he found my form repulsive, but he hadn't left my side. That counted for a lot in my book.

And in a way, I felt like we were in this together. Finian was using us both to get what he wanted. I hated that, but now I knew that Hugh hated it, too. And it wasn't just his happiness that was on the line; it was the happiness of all the primordials.

That changed things. If I pursued freedom for myself, I condemned so many others.

The thought ran through my mind over and over again as I sweated and heaved, my body returning back to its human state in slow, deliberate fashion. First my scales disappeared, then my wings sank into my back and my fangs retreated. Inch by inch, I returned to normal. Last, my claws retracted and I was left naked and shuddering and wholly human again.

I was also crouched low in front of Hugh, who was also naked. And now that I was human again? I was very aware of all this bare skin. This time, I was the one to avert my eyes, and I reached for the blanket on my bed, dragging it off and holding it against my skin to protect my naked body.

"So . . ." I said.

"Now you know," Hugh said in a flat voice.

"Now I know," I agreed. "And I understand. I really do. It doesn't make it easier for me, but I understand why you must do what you do."

He nodded.

"You understand that I'm not changing my mind, though? It makes me sad that my happiness will come at the cost of yours and so many others', but damn it, I have to think of myself. I'm not going to be some guy's stud animal. I still plan on finding a way around all of this."

Hugh looked almost amused. "I expect no less."

"All right, then." I rubbed my face, my skin aching from my hard transformation. "I think I need a shower, and a meal, and then we should head off to work."

"You lead," he said, gesturing.

"You want a shower, too? I have extra towels. And that realm you're from isn't exactly lending itself to clean and fresh skin."

His mouth twitched, as if amused. "Are you asking me to bathe?" He lifted one arm and sniffed under it. "Smells all right."

"This is coming from a man who lives in a realm without women," I teased. "Trust me. You should shower."

He chuckled. "Shall you join me, then?"

I sucked in a breath, scandalized . . . and titillated . . . all at once. "You realize men are not supposed to offer to share a shower with a woman?"

"Are we not?" He looked surprised. "Is it because your bathing pool is small?"

"My bathing pool is very small," I agreed, my cheeks flushing red. "And your skin would touch mine. And we'd rub all over. And that would be bad for my monster . . . and your vow." I shouldn't have said the flirty words, but I couldn't help myself. "Wouldn't want that."

"No," he said, and his husky voice sent ripples down my spine. His gaze rested on my face, and then he abruptly stood. "But I will bathe if you request it."

I blinked, hurt by his sudden change. One mention of my changeling side and it didn't matter how flirty I was. That stung. I sighed and headed to my linen closet. "I'll get you a towel." I thought for a minute, then glanced over at him. He was standing in my bedroom, his back to me, his tanned buttocks flexing as he poked my alarm clock. "I just realized . . . you don't have any clothes, do you?"

He snorted. "I prefer no clothes. They are annoying and they itch."

"Um, well, you need some clothes," I told him. "Unless you plan on not leaving my apartment for the next month."

"I will remain at your side."

"Well, if that's the case, then you really, really need clothing. I won't get many places with a big naked giant—no matter how sexy—at my side."

"What is this 'sexy'?"

"It means women will want to lick you up and down."

He paused. "You find me—sexy?"

Count on a man to focus on that. "I'm a changeling," I flirted back. "I'm not blind."

He grinned over his shoulder at me.

While Hugh showered, I called my bestie, Marie. To my relief, she picked up after the first ring.

"Hey! Where the hell have you been?" she said.

"Sorry, sorry."

"Don't be 'sorry' at me, missy. I've been texting you like a fiend and I've heard nothing! Nothing! Do you know how freaking annoying that is? How worried I've been? How many snarky things I've sent to you that were ignored?"

"I know. I'm a bad friend."

"The worst. It's unforgivable. So where have you *been*?"

"Been?"

"Uh, yeah. You've been MIA for the last two days."

I had? I didn't realize. Maybe with Hugh at my side I'd been ignoring my best friend. That was lousy of me. "I'm sorry. I suck."

"See? You don't even have the heart to disagree with me."

"I don't," I said with a laugh. "Listen. Can you do me a huge, huge favor?"

"Oh, boy. I guess I can. Does it involve a pinky swear?"

"It does. Are you at work at the security office? Can you go and bring me the biggest pair of Ramsey's clothing you can find? I need skin-out. We're talking underwear, T-shirt, shoes, and pants. Or shorts. Whatever he's got that's big and roomy."

"Men's clothes?" She chuckled, the sound throaty. "You little devil. Does that mean your problem—"

"Something like that," I interrupted, not wanting to get into the details. Marie knew about my issue—she was the only person who did—but I didn't want to have to explain the mechanics of the weird relationship I had with Hugh. "Can you just bring some of Ramsey's stuff over ASAP?"

"Okay. Be there soonish."

True to her word, Marie came over within an hour. I opened the door and she held out the bag of clothing she was carrying, eyeing the fact that I was sweaty and mussed, and wearing nothing but a sheet. "Is that the shower going?"

"It might be," I said, blushing.

"Oooh, girl," she drawled. "I smell a guy all over you." She wrinkled her nose. "And you smell like an old fishbowl or something. Where have you been? Everyone's been looking for you. Do you know how long—"

I cut her off with a wave of my hand. "I know. Long story. I'll tell you later."

Her eyes widened. "No *way* am I waiting for our regular lunch. We need to go out ASAP for a gossip-fest."

"Deal." I stuck my pinky out. Anything to get her off my porch and get back to Hugh. Normally I'd love to chat with Marie for a while, but I was leery of her seeing the big, naked shifter I was currently harboring.

She locked her pinky through mine. "I hope there's a good explanation for all this."

"There will be."

She shook her head at me. "Suit yourself. I have to run." Then, she waved and trotted down the stairs.

I shut the door and pulled out clothing, going through the bag. She'd brought me one of Ramsey's work uniforms. I could tell from the enormous size. The black T-shirt had the Russell Security logo on it, though it still didn't look nearly big enough for Hugh. It'd have to do. Marie was a smart cookie. She'd included some soft cloth athletic shorts and a pair of men's sandals, along with some boxer briefs. It would suffice, but one thing was sure—I'd need to take Hugh shopping. I considered his long, tangled hair and his claws. He needed a mani-pedi if he planned on blending. If I was taking him under my wing? That'd be the first thing I'd tackle.

Right after my shower.

When I got out, Hugh was sprawled on my bed, completely and utterly naked and flipping through a magazine with wonder. He stopped on a picture of a half-naked model, his hand tracing the photo. His cock was semierect, too.

"Find something you like?" I asked.

"Women are very beautiful," he said. "It gives me pleasure to look upon them. Also, your bed is far more comfortable than where I slept. I think we should trade."

"I don't think so," I said. "If you want to be in my bed, you have to take me with it."

He stiffened and sat up, a frown on his face. "You know that cannot be."

I shrugged. "You're the one with the vow, not me." *I just have a monster inside me.* I sighed. "I'm going to get dressed, and then we're taking you to a salon."

"Salon?"

"Yep," I said, wrapping my towel tighter around me and heading to my closet. "It's a place where they fix your hair and nails."

He snorted in derision. "Why is this important?"

"Because," I said. "You're going to be with me for the next month, and it's imperative you blend in. I don't want people wondering why we're hanging out together. You have to look like one of my clients in order for this to work."

"And my appearance is an issue?"

"Only to humans," I flirted. For some reason, his seeing me in my changeling form had broken the ice. The worst had happened, so I had nothing else to worry about. He'd seen me at my ugliest, and he'd looked away. He hadn't vomited at the sight of me, or screamed in horror. He'd simply looked away. It hurt my feelings, but I could handle it. It was oddly relieving to have someone to share my secret with. It made Hugh safe. Throw in the fact that he was tall, muscular, and more than a little wild? He was hitting all my buttons.

Hugh grunted. "If I must change my appearance, I shall."

"You must," I said sweetly. "And now you must get out, because I need to get dressed."

He didn't move. His heavy-lidded eyes ran over my towel-clad form. "I've already seen you naked, Ryder. And I find I like looking at women."

"Doesn't matter," I said, though I did feel a flush of pleasure to hear that he liked looking at me. "I'm naked and you need to leave."

"I am naked. You are not asking me to leave." He raised an eyebrow at me.

"Okay then, leave."

"I told Finian I'd remain at your side."

Oh, was he going to play this game? "Suit yourself," I said in my sweetest voice and dropped my towel. If he wanted to torture himself, he could. I didn't care, and I never backed down from a flirty challenge, that was for sure.

I smiled in satisfaction as I heard him give a soft groan, audible enough that even my poor senses could pick it up.

I studied Hugh, tilting my head as I considered his frame. "This might not have been a good idea."

He jerked at the tight collar of the T-shirt. "I agree. These clothes are very uncomfortable."

"It's not that," I murmured, pressing a hand to my hot cheeks. He would find most modern clothing uncomfortable, I suspected. Most men weren't built like Hugh. The black tee that fit Ramsey comfortably was skintight on Hugh, outlining his large, firm pectorals in an almost indecent way. His big arms bulged against the bands of the short sleeves, and I could even see the outline of his eight-pack abdomen. The boxer briefs he wore cupped him in rather magnificent ways, which made me blush.

I held out the shorts. "You need to put these on, too."

They were a must. I didn't want to think about his junk bouncing around all loose while I took him around town. It made me feel a little . . . flushed. Distracted. And I couldn't afford either.

I had to come up with a plan. First, disguise Hugh into normalcy. Then, work. Then, figure out how to lose my virginity.

It was going to be a busy day.

Once Hugh had (protestingly) donned the rest of the clothing, we set out. I knew just the place to take him where they wouldn't ask too many questions. After grabbing breakfast—and giving Hugh a quick lesson on debit cards and how they worked as money in exchange for goods—we drove out to Little Paradise. I lived in Fort Worth proper; my condo was close to downtown so I could be closer to work, but most of the shifters lived out in the country, northwest of the city and out in the sticks. Little Paradise was the current settlement of choice, and most of the businesses in the small town were owned and operated by shifters. Thanks to my line of work, I ended up there on a fairly regular basis.

I pulled up to Sweet Scissors, a small, bright teal building with pink curtains along a strip of Main Street. "Come on, Hugh. Let's go get you dolled up."

"What is this place?" he asked as he followed me in, ducking into the small doorway.

"It's called a salon," I told him as we stepped inside. "It's run by shifters, so they won't give you any trouble. Just follow my lead."

As soon as we entered, all heads turned in our direction. An elderly lady sat in one chair at the back of the room, her gray hair in curlers as the stylist fussed over her. Both of them had turned, as had the other woman, who was sweeping up hair from under her chair. Hugh's hulking form blotted out the light coming from the doorway, and one of the hairdressers blinked at the sight of him.

"Do you, um, have an appointment?" the hairstylist asked.

"Hi, Lisa. I'm Ryder from Midnight Liaisons." I beamed a smile at her. "I think I met you and your sister Lauren at the dance last month?"

Her wide-eyed gaze turned to me, as if seeing me for the first time. "Oh. Hi." Her voice was breathless. "Did you have an appointment, too?" Then her gaze flicked back to Hugh and I saw a frank appreciation there. "I'm sure I could squeeze you in."

The way she said that made my eyes narrow. "He needs a haircut and a mani-pedi. He looks a little too wild at the moment, and I need him to look more human."

"Why?" Lisa breathed, moving closer to Hugh, her broom still clutched in her hand. The other stylist continued to just stare at Hugh as well.

I was starting to question the wisdom of coming to a salon run by a pair of were-mink sisters. Clearly someone like Hugh was the equivalent of catnip for them. "Because he needs to blend," I snapped, crossing the room and thumping into one of the waiting chairs. I picked up a magazine.

"All right," Lisa said, moving closer to Hugh. She reached out to touch his hair—

And Hugh grabbed her arm, looking over at me, frowning.

"It's okay," I said, feeling a little better. "She's just going to look at your hair."

He released Lisa's arm. "My apologies."

"It's okay, big guy," Lisa said, reaching out to touch his hair again. She didn't look discouraged in the slightest. Her fingers brushed through his tangled locks, and she made a noise of appreciation at his streaks. "Are these highlights natural?"

He frowned. "I do not understand this question."

"Natural," I chimed in from afar and turned the page in my magazine, even though I hadn't looked at it once.

"Oh, mercy," she said, then fanned herself. "You are gonna be fun to work on."

Damn. I viciously turned another page in *Field & Stream,* wondering why it bothered me so much to watch Lisa leading Hugh by the hand to the sink, beaming all the while. Once he sat down, she spent a few minutes undoing his small, tangled braids and chattering up a storm to him while he cast helpless looks in my direction.

The other stylist seemed to recover from her trance and turned on her hair dryer.

Immediately, Hugh shot to his feet with a fierce snarl.

I jumped to my feet and crossed the room to put a hand on his chest before he attacked one of the now frightened women. "It's just a tool to dry hair," I murmured to him. "Be calm."

He looked down at the hand I'd placed on his chest, then at my face. "Calm," he repeated, glancing at the hair dryer again.

Lauren helpfully clicked it off.

"Nothing to worry about," I assured him. "Nothing to protect from here, either. I promise." I gave him an encouraging smile. "And I'll be right here."

He pulled up one of the salon chairs, dragging it closer to the sink. And he pointed at it. "You will sit right here, Ryder."

I didn't miss the annoyed look Lisa cast in my direction. I reveled in it and took a seat next to Hugh. "Right here."

And I bit back my smirk when his big hand landed on my clothed knee, making sure I was close at all times. It was just because he was sworn to keep me safe, but Lisa didn't know that.

And I kind of liked it.

A few hours later, Hugh was transformed into normalcy. His big claws had been filed down to regular fingernails, and his toes had been pedicured and buffed, which Hugh had proclaimed "ticklish." His unkempt hair had been chopped short on the sides and a bit longer on top, just long enough for Lisa to fashion into a lock that flopped onto his forehead in a most rakish fashion. She'd suggested shaving his sideburns (and had run a hand down his jaw, which I'd noticed). I'd declined.

I liked his sideburns. There was something about them that appealed to me a lot, and I didn't want him to become completely civilized.

We tipped her well for the quick makeover, and I ignored the fact that she slipped Hugh her phone number.

After all, we hadn't even gone over phones yet.

Next we headed back into Fort Worth proper and hit up the mall, where we dropped into the Big and Tall store. He didn't want the suit that I kept pressing on him or anything even remotely close-fitting. I had to settle for more loose athletic clothing: plain T-shirts and shorts, and the biggest pair of sneakers I'd ever seen. I didn't even know there was a size 18. We had a bit of a fight over the shoes; I insisted, but Hugh didn't like them because he couldn't "grip anything with his toes" with them on. I won the argument once I pointed out that every other person in the store wore similar shoes, but it didn't stop Hugh from muttering about how stupid they were.

But now that Hugh was dressed and wouldn't cause people to stop and stare when we walked down the street, it was time to head to work. I checked my watch. Almost six. We'd make it right on schedule.

I looked over at Hugh to give him one last word of caution. "Just remember to be silent if you don't want to answer someone, and let me cover it. The important thing is that we have to seem like things are normal, or else everyone's going to be up in our business."

"And that is bad?" he asked, his tone thoughtful.

"Very bad," I agreed. At least, it'd be bad for me. I was going to have to circumvent the rules and try to date a shifter if I wanted to get rid of this curse of mine. Marie had been fired for doing the same thing, and I didn't want to get fired. I loved my job. But I also loved being human way more than I did being a changeling, so something had to give.

When we entered the office, I was surprised to see Bathsheba still at work, and even more surprising than that, one of the Russell twins sat at Savannah's desk.

"There you are," Bath said, rushing over to me. "Where have you been? We've been worried sick."

I glanced at my pink rhinestone-encrusted watch. "I'm five minutes early?"

"For your shift, yes. But what about the last two days?"

Last two days? "What do you mean? I was here with Savannah at work last night."

Bath shook her head, looking frustrated. "Savannah's been out sick for the past two nights, and you were a no-show. I had to call Beau to get him to send someone over to help out. Everett volunteered, but he's still learning the systems. Marie held down the fort last night."

My eyes widened. Two days? "No way. I swear, I was here. With Savannah. It was just last night . . ."

Hugh leaned closer to me, his breath whispering in my ear. "Do you recall our conversation about time?"

I thought for a moment, distracted by his nearness, which was making my monster flicker under my skin. Time? The only time we'd talked about time was when . . .

Oh, no. When we'd talked about time, he'd said that it passed differently in the fae realm. And I'd unthinkingly demanded that he take me to see the primordials, never realizing that spending an hour there meant losing days here. "Two days?" I asked Bath again. Marie had mentioned that I'd been MIA for two days, but I thought she'd been griping that I was ignoring her. I didn't realize she'd actually meant two days had completely gone past.

"Two days," she repeated, the worry in her voice taking the snap of annoyance out. "I was about to call the police."

"I'm so sorry," I said lamely. "I guess I just . . . lost track of time."

"I see," Bath said primly, her gaze going to Hugh. She took him in, and her head tilted. "Is . . . excuse me, sir. Are you a shifter?"

"I am a primordial—"

"He's a were-tiger," I interrupted quickly. "From out of town."

"One of Vic's?" She looked over at me, her expression chilly. "Are you dating a *client* after all the agency's been through the last few months?"

"No," I said in a high, fake laugh. "Don't be silly." No one had to remind me of the chaos that had disrupted our small office when Marie had been caught dating vampires. It had nearly started World War Three between the shifters and vampires, and Bath was still sensitive that her agency had been used as the vehicle for the illegal dating. "Nothing like that at all. Hugh here is not local and he's not good at meeting girls, so I said I'd take him under my wing for a few days and show him how to flirt. I hope that's okay?"

She nodded absently, glancing over at Everett, who had a phone to his ear and was typing. "It's good that you're here," she murmured. "You can handle the Speed Dating meet-up tonight at Konstantine's. I was worried we'd have to reschedule."

Oh, rats. I normally ran the speed dating matches, but tonight wasn't great for me. For one, I had Hugh tagging along at my heels. "I'm not sure . . ."

"You said you want to date the harpy?" Everett was saying into the phone, a look of consternation on his face. "No, no, I don't know if she'll do that, sir. What she does in her personal life is up to her." He shot Bathsheba a "help me" look.

"Oh, dear," Bath said, hurrying back over to Everett's desk. "I'd better help out. Glad you're back, Ryder."

"Sure," I echoed, heading over to my desk. I set down my purse and turned on my computer, watching as Hugh took a standing stance next to my desk, since the stool had been moved. Bath was giving him an odd look as she pointed out things over Everett's shoulder. "Hugh," I whispered as I logged in to my computer. "We need to set up your profile. Can you write?"

"Write?"

"I'm going to guess that's a no. Okay, I'll help you, then." I pulled out a piece of paper and one of my pink, glittery pens, uncapping it. "What's your last name?"

"I am Hugh. You know this."

"You're not Hugh Hugh, though."

"No. Just Hugh."

"No one here has just one name," I told him. Well, unless you were a pop star. "You need a second one."

He looked puzzled. "Why?"

"You know what? Never mind," I told him, writing. "You're going to be Hugh Merino. The local tigers are all in the Merino clan." Now I just needed to hope that the tiger alpha didn't show up for any reason. Not that there was a high chance of that happening—his mate was pregnant with their first child, so it was safe to say that the odds were against him showing up at a dating agency.

I continued to fill out the form as Hugh peered over my shoulder. "Sex is male," I said, checking the box. "Age? You know what? I'm just going to put down thirty before you can give me another one of those 'time moves differently' answers." I marked religion as "other" and status as "networking," since he wasn't really seeking a woman. He had one of those waiting for him as soon as he delivered me to the fae. I wrinkled my nose in distaste at the thought.

"What does that say?" Hugh asked, and he leaned in so close that his breath whispered against my ear as he regarded the paper I made notes on. His nearness was making my skin ripple in response to him, and my nipples hardened. Eep. Under my desk, I shook my hands out and flexed them, willing my monster to stay back. I fought with it for a few moments, won the battle, and scowled at Hugh. He knew my problem.

Time for a little revenge. "Favorite sex position?" I asked sweetly. I'd intended to leave that one blank, but since he was being a jerk . . .

He jerked backward. "What?"

Both Bathsheba and Everett turned to stare at us, and I waved at Hugh. "Keep it down," I hissed. "Now. Favorite sex position."

He gave me a blank look, then leaned in again to whisper in my ear. "There is more than one?"

"Uh, yeah."

"What is it?"

I turned and stared at Hugh, who was leaning

way too close again. His cheeks were ruddy, as if he was blushing, and he looked uncomfortable. He shifted from one foot to another and gave me an expectant look. "Are you kidding?" I asked.

"No." He glanced at the others, then leaned in again, giving me a very interested look. "Tell me more. I must know these things if I am to please my mate."

I tapped my glittery pen on the desk, regarding him. Something told me I wasn't the only virgin here. "You know what? We'll come back to that later."

"But—"

"Later," I hissed. I gave Bath a sweet smile as she looked over at us and tucked her purse under her arm. "You leaving, Boss?"

"I'm meeting Beau for dinner," she said and smoothed a hand over her ponytail. "Date night."

"Don't do anything I wouldn't do," I said and gave her an exaggerated wink.

"But you—" Hugh began.

"Hssst!" I said, turning to glare at him. He was going to ruin my carefully crafted persona of office flirt if he blurted out that I was a virgin.

Hugh raised an eyebrow at me but went silent.

I turned back to Bath and gave her a cheery wave. "Like I was saying, have a good one."

"You, too," she said. "Call me if you or Everett need anything."

"Will do. Though I am sure I can help Everett with everything he needs." I wiggled my eyebrows at the handsome were-cougar at the desk across the room. "He just needs to ask."

"You flirting with me, Ryder?" Everett grinned at me.

"You know it."

I heard a low growl in Hugh's throat, and I stomped on his foot under my desk.

Everett gave us a curious look, leaning back in his office chair. "So, man," he said, turning to Hugh. "Where you from?"

"He's from Alaska," I said quickly, thinking fast. "You know how they say that there's only one woman for every eight men there? The town he grew up in was more like thirty to one, so he's not familiar with how to talk to girls. Which is why I'm helping him out."

Everett scratched his jaw, regarding us. "Okaaaay," he said, drawling the word. "And what kind of shifter did you say you were again?"

"He's a—" I started.

"Primordial," Hugh finished. "Long-tooth."

I scowled at Hugh.

"Huh? What the hell is that?" Everett looked confused.

"It's an Alaskan name for tiger," I said quickly, then turned to glare at Hugh. "Isn't that right?"

Hugh stared back at me.

"Why don't you go and get the stool out of the storeroom so you don't have to hover over me any longer?" I fixed Hugh with my sweetest smile. "And I'm going to make myself some coffee."

He considered me for a long moment, then glanced at Everett. "I will return."

"You do that," I said and headed to the coffeepot.

As soon as Hugh left the room, Everett got up from his chair and sprinted to my side. He touched my elbow—which made me glad I was wearing a daisy yellow long-sleeved cardigan over my floral white-and-yellow sundress—and leaned close. "Hey, Ryder?"

"Hmm?" I pulled out the bag of coffee grounds, noticing that we had a new coffeepot. Sweet.

"How well do you know that guy?"

I sniffed the bag of coffee, enjoying the scent. God, I loved coffee. "Why?"

"There aren't any shifter clans in Alaska. At least, not voluntarily." Everett frowned and leaned closer to me. "And I've never heard of a long-tooth. I just don't—"

A big hand shoved Everett backward. Hugh stepped between us, a low, angry rumble in his throat. "Do not stand so close to Ryder."

Everett raised his hands. "Chill, man. I was just talking to her—"

"You were standing too close," Hugh reiterated.

"It's okay," I said, putting a hand on Hugh's clothed arm and patting his sleeve. "Everett was just looking out for me. Everything's fine. Isn't that right, Everett?"

But Everett was scowling at both of us. Crap. I looked from the snarly were-saber-tooth at my side to the bristling were-cougar a few feet away. I needed to defuse this situation or there was going to be a catfight. Literally. I quickly scooped coffee into the basket and shoved it back in place, then hit the button to start the pot. "So, Everett, where's that tall, dark, and handsome twin brother of yours?"

Everett eyed us a moment longer, then returned to his desk. "Ellis? He's Lily-sitting."

"Ah," I said. Lily was the feral human girl who had been rescued from the crazy vampire at the same time as Marie. Problem was, Marie had been turned into a shifter, so she was considered "safe" and one of the team. Lily was human and completely messed up from her captivity, so everyone was afraid to release her for fear that she'd spill the Alliance's secrets. Last I'd heard, Lily had tried to escape twice now, so someone was constantly with her. Today, it seemed, it was Ellis. "Well, tell him I said hello and I miss him."

"I'm sure he misses seeing your pretty face, too," Everett teased back.

Hugh scowled at me, crossing his arms, as if he disapproved of this entire conversation.

I ignored Hugh, hovering by the coffeepot until the first cup was brewed. I took it for myself and doctored it with massive amounts of cream and sugar. Then I blew on it, humming as if this had been a normal day and a massive Ice Age shifter hadn't been hovering a step behind me. "Hey, Everett, I'm leaving shortly for the speed dating session. You going to be okay without me?"

"Lonely," Everett teased. "But okay."

Hugh said nothing, but his brows were low on his face. He was clearly not happy.

"Well, you have my number if you need me," I said to Everett. "I'm taking Hugh with me."

"And you have my number if you need anything, right?" I couldn't miss the stress in Everett's voice. It was so cute that he was being so protective.

"I do," I said with a sunny smile, and ignored Hugh's snarl.

Chapter Seven

We drove to Konstantine's, and Hugh scowled at me the entire time from the passenger seat.

"What is it?" I finally asked.

"How familiar are you with that shifter?"

I glanced over at him, juggling my coffee cup with the steering wheel. "Who, Everett? He's a friend and a real sweetie."

Hugh's eyes narrowed. "Your words to him were provocative."

"Of course they were. We have fun flirting. It's harmless."

"It is not harmless. He is interested in you."

"No, he's not," I told him, shaking my head. "Everett's a were-cougar and he thinks I'm human, so I'm off-limits." I frowned, though. Bathsheba was human, and she was married to Beau. Marie was human—once—and she was with Josh. And recently the alphas had gotten together to create a more lenient set of rules for dating humans. So theoretically, I *wasn't* off-limits to Everett anymore.

But Hugh had it all wrong. Everett was just a friend. Even as I told myself that, my scheming mind started to wonder . . . could I get Everett to have sex with me? If I told him my problem? He'd be more understanding than most.

I'd consider it. I wasn't ready to pounce on Everett just yet. He was nice, but he didn't drive me crazy. And I knew he definitely wasn't my True Love, so he was more or less just a buddy.

"You say provocative things to me as well," Hugh said, interrupting my thoughts. "Are these harmless, too?"

"Of course." My voice was smooth. "I'm destined for breeding, remember? How could I possibly say anything in a serious manner to you? And you have a primordial mate waiting."

"I remember."

"You've flirted back with me," I pointed out, thinking of our banter in my bedroom. "Were you serious?"

Hugh said nothing.

Now . . . that was interesting. I pondered this as we turned into the parking lot of Konstantine's. I parked the car, chugged the last of my coffee, and turned to Hugh. "We should talk about tonight."

"What about tonight?"

"Well, for starters, I'm running this group that we call Speed Dating. Or Speed Mating. It's for supernaturals to meet other supernaturals, and there are going to be a lot of shifters here tonight, and some vampires." I waited for his reaction. Some of the shifters didn't like vampires, and Konstantine's was a notorious vampire hangout. But Hugh didn't react, so I continued. "We have a lot of male clients, and I flirt with all of them. That's kind of who I am. So I don't want you to be surprised or getting all up in anyone's grill if they come and chat with me, understand?"

He gave me a narrow-eyed look but said nothing.

"Also. Since you're supposed to be a client, I signed you up for the speed mating." I gave him my most angelic smile. "It was kind of last-minute, but it's perfect. This way you can be at my side without seeming like a creeper."

"What is a creeper?"

I waved that off. "Never mind that. You should be asking about the speed mating."

"I am not here to mate with other females, Ryder. I am here to ensure that you remain safe—"

"Yadda, yadda, I know. But this is part of your cover. You have to do this."

"So I am to do this while you laugh and say things to other men to entice them?"

"You're not familiar with the concept of flirting, are you? It's just harmless words. Men and women do it all the time."

"Just words."

"Yep. Just words. Doesn't mean anything."

"What if they touch you while they say it?"

"Well, then that means something different."

"I see." Hugh considered this, then glanced over at me. "The were-cougar was going to touch you."

I frowned. I didn't remember that. Had Hugh misinterpreted the signals? "I won't let anyone touch me, I promise." I didn't want them to, anyhow.

To my surprise, he extended his pinky. "Swear it."

I grinned and linked my pinky with his. "Sworn." Just that bare touch of our skin made a shiver go up and down my body, though, and I recoiled away, trying to recover before we went into the restaurant. "Just . . . give me a minute."

"This swearing is not good for you," Hugh observed.

I chuckled despite the pangs wracking my body. "You started it."

"So I did," he said thoughtfully.

Speed dating? Unmitigated disaster.

I sat Hugh down and explained the concept to him. He would sit at a numbered table, where he would be given a small card. Every five minutes, I'd ring a bell and the men would sit down at a new table with a new woman. The concept was to get to know each other for a few minutes. Simple enough. At the end of the evening, everyone would write down the assigned numbers of the people they thought they would be compatible with. If there was a match, I'd set them up later in the system.

In the meantime, I made Hugh promise he couldn't talk about primordials, fae, the primordial realm, Finian, his vow, changelings, or anything along those lines. Just smile and be friendly, I assured him. And then I hurried away to explain the details of the speed mating game to the others in attendance. Hugh glared at me as I left his side; for a moment I thought he'd follow, but he didn't.

As I met one shifter, I was surprised to see he was wearing sunglasses indoors. "Hi, my name is Ryder," I told him. I gave a cheerful wave to avoid doing a handshake, but he stuck his hand out anyhow. Ah, shoot. Blind.

"I'm Brad," he said, smiling, his hand still extended. "Michigo."

Dang it. I hated handshakes. There was something inherently intimate about putting your hand in someone else's, and the closer I got to my birthday, the more the small touches bothered me. I winced and put my hand in his, shaking it as quickly as possible. Just like that, my beast reared, and I bit my lip so hard that I tasted blood. When I was calm, I said, "Pleased to meet you, Brad. Do you have any questions about the speed dating tonight?"

"Just one. Are you one of the dates?" He grinned.

"You big flirt," I teased, shaking my hands out and flexing them to will my monster away. "I'm just the organizer."

"But you have such a lovely voice," he told me, that smile still on his face. "I'm sure the rest of you matches."

"I'm sure it does," I said coyly. "But I'm human and not on the menu."

"Some of us have educated palates and aren't

afraid to try a little something new," Brad said. "But I have to say, I'm disappointed."

I chuckled. "I'm sure you'll enjoy meeting our lovely ladies here tonight."

"You'll keep me in mind if you ever decide you want to date a shifter?" He continued to smile in my direction, pulling out his white cane. "I would tell you that you have a lovely smell, but most humans don't appreciate that."

"I've been around enough shifters to know a compliment when I hear one," I flirted. "But I'll be glad to help you if you'd like assistance from table to table."

"I'd say no, but then that would deprive me of your presence, and I can't resist," Brad said with a grin. "So I'll accept."

"Perfect," I said, linking my arm through his but making sure to touch just his coat sleeve. I still had ripples of muscle jerking along my back, but I kept my fists clenched in the hopes that it'd die down. After a few moments, it did, and I exhaled a sigh of relief. One hurdle down.

I rang the bell, clicked on my stopwatch, and the speed dating started.

I knew it was going to be a problem the minute Hugh sat down at the first table. He scowled at everyone, for starters, and then proceeded to snarl at his poor date, who trembled with fear. I bit my lip, watching. Should I intervene? I hesitated.

Then Hugh turned and gave me a foul look, as if this was all my fault.

I decided to let him suffer through the entire speed date cycle after that.

I rang the bell soon enough, the five minutes passing like eternity—for myself *and* Hugh, I imagined—and then I headed over to escort Brad to his next table. "Find someone you like?" I asked him.

"Yes, but she says she doesn't date shifters," he flirted back.

What a doll. "I meant at your table."

"Ah. There's potential, but her voice wasn't nearly as lovely as yours," he told me.

"Maybe this next will do the trick," I said, steering him with my hand on his sleeve, careful to avoid skin contact. I dropped Brad off before he could flirt more and resumed my position at the head of the room, where I rang the bell again. "Date number two, start!"

Five couples immediately began talking and shaking hands. One couple did not: couple number two—Hugh and a pretty were-something. I should have guessed. She'd extended her hand for him to shake. He'd taken it, examined it for a moment, and then handed it back as if not interested. Poor woman.

As I watched the couples interact, my gaze slid back to Brad. Michigo. I recognized the name—were-otter family. I'd never met Brad before, though. I'd have remembered someone who flirted as blatantly as I did. He'd definitely seemed interested, though, and even though I hated to admit it, his blindness had me intrigued.

If he was blind, he wouldn't notice me shifting into something else if he touched me. He'd feel I was changing, all right, but there were ways around that. I could handcuff him to the headboard of my bed, for starters. Or get him drunk. Something.

He wasn't my True Love, but this had potential. I might lose my virginity after all.

I just had to ditch my big shadow.

I hid my bubbling excitement as the speed dating continued. Hugh seemed downright miserable, as did each woman he sat with. That was a shame. Maybe if I could find him someone to date, I could get him off my back long enough to hop into bed with a stranger.

Ugh. I didn't like the way that sounded, but I was running low on options.

I rang the final bell. "All right, everyone. Final round is over! Please swing by to turn in your cards." I put on my cheeriest smile. "If there are any matches, I'll notify you via email later tonight."

I collected cards as people approached me, and I noticed that a few had started chatting on their own, laughing and talking. That was a good sign. That meant we'd have a few promising matchups. The worst was when everyone filed out without talking. Then I knew the evening had gone badly.

I received eleven cards—Hugh's was blank and he gave me another obnoxious glare before moving to my side—and I glanced down the row to see that Brad was still in his seat. "Wait here," I told Hugh and set off for Brad before Hugh could argue with me. I sauntered up and noticed that Brad had turned his head toward me before I even got there, his shifter sense of smell alerting him to my presence. "Decide you couldn't get enough of this place?" I teased, putting my hand on his sleeve again. "Or just waiting for me?"

He grinned. "Waiting for the perfect opportunity to point out that the laws changed and shifters can now date humans with the approval of their alpha. Considering I'm the alpha of my group, I give myself permission. So what do you say to drinks?"

"Drinks?" I pretended to consider this, even while my heart was skipping madly in my chest. Excitement made my hands curl, and my fingers dug into his sleeve. "Don't drinks usually lead to more?"

"Only if both parties want it," he said, getting to his feet. He stood close to me—extremely close. "Why, are you interested in it being more?"

I need sex! I wanted to blurt, but I kept my voice coy. "I might be—"

One massive hand descended on Brad's chest, and one on my shoulder, and we were forcibly separated. Hugh stepped between us. "This woman is not available for you," Hugh said in an angry voice. "Do not touch her."

"Hugh," I said sweetly, my teeth gritted. "Step off. This is none of your business."

"It is my business," Hugh said.

Brad lifted his hands in the air, walking cane

tucked under his arm. "I don't want any trouble. I didn't realize she was claimed."

"I'm not," I protested. "I'm not his mate. And I do want to go out for drinks."

"No," Hugh said again and turned back to me. His cat-eyes were fierce. "I have endured this speedy dating because you insisted. Now it is my turn to insist. Ryder, you are to leave with me."

I shrugged Hugh's big hand off my shoulder, furious. "And what if I say no?"

"It sounds like the lady doesn't want to go with you, friend," Brad began mildly. Far too mild for an alpha, I thought bitterly. It was clear Brad was a bit of a liar. He gave an apologetic smile in Hugh's direction. "Perhaps you should leave her alone."

"My job is to remain at her side and protect her virginity," Hugh snarled in Brad's face. His big hand clamped down on my shoulder again.

Despite the fact that we were in a side room at the restaurant, several people in the next room turned to look over at us, overhearing Hugh's words.

"Oh, my God," I moaned. "You did *not* just say that out loud in a crowded restaurant."

"And if she doesn't want it protected?" Brad asked.

"Yeah," I said, pushing Hugh's hand off my shoulder again.

"Then I will protect it for her," Hugh said. "Against her will if I must."

"You can't make me leave," I hissed at him. "This is a public place." I was safe from him here.

Hugh leaned in to me, his face close to mine. "I am sorry for what I am about to do."

"Do? What—"

His hand moving to the back of my neck, he leaned forward and pressed his mouth to mine in a startling, fierce kiss. His lips mashed against my own, and his scent was in my nostrils, his body pressed to mine.

Then, just as quickly, he pulled away. I stared up at him, dazed.

"Now, we leave," Hugh said.

I blinked, trying to process all of this. Kiss? Leave? What? He grabbed my hand in his and dragged me toward the doors of the restaurant.

I immediately tried to jerk away, realizing what all this was about.

He was deliberately activating my changeling side. Hugh knew that if my curse kicked in, I'd have no choice but to leave with him. Anger burned inside me, but it was quickly swallowed up by the transformation spiraling through my body. My monster coiled and reared, and I felt my skin shiver with awareness. Anger at Hugh blossomed, then quickly turned to fear when others started to look at us.

Damn him! I stopped struggling and gave everyone a cheerful wave, practically running with Hugh as he stomped toward the parking lot. I had to make things seem like they were normal, or else someone was sure to follow us out due to concern for me. And that was the last thing I wanted—if someone followed us, they'd get a glimpse of my scaly side.

It was evident to me that the change was going to come whether I wanted it or not. Even now, I could feel the throb in my shoulder blades that was the onset of my wings, and my gums ached from where my fangs were about to pop. My grip tightened in Hugh's, and I knew the pressure I was exerting would soon be intense.

But if that didn't communicate my anxiety, nothing would.

As soon as we got to the parking lot, I bolted, dashing away from Hugh. He let me, and I continued on, racing for my car. My hand fumbled to find my keys, but claws were sprouting and my muscles were clenching, and it was impossible for me to concentrate. Pain erupted, throbbing through my body.

Too late. Before I could even open the door to my vehicle, my legs gave out. I crouched, huddling around myself as my changes tore through me.

Hugh crouched low next to me. His hand smoothed down my back, ignoring the fact that it was lumpy and the muscles were seething. "I am sorry, Ryder."

"You . . . suck . . ." I whispered between gasps, my hands clenched tight as my tail ripped out of my back. I gave a small cry of pain, only to have it swallowed as he pulled me against his chest, muffling my cries as he held me close.

"It grieves me to do this to you," he murmured,

and his hand stroked my hair even as he cradled me tight.

I fought him for a moment, but feebly. The transformation was happening, and I couldn't stop it any more than I could stop him from holding me close.

And what was worse? With every stroke of his hand on my hair, I didn't want him to stop holding me.

I'd never been held by a man before, after all. And since this one knew what I was going to turn into, he wouldn't flinch away. Well, not much. As the scales coated my skin and my face hardened into bumps and horns, I burrowed closer to his chest, letting him hide me away in the dark, shadowy parking lot.

And I breathed in his wildly intoxicating scent. He smelled so good. So masculine. And his arms around me felt delicious. My pulse was throbbing hard, but it seemed centered between my legs instead of its normal place. Liquid heat was pouring through my muscles and I groaned again, the presence of Hugh and his nearness sweeping away any memories of pain.

I'd take a transformation if it let a man hold me. I was starved for it. Aching. This was one of the most deliciously sinful moments of my life, and I could almost forget that I had scales, wings, and a tail.

His hand continued to stroke my hair as my body cramped and shivered through the change. "I have you, Ryder. I have you."

It was weird. Two minutes ago I wanted to smack Hugh in the face for ruining my plans. Now? I felt cherished, comforted . . . and aroused. I laid my hand on the broad flat of his chest . . . and was repulsed by what I saw. Long talons on the tip of each finger. Brownish-green scales. Bumps that crept up my arms like bizarre jewelry.

Not a pretty sight.

The moment ruined, I pushed Hugh away and averted my face, turning my back to him. "Don't touch me."

"Very well." He still crouched next to me, but he no longer held me. His hand fell away from my hair, and I could have wept from the loss.

Now that my arousal had died, though, so did the transformation. I bit down on one scaly knuckle as the reversal began to rip through me, reverting me back to my cute, blond human form. Minutes later, I stood there, panting heavily, my clothing stretched and ripped in several places.

And I straightened and glared at Hugh, adjusting my now loose cardigan. "Are you going to pull a stunt like that every time I talk to a man?"

"I don't know. Are you going to offer your virginity to every man you meet?" His voice was flat, cold.

"Does it matter?" I cried out, scooping up my purse and shoving the contents back into it. I must have knocked it over when I'd changed, and makeup had spilled out onto the parking lot asphalt. "I start to turn into a monster as soon as any man touches me. I could offer my virginity to everyone I meet and no one would be able to see past the scaly thing I turn into. They think they're getting a Barbie, and they're getting Cloverfield instead."

"I . . . do not understand these things."

I wiped at my cheeks, hating that they were wet with tears. "Just shut up, Hugh. Just shut up."

Chapter Eight

We drove back to work in silence, and I had to fake a cheery mood at the agency for the rest of the night. If Everett noticed anything weird about my now stretched-out clothing or the holes in my white espadrilles where my toe-claws had forced through the leather, he said nothing. Good man.

Hugh was silent and surly, too, though he didn't hover. Instead, he crossed his arms and sat on that stool and watched me as I worked. I pretended to be busier than I actually was, poking with flyers and updating calendars for the next five years just to have something to do. So I wouldn't have to look at him and be embarrassed that I'd cried because I couldn't have a man hold me without going all Godzilla on him.

Life wasn't fair. I'd just have to suck it up and make lemonade with my lemons, or I'd soon find myself with no lemons at all. And besides, I still had hope. My True Love could be out there. If I met him, he could solve all my problems. Hugh wasn't it, that was for sure. His kiss had triggered an instant change. Brad hadn't been it, either—I could tell that just from the handshake. So someone else was still on the playing field.

The rest of the night passed slowly, but by the time 3:00 a.m. rolled around, even coffee couldn't keep me my usual perky self. When Everett offered to lock up, I thanked him and headed out with Hugh, ignoring the strange looks that Everett was tossing in our direction. No doubt he was wondering what kind of client wanted to hang around until three in the morning, but he didn't ask.

That was the good thing about working with shifters and supernaturals in general. They tended to be a secretive lot, so if you were equally secretive? They didn't pry too much. Just a side perk of the job, I supposed.

My stomach growled, and as I pulled out my car keys, I looked over at Hugh. "There's a twenty-four-hour Chinese takeout place nearby. How do you feel about fried rice and mu shu pork?"

"I have no feelings for them."

I chuckled despite myself. "Then you don't mind if I order them. Get in the car."

We drove to the place. Since I had company, I ordered two family-sized meals, complete with a myriad of dishes and all the rice and hot and sour soup a person could possibly want. When we got back to my condo, I took the food into the kitchen and began to unpack tray after tray of steamed vegetables, lo mein, rice, chicken, and pork. It all smelled delicious, and I was starving. Hugh arrived at my side to sniff everything.

"Help yourself," I told him. I made myself a plate and sat down.

He followed my lead, and I couldn't help but giggle when he sat down with three of the cartons in front of himself and a spoon (Hugh didn't like forks). He'd gone straight for the main course. Couldn't blame him. I studied him as he ate, noticing the way his eyes widened as he took a bite of General Tso and then ate more of it. Seemed like my were-saber-tooth liked spicy food.

"So. You knew that kissing me would change me," I pointed out. "I don't think I ever told you that."

He looked uneasily at me. "It is common knowledge that fledgling changelings are unable to control their sexual impulses."

Oh, great. "I like how that is common knowledge to everyone but the changeling herself. I had to find out the hard way. What else do you know about changelings?"

He hesitated.

"Oh, come on," I said, getting annoyed. "What's the harm in telling me? It's pretty clear that I know some of the basics. I just want to compare notes. That's all."

He took another big mouthful of General Tso and chewed, thinking. After he swallowed, he looked over at me. "*Changeling* is a human word. The fae have adopted it because it amuses them, but when I was young, your kind were called *fionn gainne*. It means 'pretty scale.'"

I snorted. "Nothing pretty about it."

He looked amused at my reaction. "Your kind are quite prized."

I waved my chopsticks in the air. "So I'm told. Go on."

"*Fionn gainne* are very rare, and in childhood, very fragile. The fae realm is harsh and unforgiving, which is why the fae have flourished despite human encroachment. Their realm is safe for them precisely because it is so dangerous. No one else would dare live there."

I said nothing. I'd had my taste of primordial town and had agreed that it wasn't for me. "So the fae leave the baby changelings with humans because it's too dangerous on home turf?"

"The children are glamoured to look human and hide their natural form. And yes, then they are exchanged for a human child."

My eyes widened, and I shoved my chopsticks onto my plate, my stomach suddenly churning. "What happens to the human child?"

"The fae are callous with life," Hugh said in a flat voice. "They think nothing of toying with others as long as it serves their purposes."

I wanted to touch the brand on the inside of my thigh, the mark Finian had left so he'd recognize me as "his" property. The more I found out about the fae, the less I liked. "So I was left out here. Does . . . does this happen often? The baby switching?"

He shrugged. "I have heard rumors, but the news we get from the fae realms consists mostly of what they choose to tell my kind." His expressive mouth grew wry. "Luckily, they like to brag."

"So it seems." I studied him curiously. "You've seen another like me, though, haven't you?"

"I have," he agreed. "It was some time ago. Months. Perhaps years. The fae thought she was very interesting. She had a very wild streak until they settled her down and bred her. You might even be one of her pups. I think her name was Jer-See Dayvil."

"Jer-See? Oh, my God. The Jersey Devil?" My mouth dropped open in horror. "I'm related to that?" Every kid had heard of the Jersey Devil—the big, scary, winged monster in the woods that terrorized early settlers of America.

Hugh looked uncomfortable. "It's possible. There are not many of your kind. That is why you are so highly prized. I know of less than a dozen. Owning a changeling is quite a status symbol for the fae. Finian has been waiting for you for many years."

I blew out a breath. "So the Jersey Devil, huh? I guess she never found her True Love."

Hugh turned his catlike gaze to me. "You speak of this, but I am not familiar with it. What is this 'true love'?"

"A fortune-teller that had fae blood told me that there was one person on earth that is my perfect match. My True Love. If I find that person, I will succeed in circumventing my curse and won't transform when he touches me."

Hugh gave me a pitying look. "Ryder. You are not cursed. The other form is what you *are*. That *is* your real form. There is no true love that can fix it. She lied to you."

I swallowed hard. "No. That's not true." It couldn't be.

"It is true. Your real nature overcomes the glamour when you get excited. That is why you lose control of it. That is who you are. You are not a human with a creature side. You are a creature who pretends to be human."

Hot tears pricked my eyes as desolation sank in. What he said had the ring of truth, and Hugh couldn't lie to me. "So there's no one who can save me?"

"I have never heard of such a thing."

I wanted to bawl like a baby. It felt as if the rug had been dragged out from under my feet. All hope, vanished in an instant. "Then I'm screwed."

"I am sorry, Ryder." Hugh set his food down and his big hand clasped my shoulder again. "I know you think I am cruel, but if there were another way for you, my task would not be so easy."

This was easy for him? I felt bleak. "Well," I said. "Thanks for the kiss, at any rate. The ones I get are few and far between, and they always end badly."

He gave me a curious look. "Was it a good one?"

"To be honest, it was so brief that I didn't exactly critique it."

Hugh stared at me for so long that it made me nervous. Finally, he said, "Are . . . are they longer?"

"Kisses?" I was so surprised for a moment that I couldn't answer. My body felt suddenly flushed with arousal, but I didn't transform. He hadn't touched me, after all. I could get turned on, as long as I wasn't triggered by touch. "There are lots of different kinds of kisses, Hugh. Some are short and sweet, and some take so long that they leave both parties breathless at the end."

Or so I'd heard.

His gaze went to my mouth, and I felt my nipples harden in response. "Breathless? By merely pressing mouths?"

"It's not just that," I told him, licking my lips. "That's not the only way you kiss. You can nibble on the other person's lips, or suck on them, or you can use tongue."

"Tongue?"

"Yes. You . . ." I blushed. "You thrust tongues into each other's mouths. It's very erotic."

"Tell me more about this. Are you very experienced?"

My mouth twisted into a wry smile. "Not at all. I have a problem, remember?"

He looked skeptical, one heavy eyebrow arching. "Then how do you know how it is?"

I laughed, because he looked so very put out at the thought that I might be lying to him. "I have eyes, of course. I see what people do. And then there is always the television." My eyes widened and I stood up, forgetting about dinner. "Holy cow, I haven't shown you the television, have I? Come on, follow me."

He did, carrying one of the cartons of takeout with him as he followed after me. "What is this 'television'? You will explain it to me."

"I'd be better off showing you," I told him. "Sit down and I'll get the remote."

He thumped down on one end of my sofa, still eating and watching me with curiosity. I noticed that his gaze was following my figure and that it focused on my behind when I knelt to pick up the remote from its place on the TV stand. So Hugh was checking me out? Must have been because we'd been talking about sexy things and his experience with women was limited. If I had no experience with men and one was right in front of me, I supposed I'd stare at him, too.

Still, it made me feel warm, and I might have rolled my hips a little more as I strode back across my living room to sit next to Hugh on the couch. I pointed the remote and immediately the TV clicked on, the news blaring. I appreciated the way that Hugh jumped, startled, at the sight, his eyes going wide. I glanced at the TV, trying to see it through his eyes. Nothing exciting was on, just a weather report. "It's a box that transmits pictures," I explained to him. "And we can pick what we want to watch. Let me see if I can find something with kissing."

I flipped to the next channel, and Hugh jerked as horses galloped onto the prairie—an old western. I flipped past it again, and Hugh turned to stare at me.

"Where were those horses going?"

I shrugged. "I don't know. It's just an old western clip."

"Western?" He pointed his fork at the screen again. "I wish to see more of the horses. They are tasty eating and rare creatures in my world."

"They're not rare here," I told him. "And no one in the United States eats horses."

He snorted. "Then they are fools."

I clicked past a few more channels, ignoring his sounds of protest as we passed by interesting item after interesting item. But I needed to find kissing, darn it. Why was it that I couldn't find anything remotely romantic at three in the morning? I looked over at Hugh, who was shoveling General Tso into his mouth, his wide eyes fixed on the TV as someone held up a hand mixer on a shopping channel.

I glanced at my small DVD collection, but I didn't see anything that screamed sexy moments. Time for desperate measures. I clicked over to a paid channel and selected the first porno that came up. "We're only going to watch the first few minutes of this, okay?"

"What is it?"

"You'll see," I told him and clicked Play.

I winced as cheesy music filled the room and a pizza boy walked down the hall of an apartment building. I wanted to cover my face with shame over the cliché, but I snuck a peek at Hugh instead. He watched, rapt, no longer eating, as the pizza guy rang the doorbell and began to converse with the scantily clad blonde who answered the door.

Then his eyes bugged.

I stifled my giggle at his look of shock and peeked at the TV again. Sure enough, the blonde had the pizza boy by the collar of his shirt and was dragging him into her apartment, her mouth locked on his. There was lots of tongue, and deep, breathless moans coming from both of them as they smooched loudly and made tons of noise. The girl kept making this high-pitched whimper in her throat as she kissed the man. The sound both embarrassed me and fascinated me, and I felt my monster prickle. I bit the inside of my cheek to hold it back and glanced over at Hugh.

His eyes had narrowed, and he stared at the TV so hard that his face was drawn into stark lines of concentration.

For some reason, that made my changeling side prickle harder, and I felt my body begin to ache with the need to transform. I quickly lifted the remote to turn the TV off again.

Hugh stilled me, careful to grasp my sleeve and not touch my skin. "I want to see." His gaze remained locked on the TV screen.

I lowered my hand and left the TV on, but I didn't look at the screen. I couldn't look at it any longer. I stared at Hugh instead, trying to blot out the noises coming from the TV as I watched his profile.

He was utterly fascinated, his eyes shining with the reflection from the screen, every muscle locked rigidly in place as he continued to watch.

It occurred to me that this might have been his first experience with any sort of sexuality, given that his people—the primordials—had no women in their little dimension. I wasn't sure that a porno flick should be his gateway to carnal knowledge, but I didn't know what else to do.

"Yeah, you like that, slut?" one of the voices on the TV said.

That caught my attention, and wide-eyed, I turned back to the screen. The man on camera had his pants unzipped and his dick out. The woman was kneeling in front of him, and as I watched in a mixture of arousal and horror, he took his penis and smacked her face with it.

"You want that, slut?" the man asked again, and the woman on TV moaned and rubbed her face against him.

I felt a hot pulse scorch through my body. "I can't sit here," I told Hugh and jerked to my feet. It was too awkward. And arousing. One touch from Hugh and my wings would burst out of my back. I left the remote on the couch.

If Hugh noticed my hasty retreat, he certainly didn't follow.

I suspected I wouldn't see him until the movie was over. I shook my head to clear it. A nice, cold shower, and then I was off to bed. I'd try my hardest not to think any more about Hugh watching porn in my living room, his eyes gleaming catlike as he watched people fuck on-screen.

I certainly tried not to think about what would

have happened if I'd stayed in the room with him. Would he have looked over at me at some point? Wanted to try something out? My breath quickened and I touched my cheek . . . and imagined him feeling my ugly scales.

Sadness washed over me. Yeah. Not in this lifetime.

Chapter Nine

My calendar was all messed up, thanks to the missing days, but I prioritized things, and first on the list was a make-up lunch with my bestie, Marie.

Marie Bellavance was a few years older than me and pretty much my polar opposite. She was snarky and sarcastic, where I was cheery and happy. I liked makeup and cutesy things. Marie wore big nerd glasses, did nothing with her dark, curly hair, and had the most boring wardrobe possible. She also cussed like a sailor, always in French. And as of last month, she was a newly turned were-cougar.

But I absolutely loved Marie. I'd adored her since she'd first walked into Midnight Liaisons. Despite her sour personality, she was a blast to be around. She had a sharp mind and a sharper tongue, and I'd loved watching her wield it against the unsuspecting. Sitting across from her every night at work had made the time pass fast, and we'd had so much fun together. During slow periods, we'd chatted for hours about everything in the world.

Marie also knew my secret side. After a client had gotten a bit too fresh with me once and mistaken my casual flirting for genuine attraction, he'd grabbed my hand. I'd twisted free and retreated to the back conference room while Marie had shown him out, and she'd caught me mid-change. Instead of flipping out, she'd calmly shut the door again and waited until I'd returned, then she'd asked me if I'd needed a drink of water. I'd begged and pleaded for her not to say anything, and we'd made our first pinky swear that night. I hadn't realized that Marie's dark, sad eyes had been so accepting because she'd had secrets of her own, and when she'd gotten sicker and sicker, I'd realized that I could keep her secrets, too.

Those mutual secrets had cemented our bond. And even though Marie had been fired from the agency and was now working as Beau's personal assistant, we were still best friends. I missed seeing her sitting across from me every night, though. Savannah was a sweet girl, and quiet, but she wasn't Marie. Work hadn't felt the same since Marie had left.

Now that Marie worked days and I was still stuck on nights, we didn't have the chance to get together as often as we'd have liked. Our regular weekly lunches were to catch up on gossip that was too long to text to each other. Today's lunch, though, was to catch up on everything since I'd been flaking out on her. She didn't want to wait for our normal date to get filled in, and I didn't blame her.

For our meeting, I'd changed into floral jean capris and a pink sweater crop top (with matching pink sandals, of course). My blond hair was twisted into two topknots, and I'd paired my ensemble with my favorite Hello Kitty purse.

The only thing marring my cute perfection?

My big, scary shadow, Hugh, who'd was coming to lunch with me.

Between text messages, Marie and I had agreed to meet someplace slightly different for lunch today—a café in the mall. I hoped I could give Hugh a few dollars and turn him loose so he could explore while I chatted with my friend. Surely I'd be completely safe out in public, right?

Hugh wasn't buying it.

"No," he said when I sweetly suggested that he take off.

"Just for an hour," I pleaded. "Come on."

"No."

"I'm going to be in the middle of a busy café. It's not like anyone's going to try anything. You don't have to hover over me!"

"That is my job." He frowned as I slung my purse over my shoulder. "It is especially important I hover today."

"Why?"

"Your clothing is inappropriate."

Was he joking? I glanced down at my outfit. "What's wrong with what I'm wearing? It's cute."

He ran a hand over his mouth. "Your . . . stomach is exposed."

"I know." I wiggled a little in display. I had a nice stomach . . . in human form anyhow. "That happens when you wear a crop top."

"It will be . . . enticing to men." He couldn't stop staring at my stomach.

My skin prickled and I was reminded that I'd left him last night in the company of a porno flick. What had he seen? What was he thinking? I felt my monster surge and fought it back. "All this modesty coming from a man who tends to walk around naked?"

To my surprise, he scowled. "That is different."

"Don't go all chauvinist on me, Hugh. I'm allowed to wear what I want."

"And I am allowed to stay at your side."

I sighed. "If I wear something more modest, do you promise to leave me alone for a few hours?"

"No."

"Then the crop top stays."

"As do I."

I took a long, steadying breath and jingled my car keys at him, knowing I wasn't going to get anywhere. "Then come on. I don't want to be late, and we're going to need to set you up nearby without freaking Marie out."

As we drove to the mall, both of us were silent. It wasn't like me to remain quiet when I could flirt, but things were feeling weirdly awkward with Hugh. For starters, he'd watched porn last night. His first porn. I'd never made it through one myself, because even a few seconds of a skin flick gave me the uncomfortable urge to transform, and I loathed the helpless feeling that gave me.

But that didn't mean I wasn't envious of his porn watching. I was so curious. Had it been sexy? Had he been aroused by watching it? Had he mentally taken notes for things to do to his mate when he got her?

And then I pictured him giving a tall, feline-looking woman those deep tongue kisses like in the movie, and I frowned to myself. I didn't want to think about that. For some reason, the thought irritated me. Maybe because by him getting his mate, I'd be completely screwed over.

It didn't seem fair. For him to get his fantasy, I was going to have to live a nightmare. I glanced over at Hugh as I drove and found his gaze on me more than once. Each time I saw it, though, he jerked away again, as if embarrassed to be caught.

And it made me wonder.

The local mall wasn't all that busy at lunchtime on a weekday. There was a moderate crowd, and I parked the car and headed in. Hugh got a few stares, but I guessed it was mostly due to his size and not his slightly furry arms and legs, or his fangs and catlike eyes. I knew those were there, but strangers might not think anything of it unless they stood very close to him. With Hugh's intimidating size, that wasn't likely.

"Now here's the thing," I told him as we entered the café fifteen minutes early. It was a cheery little chain bistro with tiny tables and lots of kitsch on the walls. It wasn't a favorite of mine, but we couldn't have picked a better place to blend in. I scanned the room and headed to the back, Hugh trailing a step behind me. There was a big crowd, thanks to lunch, but I managed to find two tables reasonably close together. "You can't sit with me or you're going to drive me insane. So I need you to sit at this table here." I pointed at an empty table in the corner. "And I'm going to sit here."

The table I pointed at for myself was two tables away.

Hugh frowned. "No."

I turned and gave him an exasperated look. "Come on. I'm in earshot. You'll be able to hear everything we say without hovering over me like an overprotective mother hen. Meanwhile, I'm going to have some semblance of privacy. Understand? I need this or I'm going to lose my cool."

He studied me for a long moment, then gave a short nod. "Very well."

I gave his shoulder a happy little squeeze through his sleeve. "Thank you, Hugh! You are the best."

Hugh gave me a gruff nod and sat at the table, looking momentarily lost. He picked up the napkin roll of silverware and examined it curiously.

"Just sit here and order some food," I told him. "Tell them I'll pay for your bill." I reached over the table to pull the menu out, and when I leaned back, I noticed that Hugh jerked backward as well, his nostrils flaring. "Did . . . did you just sniff my hair?"

He wouldn't look at me. Instead, he glared at the menu I handed him.

That made me feel a little . . . funny. Fluttery. "The menu has pictures," I told him breathlessly. "Just point at something that looks good and don't worry about the cost. The bathroom is across the room if you need it." I hoped I wouldn't have to show him how the flush handles worked—again.

"I'll be fine," he said in a low voice, his gaze flicking to my bare stomach.

Again that weird flutter in my stomach. My monster prickled but didn't rise to the surface. Just nerves? Anxiety? Something. The way he was looking at me seemed very personal, though. And he hadn't answered me when I'd asked him if he'd sniffed my hair.

Which meant that he *had* sniffed my hair and didn't want to admit it.

I sat down at the nearby table, waiting for Marie and pretending to look over the menu. My thoughts were whirling, and I was distracted until Marie plunked into the seat across from me. "Earth to Ryder, come in, please. I've said hello to you twice."

"Oh!" I jerked up and hastily slapped the menu down. "Sorry. I was lost in thought. Hey, girl."

"Clearly." Marie grinned and tossed her messy hair back over her shoulder. "Good to see you, silly. Where've you been hiding out?"

"Hiding out?" I asked absently.

"You disappeared for days," she said with a frown. "Didn't answer my calls or texts or anything. I was worried sick."

"Oh. Stuff came up." I wiggled my pinky at her.

"Stuff," she said blankly, unrolling her silverware and giving me a skeptical look that said she clearly didn't believe my too-simple answer. "You have a lot on your mind or something?"

"Something like that," I said.

Her nostrils twitched, and she rubbed her nose. "You smell like cat. I don't know what kind, but cat, definitely." She lifted her head and glanced around. "A cat that's here." Her gaze scanned the room and stopped two tables over, on Hugh. Then her gaze whipped back to me. "Don't tell me that you're hooking up with Tall, Dark, and Behemoth over there?"

"I'm not hooking up with anyone," I whispered. "You know that."

"But that's who you needed the change of clothes for the other day?" She peered at me from over the glasses sliding down her nose. "That guy?"

I gave her a helpless look and stuck my pinky out.

She sighed heavily. "*Voyons*. I'm starting to hate the pinky swears." She hooked her pinky in mine, though. "So tell me about work. How's Savannah doing?"

"When she's there, she's fine," I said. "But she's been really sick with the pregnancy. I came in the other day and Everett was filling in. I don't think he was a big fan of it, either."

She chuckled, glancing over the menu. "No, I guess not."

The waiter arrived, a teen girl that was all smiles. "Hi, what can I get you ladies to drink?"

Marie ordered a water, and I took a coffee, then gestured at Hugh's table. "I'm paying for that one, too."

"Oh." The waitress gave me a confused look. "Okay. I'll be back in a minute to get your orders, then." She sauntered over to Hugh's table and greeted him.

Marie pushed her glasses up her nose and gave me a skeptical look. "Call me crazy, but did you hire a gigolo or something to solve your little problem?"

"What? No! You *are* crazy." And God, that made me blush. Not only because it was embarrassing but also because I was pretty sure I was going to have to explain *gigolo* to Hugh later. "It's a long story. But I'm paying for his meal, and no, I won't say more than that."

"Oookay," Marie said. "So let's go back to Savannah. She talking to Connor yet?"

"Only when she has to. At least that's my understanding."

"Poor guy. Poor Savannah, too. He's miserable with love for her and she's just miserable." Marie shook her head. "Beau's all tied up in knots about it, too."

"Why? Savannah's his cousin." I didn't understand why Beau—who had a nice, sweet human wife in Bathsheba—would be so very stressed about Savannah's love life. "She's an adult, right? She can date who she wants."

"Yeah, but Connor's a wolf. You know how tense things are with them ever since the Sara thing."

"Ah." As I was human, no one had ever given me tons of details on the "Sara thing," but from what I could tell, one of the nearby wolf packs had tried to claim Bath's sister, Sara, as their own.

It had gone over about as well as could be expected. Some wolves had been exiled, pack leaders had changed, Sara remained free, and most Alliance members gave werewolves an even wider berth than before. Wolves were not well liked in Alliance territory.

Which made it harder for Savannah, because she'd gone into heat a few months ago and had been impregnated by Connor. A wolf. It was all really messy. From what I could tell, Connor was desperately in love with Savannah, and Savannah resented Connor for knocking her up.

Yeah. Complicated.

"Beau wants the wolves to be welcome so they can continue to make inroads with the packs, but the whole Savannah-Connor thing is still unresolved, and with Sara's history with the packs, it's just a weird time right now. Beau just tenses up every time we get a call from a local wolf, though most of them are benign sorts of questions." She shrugged. "I can tell when a problem is wolf-related just by the stress lines in his forehead."

"Do you like working for him?" I asked her as the waitress stopped by and dropped off our drinks, then took our orders. I had a salad, and Marie ordered the same. She'd told me that meat sometimes made it difficult to control her new shifter side, so she went vegetarian when she could. I understood that. I lived a life of avoiding triggers.

"I do," Marie admitted once the waitress was gone. "Bath's there so often and I see so many of the same people that it's almost like being in the office again, except I'm working days now instead of nights, and you aren't there." She gave me a sad frown and pantomimed a tear going down her cheek.

It was then that I noticed the big flashing rock on her finger. I gasped and grabbed her hand. "Holy crap, what's this?"

She gave a happy little hop in her seat. "What do you think it is, silly? Josh proposed!"

We shared a girlish squeal, and I squeezed her hand happily. "Oh, my God! I'm so excited for you!"

Marie seemed unable to stop smiling. "Thank you! I'm so excited. It happened about two days ago. I tried to call you, but you didn't answer." She gave me another curious look.

I waggled my pinky at her.

She rolled her eyes.

"Just give me the deets and spare not a single detail," I told her, leaning forward and resting my chin on my hands dreamily. "I need to know everything."

Over the next half hour, we picked at our salads and Marie talked in happy, animated gestures about Josh and his moving into her apartment. She acted exasperated when she talked about their bickering in regards to whose laundry went where (Marie was a neat freak and Josh was apparently a slob), but every time she said his name, it was with a note of affection. Then she told me all about the engagement. How they'd gone to Konstantine's and he'd taken her into the alley (which apparently meant something to the two of them) and showered her with flowers and had a band there to serenade her. He'd gone down on one knee in the midst of the dirty alley and proposed to her, and she beamed, like it had been the most romantic thing ever.

Weird, but Marie loved it, so I couldn't protest.

Then she talked about their plans for the future. They would get married at some point next year, and then maybe look at getting a house in Little Paradise to be closer to Josh's family; he was one of many Russell were-cougars in the area, and Marie naturally fit into their clan well. Her father wanted to pay for the wedding, and the two families were already bickering about location and catering.

"It's only been two days," she said with an exasperated smile. She forked another mouthful of lettuce into her mouth and added, "I can only imagine what the next year is going to be like."

"Oh, you're eating up every bit of it," I told her with a smile. "Admit it."

"Maybe just a little."

I smirked to hide my wistfulness. Marie was so happy and animated. I was used to pale, sarcastic Marie, but the Marie of the last month had truly come out of her shell. She was lively and had color in her cheeks for the first time since I'd known her, and she looked healthy and oh-so-happy. She was beaming.

I was insanely envious of my friend. Her life was perfect and on track.

Mine was in danger of running off the rails.

"So you'll come to the engagement party? It's a week from tomorrow. You can even bring your date." She winked and nodded her head at Hugh. "It'll be so much fun."

"Of course I'll be there," I told her, sharing her excitement. "Do you need me to do anything? Help with anything?"

"It's a pretty informal get-together," she said. "We're renting out a barbeque place over in Little Paradise, though I personally thought a pizza or two would be great."

The sound of breaking glass made me jerk in my seat, and Marie winced, clapping her hands to her sensitive were-cougar ears. I looked over at the direction of the broken glass . . .

And saw Hugh sitting at his table alone, his drink spilled all over the table, the broken glass in his hand. He was staring at me with an intense look on his face, and his cheeks were bright red. Blood covered his hand.

He'd smashed his glass in his fist by accident as soon as he'd heard the word *pizza*. And I knew why, and the thought filled me with heat.

It seemed the porno viewing last night had affected Hugh more than he'd let on. I got up and hurried to his table, bringing my napkin even as the waitress rushed over.

"Oh, my goodness," the waitress gasped, plucking glass from the table and putting it onto a tray. "I am so sorry, sir. Let me get you another drink and some napkins. Are you okay?"

I peered at his hand. "Did you hurt yourself?"

He glared at me. "My drinking vessel broke."

"I see that," I said mildly. "Did you want me to help out?" I held my napkin out to him, intending to dab at his hand.

"No," Hugh said as he snatched the napkin from me.

"Fine, be that way." I went to sit back down with Marie.

She watched Hugh with confusion, a frown furrowing her brow. "He okay?"

"He's fine," I said cheerfully. "Just not good with fragile things."

"Then it's probably good that you're not dating him," Marie said.

For some reason, I didn't like that comment. I wasn't that fragile. I glanced over and noticed that the waitress had remained at Hugh's side and was wiping his hand, taking it in hers and dabbing at the blood as she babbled about how very sorry she was. Hugh looked . . . confounded. Like he wanted to jerk his hand away but couldn't. He stared at the woman, fascinated, as she fussed over him.

Was he thinking of his mate? I felt another envious surge. Everyone was getting their happy ever after but me.

"Oh, crap," Marie whispered as I picked up my

fork again. "Don't look now, but things are about to get really crowded in here."

"Huh?" I looked up and found she was staring over my shoulder. I glanced behind me and froze.

A celebrity with a pretty-boy face and tousled curls was sauntering through the café. He waved at people while giggling women pulled out their camera phones and snapped pictures of him. A *famous* celebrity. At the mall I was having lunch at. What a remarkable coincidence.

Yeah, right.

My heart sank. One of the fae was here. Just what I needed. While this man had the face of a lesser-known actor from a recent pirate movie, I knew it had to be Finian, checking up on me. The fae could take on any appearance they wanted, and they often switched between a few choice celebrities.

My salad suddenly tasted like dirt in my mouth. "I should probably go," I told Marie as I raised a hand to flag down the waitress.

"Go? But we've barely talked," she said, giving me an odd look.

"I know." I glanced at the fae man again as he declined autographs and posed for photos at the far side of the room. Was it my imagination, or was he swinging around to this end of the café? Or was I just paranoid?

Turned out that nope, I wasn't paranoid; the fae made a circle around the room and began to head unerringly in our direction, his gaze focusing on me. A cool smile crossed his face as he hurried toward me.

I was trapped.

Marie continued giving me that odd look as I jerked to my feet, fumbling for my purse. "I need the check," I told her again. "I have to go. I'm sorry."

"It's okay," she told me. "I can get the check."

I gave her a grateful look and moved to head to Hugh's table.

The fae stepped in front of me. "Hello, delicious. What have we here?" He tilted his head, staring at me with fascinated eyes. "Is this my lucky day?"

I kept my voice low. "How did you find me here?"

"Oh, it's obvious, my darling," he said in a smooth voice. "You're positively clouding the air with pheromones."

My eyes narrowed at him. His voice seemed a bit smoother, more urbane than what I recalled. "Do we have to talk about this now, Finian?" I asked, my heart hammering in my throat.

"Finian?" His eyebrows arched. "So that's who's been hiding you away?" He *tsk*ed. "What a naughty boy. I had no idea he was holding such a delicious prize . . . and so close to ripening." He plucked an imaginary piece of lint off my shoulder. "Too bad for him, though. You're coming home with me."

If he wasn't Finian . . . who was this? "I'm not going anywhere," I told him, a little clench of fear settling in my stomach.

"Oh, but you are," he said in a low voice and leaned in. "Look at all this skin you have exposed. I'd hate for you to have an accident and show your true side to all these people. They might not understand what they're looking at . . . and then what would happen to you?"

I remembered Hugh's story about the Jersey Devil, and I shuddered. No one here would understand. The strange fae was blackmailing me. I was so afraid that I took a step backward, only to have his hand remain on my shoulder. He pulled me closer, his arm going around my shoulders. "All these people think you're so lucky to be getting my attention. Every single one of them has a camera phone trained on us. I'd hate for you to end up on a YouTube clip, dearest."

I shuddered. That was my worst nightmare. "Just . . . please don't."

A big hand clapped down on the fae's shoulder and jerked him backward a step. The fae's hands flew off me. To my relief, Hugh had appeared behind the man and had pulled him away. He leaned in, his feral eyes gleaming. "She is not yours to touch, friend. She is spoken for."

The fae's gaze remained on me, though his mouth twisted into a bitter smile. "I should have known that Finian would set a watchdog on you."

"The biggest," I agreed, relieved to have Hugh at my side.

Everyone at the restaurant was now staring at us. Phones were raised into the air, and I knew several people were recording. My skin prickled—not with my monster but with fear. I just wanted to get out of here.

And the fae was not leaving.

"Let's go, Hugh," I told him. "Please. I just want to leave."

Hugh growled, causing a few people nearby to jump in alarm.

"Do as your little friend says," the fae said in a charming voice. "I'd hate to make a scene. I don't think anyone wants that."

"We don't," I said desperately. "Come on, Hugh. Let's just go, okay?"

But Hugh's eyes were gleaming, and as I watched, his fingernails seemed to grow past the manicured, blunt ends, forming claws again. He was losing track of his human side smack-dab in the middle of a crowded mall café. As I watched, his teeth elongated, poking out from under his upper lip.

This was a nightmare.

What was I going to do if Hugh changed into a saber-toothed tiger in front of all these people? It would be as bad as my own change. Worse, maybe, because if something happened to Hugh, then who was going to protect me from the fae that wanted to kidnap me?

I had to stop him. My hands went to Hugh's sleeve, and I stepped forward and tugged at his arm. I looked up into his eyes. "Please," I whispered. "Please stop. For me."

Hugh looked down at me. His hard, rugged face twisted a bit. He shook himself, and I watched the long fangs slowly retract. He nodded. "Very well. We are leaving." His eyes hardened as he focused on the fae stranger. "Do not follow us."

"Wouldn't dream of it," the man said, far too easily. He gave me an unctuous smile. "See you later, dearest."

I shuddered and clung to Hugh's sleeve as we pushed out of the café. People were milling around us, drawn by the celebrity, but luckily we only got a few stares and no followers. As soon as we were out of the café and in the parking lot, I breathed a sigh of relief and slowed my steps.

Hugh, however, didn't slow down. He placed his hands carefully on my shoulders and continued to propel me forward. "Keep walking, Ryder," he said. "We must get into your cart and drive immediately."

"Car," I corrected. "What's wrong?"

"I do not trust him not to follow us." Hugh headed to my side of my car with me, and he didn't leave until I opened the door and slid inside. He shut the door behind me, then moved to his side of the car and got in.

I was getting more scared by the minute. Hugh was on high alert, his nostrils flaring as he rolled the window down a crack and scented the breeze. He gestured for me to start the car, and I did so, pulling carefully out of the parking lot.

"Is there more than one road to your home?" Hugh asked, still scanning the parking lot as we pulled onto the highway.

I could hear my cell phone buzzing in my purse, and I knew Marie was texting me, wanting to know what the hell was going on. I couldn't answer her right now, though. I was too busy driving and being wigged out by Hugh. "There are lots of roads," I told him. "I can take several routes. Why?"

"He will not be deterred by a public scene," Hugh said in a clipped voice. "He will attempt to come after you tonight, once he has determined where you live."

My eyes widened. I swallowed hard, forcing myself to stare at the road and not at Hugh. "I don't understand. How will he know where I live? Is he going to find me by tracking my scent?"

"By your pheromones."

"If I'm giving off all these pheromones, how is it that all the other shifters aren't going nuts around me?" Panic striated my voice.

"He does not have the same senses that the primordials do. He does not need them."

"Then what do we do?" There was a panicky note in my voice, and I made a left at the next light instead of a right, because a right would lead me closer to home. "Can you put another one of those magic seals on my front door so he can't come get me?"

"And then what?" Hugh snarled. "Let him take you as soon as you go out again?"

"I don't know," I bit out. It was getting harder to concentrate. I pulled off the road and cut through a grocery store parking lot just because it was random. "I don't know about any of this. Aren't you here to protect me? Can you stop him?"

"He knows I am here. He will seek to go around me. Or to eliminate me." Hugh sounded grim.

I shot a horrified look in his direction. "Eliminate you?" Someone honked at me, and I forced the car back into a straight line. "What do you mean?"

"Exactly that," Hugh said. "We need a new plan."

"Where do we go?"

"Somewhere new. Someplace that you have not been before so there is not a thick concentration of your pheromones. He will find your home because your scent will be imprinted in your things."

"So we get new clothes," I said, thinking quickly. "And stay at a hotel for a few days?"

"Hotel?"

"It's a place where they rent rooms," I told him.

"Are there many of these? We will need a new one every night. We do not want to take chances."

I was beginning to freak out, but I forced myself to remain calm. "Okay. Okay. New hotel every night. We can do that. And some clothing changes. No problem. I have room on my credit cards."

Hugh grunted. "Good. We will start with that."

My bodyguard continued to peer out the windows of the car as I drove—aimlessly—around the city. I eventually settled on a downtown hotel, just because it seemed more public than most and the roads here would be more heavily traveled. If I'd left a scent trail, hopefully it'd be covered up by exhaust and afternoon traffic before long.

I parked in the parking garage and we briskly walked the block to the hotel. Hugh kept his arm around my shoulders as I clutched my purse close, and I did my best not to stare around me.

The fae could glamour himself to look like anyone. I'd have no idea who he was until it was too late. He could even look like Hugh, really. Suddenly the concept of Hugh not leaving my sight didn't seem like such a bad idea after all.

My hands were shaking by the time I went to the front counter and got us a room with two full-sized beds. We rode the elevator to the fourth floor, and luckily, Hugh didn't ask any questions. In fact, he didn't say anything until we shut the door behind us.

Then he took out his necklace charm and began to run it along the edge of the door, magicking it to lock me in.

I collapsed on the edge of one of the beds, my thoughts in turmoil. Another fae wanted to nab me. It didn't matter if the fae was Finian or a stranger—both wanted the same thing. They wanted to turn me into the changeling version of a puppy mill. If I disappeared with one of the fae, I was done for. There'd be no second chance for Ryder. No hope of ever escaping my changeling fate.

And the fact that I now had a second fae prince pursuing me? It was like the icing on top of a very crappy cake. The weight of it all felt like it was pressing on my shoulders. A small sob escaped my throat, and I sank to the floor.

"Ryder?"

I looked up to see Hugh looming over me, his necklace hanging from one big hand.

He frowned down at me. "Why do you cry?"

"It's nothing," I said, wiping at my cheeks. "I'm just . . . stressed. That's all. Pay no attention to me."

"You are upset," he said, glowering down at me.

"Of course I'm upset. You would be, too, if you were in my situation. One guy wants to turn me into his own personal exotic pet and stud me out so I can breed him more little exotic pets, and the other guy wants to steal me from guy number one. I don't have a way out, the True Love thing is bunk, and I'm going to spend the rest of my life as someone's pet monster." Just letting it all erupt out of me made fresh tears crop up, and I continued to wipe at my cheeks. "Now I'm hiding out in a hotel with some big jerk that doesn't even like me, and my best friend is getting married to the love of her life."

He said nothing, which only made it worse.

I put my head down and continued to weep, feeling sorry for myself. The situation just continued to swirl in my mind, all the pieces interlocking. Just as Marie's life was coming together, mine was falling apart. My best friend was happy and engaged and radiant with joy. I was having to overnight it in a hotel with a stranger because I couldn't go home thanks to the fact that I was being hunted.

Yeah, there was no way I could put a happy spin on this.

To my surprise, the bed shifted and Hugh sat down on the floor next to me, leaning up against the bed. He sat close enough that our shoulders rubbed, and then he awkwardly patted my shoulder. "I will not let anything happen to you, Ryder."

For some reason, that quick, impersonal touch just made things worse. I only cried harder.

"You are not comforted?" He sounded chagrined.

"You're trying, and I appreciate that, but . . ."

"But it is not how a man comforts a woman," he guessed. "And this makes you sad."

Hearing it said aloud made a sob catch in my throat, and I nodded miserably. "I . . . can't . . . even . . . be . . . held," I choked out between sobbing hiccups. "It's not fair! Why can't I be normal?"

One big hand landed on my hair, and the next thing I knew, my face was mashed against Hugh's broad chest. He rubbed my shoulder, and his arms went around me. "I will hold you."

My heart melted at his thoughtfulness. "Thank you," I said around the knot in my throat. I leaned against him, careful to avoid his skin. "You're sweet."

"I am sorry you are sad."

I sniffled. "I just . . . want to be normal. I want a boyfriend. Someone that will hold me when I'm scared and love me for me." I thought of Marie's engagement ring with a pang of envy. "Someone to share my life with."

Hugh said nothing. He simply continued to stroke my hair.

That was fine, really. It wasn't a situation that could be solved by kind words. It was just me, full of self-pity that I normally didn't allow myself to indulge in.

We were silent for long moments, my head snuggled against his chest as his hand slid over my hair. "I know how you feel," he said after a pause. "This world . . . I see people together, and it makes me envious. I see men walking with their women, and holding their hands. I see the easy touches of couples. I see their children. I see families, and I realize that my men have nothing. We have nothing but a bare, lonely existence in our realm. And . . . I want things, too." He sighed, the sound heavy and sad. "I cannot help but want more."

I felt a weird kinship with Hugh in that moment. He was just as lonely as I was, just as stranded and isolated in this sea of happy, normal people. He understood how alienating it felt to watch someone casually caress a loved one's cheek and know that you could never have the same.

He got it. And he got me.

The thought was so incredibly warming that I lifted my head from his chest to look up at his face, to tell him that I understood. That I knew what he was talking about and how he felt.

And when I looked up, I realized that his face was mere inches from mine.

Hugh's gaze dropped to my mouth, and my breath quickened when I realized what he was thinking. He was thinking about kisses. Hot, wet, delirious kisses like he'd seen in the movie. I knew this, and knew I should pull away.

But I didn't. I pressed closer to him, my breasts brushing against his chest. My hand clutched at his T-shirt, and I tugged myself up against him, my mouth angling closer. Any second now, he'd push me away. Demand that I cease. So I figured I'd get as close as I could before he did so.

Yet as my mouth moved closer to his, my breathing escalating into small, excited pants, I flicked my gaze to Hugh's. Wasn't he going to stop me?

The look in his eyes was scorching with heat. It made me suck in a breath to see all that desire storming through those catlike pupils, to see the ache in them.

He wanted to kiss me. He wanted it just as badly as I did. My pulse settled low in my thighs and I whimpered, even as my other hand dug into his shirt and I slanted my mouth down over his.

And then, I was kissing Hugh.

Our teeth banged together, startling me. I wanted to pull back and apologize; I wasn't very good at this, and my experience was limited. I was good at letting others kiss me and then running away. Me starting the kiss? Clearly I needed work.

I moved to pull back . . . and Hugh's hand was on the back of my neck, suddenly, holding me against him. His mouth slanted over mine, shocking me with the heat and intensity of it.

I melted against him. The feel of his lips against mine was stunning . . . and wonderful. Hugh was clearly a quick learner; I felt his tongue press into my mouth, seeking entrance. I opened to let him in and was shocked by the wave of arousal that swept over me when his tongue touched mine. I licked him back, and when he retreated, I grazed my tongue over one of his extra-long canines, earning a throaty groan for my efforts. Then he was tonguing me again, stroking into my mouth.

His body was rigid under mine. Even as our mouths meshed, I could feel under the throbbing of desire the prickle of my skin as I transformed. The hands digging into his shirt were turning to claws, and my back ached, my wings thrusting out of my skin even as Hugh's tongue thrust into my mouth again. It left a wild ache between my legs, and I moaned.

The sound was gutteral; inhuman. During the kiss, I'd transformed into my changeling form. Even now, I could feel the scales over my nipples pushing against his chest. The feeling was oddly erotic. I wanted more of it, and I brushed up against him as he continued to kiss me.

But just as quickly as the kiss had started, it ended. The hand that had landed on the back of my neck to pull me toward him? Suddenly pulled me backward and jerked me away. My eyes flew open—I didn't even realize I had closed them—and I stared at Hugh in surprise, panting.

He'd transformed during our kiss, too. His face had changed, his nose flattening, the whiskers along his sideburns becoming more prominent. His fangs had extended and his eyes had no whites, and I could feel his claws pressing against the now scaly skin of my neck. It was like he lost control of his humanity when he got turned on. Seeing that gave me pleasure. He was just like me.

I leaned in to continue our kiss.

Hugh shook his head, jerking away. "No."

"No?" He shook his head again and shoved backward, the bed sliding across the room. Hastily, he stood, spilling me to the ground. He wouldn't look me in the eye, either. Instead, he went to the window and peered out the curtain.

And I was left sitting there, my tail and wings lashing through my clothing.

Utterly humiliated.

Utterly devastated.

He saw my transformation and didn't want to kiss me anymore. It was okay that he'd turned more tigerlike; I'd actually found that arousing, because I'd known it had meant he was losing control. But me? I didn't turn into something pretty. I turned into something ugly.

And he didn't want to put his mouth on that.

The tears returned, and with a choked sob, I fled to the bathroom and slammed the door shut behind me, then locked it and leaned against it. The mirror was to my side, but I turned away, not wanting to see my hideous reptilian face.

I was so ugly I was beyond kissing, even to a shapeshifter like Hugh.

I was doomed.

Chapter Ten

When I'd composed myself, I sucked in a deep, steadying breath and studied my face in the mirror. I'd transformed back to the old, familiar, human Ryder. My blond hair was delicately mussed, my bangs shifted over to one side of my forehead. My eyes were red-rimmed and puffy from crying, and the tip of my nose was red as well. Not a cute look, but better than the alternative.

I headed out of the bathroom and shut the door behind me. No more hiding.

Hugh turned away from the window and looked over at me. "Is everything well, Ryder?"

Was everything *well*? Was he just messing with me now? I ignored his question and grabbed the remote, flopping onto the side of the bed and clicking it on. Screw him. I turned on something boring. It looked like a home improvement show. Whatever.

"Ryder?" He moved to the other side of the bed and sat down on the corner. "Are you ignoring my questions?"

I shot him a glare. "What does it look like?"

He seemed astonished by my reaction. "You are upset?"

Why was he surprised by this? "Why wouldn't I be?"

"I do not understand." He got up from the bed and moved around it to my side. Then he leaned over and peered at my face. When I scrunched down, scowling, he frowned. "Have you been crying?"

"Of course I've been crying," I said bitterly, trying to avert my face from his inquiring gaze. "You would be, too, if you were in my situation. And for the record, I'm sorry I pushed my gross mouth on yours. I should have remembered how disgusting I am. It won't happen again."

Silence.

Then, to my dismay, Hugh sat down next to me on the bed, blocking out my view of the TV. "You think you are disgusting?"

I jerked my gaze to his. "I have a mirror, Hugh. I know what I turn into."

"That is what you turn into right now," Hugh agreed. "The closer you get to your peak, the more you transform. Or didn't you notice?"

"I try not to look in the mirror," I pointed out stiffly. "I don't like what I see."

"I do not think you are hideous, Ryder," Hugh said in a low, gentle voice. "If I did, I would not have kissed you. And make no mistake, it was *I* that kissed *you*. I did not forget who and what you are. I pressed my mouth to yours knowing this. I touched my tongue to yours fully aware of this."

That hot look returned to his eyes. "And I pulled away not because I forgot what you are but because I did forget what is waiting for me should I fulfill my vow."

A knot of emotion choked my throat. "A mate for you."

"A mate for *all* of my men. An end to our loneliness. If I deliver you, there will be children for my people. Mates to warm us at night. It is the thing we dream of most. How can I deprive my men simply because I am selfishly attracted to you?"

I felt curiously warm. "You're attracted to me?"

His gaze was deadly earnest. "I am."

"Even knowing what I turn into when I'm touched?"

"It does not offend my senses. It is simply part of who you are, and I like all of you." His expression became rueful. "And you are not the only one that transforms when you are touched."

I sat up, suddenly fascinated by this conversation. He . . . didn't find me revolting? In my monster form? My touch made him shift into his form a bit more because he lost control? "I noticed that. It was because you got turned on?"

He nodded.

"You're not just saying this to make me feel better?"

"I never lie." He looked affronted at the thought.

I waved a hand at that. "I know, I know. But you also didn't say anything just then. You just kind of nodded."

"I am attracted to you," Hugh said gruffly. "In either form. Does that satisfy you?"

It made me giddy, actually. "But you won't touch me because of your vow?"

"That is correct."

"Then why did you kiss me?" I asked, feeling a little breathless. My gaze went back to his mouth, fascinated by the tension there. "Why didn't you pull away when I leaned in?"

"I wanted to see what it was like," he admitted. "This kissing with tongues."

"We can practice some more," I said eagerly, sitting up on the bed. "You probably want to have more experience for when you get your woman—"

Hugh shook his head, his gaze hot and dark on my face. "I dare not." He stood. "And you should get some sleep. I will keep watch."

I settled back down into the blankets, feeling oddly pleased with this turn of events. So Hugh didn't find me disgusting after all? That was fascinating. He'd pulled away only because he'd wanted more, and he was trying to remain true for his upcoming bride. Mate. Whatever. I fluffed one of the pillows and snuggled it, turning back to the boring home improvement show but not paying a bit of attention as they waxed rhapsodically about resurfacing cabinets.

Hugh was attracted to me. I hugged the thought close, happy.

Then I stopped. I was thrilled that Hugh liked me . . . at the expense of his own happiness? It was clear that he was tormented by his attraction to me because it carried such heavy ramifications. If he made me happy, he made so many others miserable.

The thought was not an encouraging one, and for the first time, I felt jealous of the nameless, faceless female that had been picked out for Hugh's mate. He'd treat her like she was the most amazing, incredible thing in the world. He'd be ecstatically happy.

And I'd be miserably busy breeding little changelings for my fae master.

The night passed uneventfully. No fae showed up to bust down the doors of the hotel room. It was as if nothing had happened and we were just being silly and paranoid. Of course, I imagined that was what I was supposed to think. I would let down my guard, and as soon as I did, I'd be snatched. I knew how the game went. I wasn't stupid.

I was, however, utterly distracted.

All night, I'd dreamed about Hugh. Delicious, sexy dreams in which we were in the primordial lands, all alone. Just the two of us and misty, wild trees all around. I was naked, and so was Hugh, and when he stepped close to me, I couldn't resist brushing my hands over his body to see his reaction. And he always, *always* reacted.

I woke up with a little shiver and looked over at Hugh, but he'd maintained his post at the window. Darn.

Still, for all that it had been a naughty dream, it had been a good one. I yawned and stretched, then swung my legs out of bed, surprisingly cheerful. Tonight after work, I decided, we'd get a nice, swanky hotel room. After all, if I was going to end up in the fae realm for good, I might as well go out in style. I kicked off the covers and bounced up. "Morning, Hugh."

He grunted.

"Someone clearly needs his morning coffee," I teased, then glanced at the alarm clock. One in the afternoon. "Afternoon coffee," I amended. "Do you mind if I shower before we head to work?"

He turned and gave me an incredulous look. "Work? We are not leaving safety so you may play at your desk."

It was my turn to frown. I put my hands on my hips. "You're kidding, right? I have to go to work. I don't want to lose my job. I've already missed two days."

Just in case I managed to wriggle myself out of this mess, I'd want to have my job to pay off the credit card bills this week was going to cost me.

Hugh shook his head. "It's not safe."

"But—"

"I have decided," he said in a snarl, glowering at me.

Someone was definitely cranky. It didn't deter me. He could snarl at me all he wanted—I knew he wouldn't harm a hair on my head. And layered with the knowledge that I knew he found me attractive? Yeah, I was going to get my way in this. "But Hugh," I said pleadingly as I put a hand on his sleeve, "I need to go to work or I'll go stir-crazy, waiting for something to happen."

When he looked over at me, I gave him my most innocent, vulnerable female look. And then I licked my lips.

His gaze went to my mouth and his eyes softened. Poor man had no chance against a woman's wiles. "I—"

"And I need to work in order for us to stay in these rooms," I told him. "Otherwise we won't have the money. And I'm sure I'll be safe with you around." I ran a hand along his bicep and gave it a bit of a squeeze. Just a bit. "You're strong. And capable."

He sighed. "Do you say these things in a sweet voice to coax me, female?"

Maybe Hugh wasn't as clueless as I thought. I grinned up at him. "Perhaps? But it's all true. I do feel safe with you."

He grunted. "And you must go to work to get money? For the rooms?"

Well, I did have a nest egg, but what he didn't know wouldn't hurt him. "Yep."

"Very well."

"Wonderful!" I gave a happy little bounce and headed for the shower. "Just give me ten minutes to get ready and we'll head out, okay?" I didn't stick around for an answer.

I took the world's fastest shower and just as

quickly toweled off, tossing aside the small, rough towels as soon as I was dry enough. My hair was a wet, tangled mess, though, and I hated the thought of going in to work with it laying flat against my head. There was a hair dryer attached to the wall, so I pulled it off and flicked it on, aiming it at my hair.

The door to the bathroom slammed open and Hugh thundered inside, eyes wild.

I froze in place, staring at him in shock. "What is it? Who's here?"

"That noise . . ." He made a weird gurgle in his throat and fell silent, staring at the hair dryer.

I flipped it off, straightening. "Oh, I'm sorry. I must have panicked you. I—" I stopped, realizing that he was staring pointedly at the now broken door that was hanging off its hinges and avoiding looking at a very naked *me*. His face was bright red. "Hugh?"

"You will put on a towel, female."

Oh. So it was my nudity that was bothering him? I smothered a laugh. The man was the biggest, most dangerous person I knew . . . and he was blushing like a schoolboy because I was naked. "You're the one that barged into the bathroom," I told him. "You shouldn't be surprised at what you see if you do."

"I thought you were in danger."

"Only in danger of having flat hair, sweetie," I told him and put the hair dryer down. "You've seen me naked before, Hugh. Back when I transformed in the primordial lands, remember?"

He continued to stare at the broken door. "I did not look. I would not look. It is not . . . polite."

Oh, my Lord, this was cute. I tousled my wet hair with my fingers. "What do you think? Is this a good look for me?" I teased him.

He refused to look in my direction, glowering at the wall.

"Or maybe I should pull my hair up. What do you think?"

"I think you should put the towel on."

"Really? Because I was thinking you should kiss me again."

He looked over at me then, and oh, his eyes were so dark that I could see no whites in them. He was close to transforming.

And God, that made my skin prickle with excitement.

"Put the towel on," he said, his voice flat. His gaze remained locked on mine.

"Give me a kiss and I will."

Hugh glared at me and spun around, storming out.

I felt a twinge of guilt at his anger. Of course he was mad at me. I was blatantly trying to get him to break his vow. I was putting my needs in front of the needs of twenty-four men waiting for their mates . . . to say nothing of the women waiting for the men. Was I that selfish, truly? Could I continue with this plan knowing I was going to keep a faceless band of people from their happiness?

But . . . what about me? Didn't I deserve happiness, too? Biting my lip, I tamped down the guilt

I felt and pinned my sultriest smile to my face, following Hugh into the hotel room. "Where are you going to go, Hugh?"

He had the same problem I'd had last night when I'd wanted to hide—there was no place to go. I trailed behind, my hands on my naked, slightly damp hips, and watched him.

Hugh had sat down in one of the two small chairs at the table near the window. I knew it wasn't comfortable for him; it was obvious in his body language and the stiff way he sat. He'd turned the chair toward the wall, as if that might somehow save him from my naked guerilla tactics.

I moved around to the front of the chair, ignoring the fact that Hugh's knees were practically pressed to the wall. "Nowhere to hide," I teased.

He blanched at the sight of me and my damp breasts moving closer to him. "Ryder, don't—"

I sighed, incredibly disappointed. "But you said you wanted to kiss me, right?"

"I do. But you know why I cannot."

"But it's just a kiss," I coaxed him. "It won't mean anything. And you need practice, and I, well . . . I want to stockpile the good things before all the bad stuff happens." And before he could protest, I sat in his lap.

Hugh's hands clenched the arms of the chair and he looked braced, ready to leap up and dump me on the floor.

"What's so bad about a kiss?" I asked him. "Can I help it if I want one more?"

"No."

I decided to tease him. "It's because I'm ugly, isn't it? I—"

I wasn't able to get another word out, because Hugh snapped. His arms locked around me, his hand going to the back of my neck, and he dragged my mouth against his, as if he'd been a drowning man and I'd been the breath of life. I gasped as his tongue licked into my mouth, all need and savagery, and then I moaned, leaning into him, my skin pressing against him.

His claws dug into my bare skin—which was quickly scaling over—and I took it as a sign that my own claws were okay, too. I raked my hand down his chest, ripping at the hard slabs of muscle there with delicious need even as his mouth savaged mine. He wasn't gentle with me. His mouth moved over mine hungrily, and I felt his teeth against my skin and lips—and I loved every bit of it.

I whimpered low in my throat, my tongue moving against his. My nipples were so hard that they ached, and I longed for him to touch me. I wanted those big, rough hands on my skin, the claws dragging against my scales. I wanted his fierceness.

He pulled away from me just when I was breathing hard against him. And he looked just as dazed as I felt. "Your kiss is finished. Dress yourself." His voice was surprisingly calm.

"Thank you," I said breathlessly. "That was very . . . kind of you." I wriggled off his lap, feeling my pulse pounding between my legs. I felt weak in the knees, like all the strength had been kissed out of me. My claws touched my scaled breasts, and I looked over at him as he stood up.

Hugh was sporting a very large tent in the front of his pants, and there were no whites in his eyes when he looked over at me.

"Dressed. Now."

"Very well," I said, ignoring his irritated tone. I sauntered back to the bathroom, taking great care to swing my hips as I walked. I sighed when he didn't follow me and glanced up at my reflection in the mirror.

The same changeling face stared out at me. The eyes were mine, but the skin was still scaled, the horns twisted. I ran a long-taloned hand down my cheek thoughtfully. Were the ridges on my cheekbones less prominent? Were my scales a less muddy shade of green? I turned to the side and examined my wings. Still crumpled and batlike, but they seemed less wrinkled than before.

Huh. I reached back and grasped one in my hand, spreading my wing. It twitched in my grasp, but it definitely seemed . . . smoother? Maybe someday it'd become a real, usable wing. And maybe Hugh was right, and my appearance would change over time. Maybe that was why Finian and the other fae kept talking about me "ripening."

Maybe the ugly caterpillar would turn into a butterfly after all.

Or maybe I was just grasping at straws. After all, turning into a butterfly would do me no good.

I'd still be treated like an animal—an object to be bought and bred simply to produce young.

I'd be better off ugly.

We headed to work as if nothing weird was going on. When Hugh suggested we drop by my apartment to scope out the area, I quickly agreed; I needed a change of clothing, and so did Hugh. I might have been off work yesterday, but I still felt out of sorts today, dressed in yesterday's wrinkled, stretched-out clothes. I changed as Hugh checked out my apartment, but the findings were perplexingly dull. No sign of fae or any sort of follow-up.

"Does this mean we can stay home tonight?" I asked him.

"No. Better to assume the worst. We will sleep in the public bed tonight."

I chuckled at his words, had a nice conversation about the word *hotel* and how he should use it, and packed extra clothing for both of us into a pink vinyl backpack.

A short time later, we walked into work, and I was pleased to see that Savannah was back. "Hey! I'm glad to see you. How are you feeling?"

She gave me an easy smile and put her hands on her only-slightly-rounded stomach. "I'm managing. This one's making it difficult, though. How are you?" She gave a curious look to Hugh, then back at me. "Still working on a special project?"

"Special project," I agreed. "Yup. Still showing

Hugh the ropes of how to woo women." I turned and gave Hugh a meaningful look. "I think we've made great strides lately, don't you?"

He said nothing—he simply scowled at me.

I grinned and bounded to my desk, setting down my purse. I'd chosen something simple but full of color to wear today. I wore stretchy pale green capri pants, a pink peplum top, and my favorite pair of pink Keds. I hadn't done a thing with my hair, so I'd pulled it up into a clip and slicked on a bit of pink lip gloss. After all, if I dressed down too much for work, they'd start to suspect something was going on.

And my goal was to be business as usual, even if my mind was on anything but business. In fact, I couldn't stop thinking about those kisses. My mind was constantly on Hugh's firm, delicious mouth. Even when I sorted through the mail and opened envelopes and chatted with Savannah, my thoughts fixated on Hugh. It didn't help that he'd gotten the stool out of the storeroom and sat a few feet behind me instead of across from me. I felt his gaze on the back of my neck, making my skin prickle with awareness.

What was he thinking? Was he as rattled by our kisses as I was? Was he thinking—no, *obsessing*—about the next one? I was dying to know, but this wasn't the place to talk about it. So I gave Savannah a sunny smile. "How far along are you with that baby?"

She patted her stomach again, as if to reassure it. "It'll be five months next week."

"Wow, that far? And you're still getting morning sickness?"

Savannah gave a small grimace. "Morning, noon, and night." She adjusted her computer monitor in a fussy motion. "I'm getting used to it. Everyone tells me it's normal."

"Do you feel up to working? I'm totally okay if you want to bail out early."

She gave me a grateful look but shook her head. "I'm fine. And I need to work. I need the money. I'll be raising this little one on my own." Her hand went to her stomach again.

It was on the tip of my tongue to ask about that. Everyone who had any sort of dealings with the Alliance knew that Savannah had been knocked up by one of the Anderson wolf pack. I looked at her belly with some trepidation, wondering how mine would look if I had a child.

And then I wondered how long I'd get to keep that child.

I shuddered.

"Well, you have a big family," I told Savannah brightly. "I am sure one of those brothers or cousins of yours would be happy to babysit if you asked."

She laughed. "You'd trust those men with a baby?"

"Good point." I picked up my day planner. "Anything special on the dating books tonight?"

She shook her head. "Just more training, if you're up for it. I still need to be shown some of the match-generating jobs Sara was talking about. She started saying words like *macro* and *SQL* and *database*, and I tuned out."

"Yeah, that sounds like Sara. All I know how to do is punch buttons, but I can show you that," I told her. I looked over at Hugh, and an idea popped into my head. "Why don't you put on my headphones and watch this nice dating video?" I said to him.

He gave me a quick nod, and I held a finger up to Savannah, indicating that I'd be just a moment. I put the headphones on Hugh and showed him how to adjust the sound, then leaned over the desk to pull up my movie rental account.

And I pulled up a porno and purchased it, just because I had a mean streak.

I hit Play. The music started and was immediately swallowed as Hugh put the headphones on. His expression showed no change. He hadn't realized what I was up to. Yet.

"Enjoy," I said with a pat on his shoulder. I hurried over to Savannah's desk and pulled my chair close so I could show her how to manage the programs. A few minutes later, I peeked over at Hugh from across the office.

There was a look of sheer horrified fascination on his face, and I had to smother my laughter.

By the time three in the morning rolled around, I was yawning and ready to call it a day. Hugh wasn't talking to me—no shock there, considering that I'd slipped him a surprise porno. Given that movie and our shared kisses from earlier, he was probably all bothered to hell right about now.

Which fit my plans perfectly.

Because I had a new master plan for how to save my hide.

Hugh was a virgin. I was a virgin. Hugh was attracted to me. Hugh didn't mind that I had a monster side. In fact, Hugh changed when aroused, too. It seemed that we could help each other out with things. I could fix his virginity for him, and he could fix mine. Win-win situation. There was the little issue of his vow, but I wasn't too worried. I could be very convincing when I wanted something.

And I wanted this. I wanted Hugh. I wanted my freedom, even if it came at the cost of the happiness of the primordials. I thought of the men in the primordial realm, with their avid, too-hopeful eyes, and felt a fresh surge of guilt. Damn it. I couldn't think about them. I had to think about me. Did I deserve to be a sacrificial lamb just because some guys wanted wives? It didn't seem fair.

There was no right answer. I'd just have to trust my gut and continue on the path I'd chosen, no matter how unhappy it made the other primordials. I . . . just wouldn't think about them. I couldn't.

I formulated my attack plan as I drove to a new hotel for the evening, since we were still playing it safe. The good thing about the hotel hopping? We'd have to share a small room. Unlike my condo, a hotel room was one single, solitary bedroom. Some nice, slinky lingerie—I didn't have any, but my bra and panties were pink and lacy, so they'd do. Some mood music. More demands for kisses, and then I could be more aggressive. Show him exactly what I wanted. He'd resist a little—after all, he was committed to his course of action—but I figured I could convince him. Most men didn't need much convincing for sex, right? Just touch them in the right places and they'd turn into putty in my hands. Or so I'd heard. Granted, I had no personal experience in these things, but I read *Cosmo* faithfully every month and had memorized several "tricks" that they'd suggested.

I figured all I had to do was put us in the situation and hormones would take it from there.

The hotel I picked for tonight was a big, expensive one situated in downtown. It was the type of hotel that catered to upper-echelon tourists and business conferences and I'd never have considered for a simple overnight stay. I hefted my pink backpack over my shoulder and felt a little silly walking across the gleaming marble floors and heading to the beautifully polished wood check-in counter with ultracasually dressed Hugh at my side.

"Hi, there," I said to the girl at the counter, pulling my wallet from my purse. "Is your honeymoon suite available tonight?"

Her gaze flicked to my casual clothing and the large man at my side, and I saw her wondering about us. I could guess what she was thinking. Cute young girl, big dude, three-in-the-morning need for a hotel room equaled possible hooker scenario.

"My apartment's got no air right now," I lied.

"We can't sleep in the heat, so we figured we'd get a nice hotel room."

Her face relaxed into a smile, and I realized that I'd said the right thing. "It's the worst when your air conditioner breaks down, isn't it?" She began tapping on the keyboard, peered at her monitor, and nodded. "Honeymoon suite is available tonight."

"Perfect," I said cheerfully and handed over my credit card.

Ten minutes later, we were heading up to our floor, key card in hand. I hummed a happy tune to myself as Hugh stood at my back, acting as if nothing was weird about this at all. Casual, I told myself. I was being casual. I faked a huge yawn and looked over at Hugh with a smile, pleased when he repeated the motion. Yawns were always catching. "Tired?" I asked sweetly. "You didn't sleep at all last night."

"I must remain vigilant," he told me. He didn't look me in the eye.

"Suit yourself," I told him. "But that's what that spell on the door is for, I thought. You won't be able to protect me very well if you don't sleep. Think of how much better you'll be if you're well rested."

He considered this, then gave me a quick nod. "You speak the truth. But there is only one bed."

"Of course I speak the truth." I slid the key card into the lock and waited for the green light to click on. "And I'm sure the room has two beds tonight," I lied, then pushed the door open. I stepped into the room and admired the suite.

The first thing I noticed was the big bed in

the center of the room. A huge square mahogany headboard dominated the far wall, looming over the king-sized bed, which was covered in pillows. There were delicate upholstered chairs, an antique-looking sofa, and decorative tables in the room—all of which looked too flimsy to hold poor Hugh. A bouquet of roses had been left on one table nearby, and in one corner of the room was a massive jetted tub big enough for two. I blushed at the sight of it.

Okay, I was brave, but I wasn't sure I was that brave. I glanced over at Hugh. "Home sweet home for the evening."

He frowned even as he shut the door behind him. "There is only one bed."

I shrugged. "Don't worry. We'll just share. I promise not to steal the covers."

He looked as if he wanted to protest but then thought better of it. Success, I told myself. Now to lay out the rest of my plan.

I slung my backpack off as Hugh pulled off his necklace and began to run the rune around the edge of the door. "Mind if I get comfortable while you seal everything off?"

"I do not mind," Hugh said, distracted with his task, his back turned to me.

Perfect. I stripped off my peplum top and wriggled out of my tight capris, folding them neatly and stuffing them into my backpack. "Whew, it's hot in here, isn't it?" I commented, setting up phase two of my seduction scene. "I don't know if I'm going to be able to sleep in this kind of heat."

And I adjusted my pink and white bra, plumping my breasts.

No response from Hugh. That was okay; he was still busy on his task. I slipped off my shoes and moved onto the bed. I didn't pull the covers back; instead, I lay on my side and shifted one hip, posing as sexily as I could.

Then I waited for him to turn around.

It took a few moments. He finished running the rune around the door and looped the chain back onto his neck. Then he studied the door, running a hand along the edge and watching the magic flash in response. Satisfied, he let his hand drop and glanced over at me.

His eyes widened.

I pretended to fan myself with one hand. "My, it's warm. Don't you think?"

Hugh moved closer to me, still staring. "Do you . . ." He swallowed. "Do you get under the blankets now, Ryder?"

"No," I said and stretched languidly, the motion making my breasts bounce in what I hoped was an attractive manner. "Too hot. I'm comfortable like this." I ran a hand down my side. "Why don't you get undressed and come to bed?"

Was that sweat breaking out on his forehead?

Hugh remained in place, clearly trying to determine what to do. I saw his gaze flicking around the room. Sit in one of the dainty chairs that wouldn't hold his big body? Sit on the bed with me and all my mostly naked glory?

"Oh, come on, Hugh," I said in a low, flirty purr and patted the bed. "I don't bite . . . unless you want me to." And I winked at him.

The breath hissed out of his lungs. He collapsed on the corner of the bed and turned his back to me. "Ryder . . . please put clothing on."

"Don't you like looking at me?"

"More than I should. That is why I ask you to dress." His voice was tight. "For my sake."

"I'll do lots of things for your sake," I told him flirtatiously. Truth was, I was getting rather excited about the thought of doing naughty things to Hugh. "I'd love to run my mouth all over your skin," I told him. "Lick your fangs. Dig my claws in."

A low groan escaped his throat.

Yes! Excitement flashed through me, and my hands curled into the blankets. I wiggled a bit closer on the bed. "What do you say? Want to do a little mutual exploring? Figure each other's bodies out and see what the other likes?"

"You know I cannot."

"Why not?"

"My vow." He still didn't turn around to look at me.

That darn vow. "Listen, Hugh." I made my voice as persuasive as I could. "You're a virgin. I'm a virgin. Why not take care of each other's needs?"

"Because my mate is waiting for me," he said in a harsh voice. "Not just my mate but the mates of others who are depending on me. I will not rob them of their chance at happiness and family simply because I gave in to my own desires."

"But you do desire me?" I focused on that single word, ignoring the guilt I felt at pushing for something I shouldn't have wanted so desperately.

"You know I do." His voice was ragged, his face averted.

"Then why can't we play a little?" My tone was coaxing. "You want to please your mate, don't you? You want to know how to make her body respond to you. I bet she's a virgin, too. And she's going to look to you to make sex delicious for her. How are you going to do that if you don't know how a female body works? You're a big, scary guy. She'll be frightened of you. *And* of making love, unless you're totally skilled with her."

Hugh said nothing . . . but he wasn't protesting any longer, which I took as a good sign.

"I could show you," I said in a cajoling voice, lightly running my fingers along the bedspread, since he was too far away to touch. I was totally aroused at this point, my breathing quick, my nipples hard. The slightest of touches from him would turn me into full-blown monster-girl. "You can use me as a test of sorts. We can figure out what you can do to make her respond to your touch. And . . . we can experiment on you, too. You can show me what you like. After all, I'm going to need to learn these things myself."

"I have . . . seen the picture stories. I have learned plenty."

"Those movies aren't how things really are." I couldn't help the throaty laugh that escaped me.

"Those are just materials used to arouse. They're blatant and not romantic in the slightest. If you want your woman to crave your touch, you're going to need to be sexy. I could show you how to do that. How to touch her. You could touch me."

And I quivered at the thought of him touching me. At the thought of one of his big hands cupping one of my breasts.

He inhaled sharply, then shook his head and jerked to his feet. "Get some sleep." And then he retreated to the bathroom. A moment later, I heard the shower running.

I frowned. Damn him. He'd been so close to giving in. I'd clearly started with the wrong tactic by suggesting the mutual loss of each other's virginity. That was a nonstarter. He'd hesitated when I'd mentioned learning each other's bodies, though. That was the key.

Because Hugh clearly wanted to please his mate, I thought with a sour jealousy. And by keying in on that, maybe I could get him riled enough to seduce him fully and make him forget his vow.

The prospect was an exciting one, I had to admit. It would take some serious courage on my part, as well as some strategic planning, but I could do it.

I'd just have to ignore my niggling conscience, which told me I was pursuing my own happiness at the expense of so many others.

Chapter Eleven

I deliberately slept on top of the blankets, part of me hoping that I'd wake up and find Hugh touching me, unable to resist my allure. Instead, I woke up to find that Hugh had tucked a blanket around me as I'd slept. I wasn't sure if I found that sweet . . . or utterly frustrating. Surely I hadn't been stuck with the one man immune to my charms? Maybe I just wasn't trying hard enough.

I resolved to try harder and brainstormed for ideas. I could prance around him naked, but he just wouldn't look. I could rub myself up against him, but he'd just move away. Or forcibly move me away.

Seducing Hugh would require stealth and wiles. And since I was a virgin, I was low on these things. I could flirt with the best of them, but when it came to outright seduction? I had no ammo in my armory. Add that to the fact that Hugh was constantly at my side? I couldn't even research a dirty movie or two without having him catch on.

I considered this as we went to work together a

bit early the next day. I told Hugh I had a big, important project I was working on.

That wasn't really true. I just wanted to talk to my friends and get some advice. But with Hugh hovering, I had few options. I could have texted, but Marie sucked at checking her phone, so I thought I'd use the office chat programs.

Sara was surprised to see me. She had on a pair of massive headphones and was typing frantically into her computer when we walked in. "Hey, Ryder," she yelled, clearly unable to tell that she was shouting. She pointed at her headphones. "Give me two seconds and I'll get to a safe spot in my game."

"No rush. I just came to work on a project," I yelled back and headed to my desk. I gestured for Hugh to take a seat anywhere. He went to the back and got his stool, and as he did, I craned my neck and peeked at Bath's office. Not in. The only person in was Sara. Huh. I thumped into my seat and pulled up the chat program on my computer. We were linked to Beau's office, and I frowned to see that Marie's status was set to Away. Probably in a meeting of some kind. When Hugh sat down across from me, I gave him a tabloid magazine to "research" while I worked.

My mind still on the topic of advice, I decided to ping Sara first. *Where's your sister?* I typed.

She's scoping out locations for a sock party, Sara typed back. *She just came up with the idea and was all excited. Wanted to get started.* She was sitting across the room, so she could have just taken off her headphones and talked to me, but I preferred the chat program. Hugh wouldn't be able to eavesdrop on the conversation this way.

Sock party? I typed. *Dare I ask?*

It's a match-up gig. You're given a sock when you come in and you have to go around and meet other people while looking for the match to your sock. She thought it was brilliant.

It sounds kinda weird.

Across the room, Sara giggled at her monitor, then continued typing. *I suggested a lock-and-key party, but she thought that was too suggestive.*

Mmm, she might have a point. Say . . . since you're in. I wanted to ask you something . . . about guys. Sara was mated to Ramsey, so she might be a good one to ask. Ramsey was big and surly and silent, but somehow Sara had wriggled her way into his heart. The were-bear was utterly devoted to her. I figured she had some sort of mojo going on that I could get pointers on.

ME? Really?

Yes, you.

Dude, okay, but I'm not sure I'm the expert. You're the flirt around here! I should be asking you!

She had a point. *Yeah, but the guy I'm interested in seems to be immune to my flirting. I'm baffled and not sure what to do. I'm not sure how to let him know that I'm interested.*

How about telling him?

Tried that. Don't want to take no for an answer.

I see. She drummed her fingers on her chin for a

moment, thinking, and began to type furiously once more. *How serious are we about this guy?*

Let's just say I'm trying to get him into bed and he's ignoring all my attempts.

Uh-huh. Is he a shifter?

I frowned at my computer. *Is that important? But yes. I'll get it approved before we go anywhere with things.*

You're in the Alliance. Remember that hubbub with Marie's turning? They changed the rules on the human thing. As long as you don't suddenly start to grow a tail, no one will care.

I forced myself to type in an *LOL* in response, even though her remark was too close for comfort. I did grow a tail in my changeling form.

Here's the thing with shifters, she sent back quickly. *They're super scent-attuned. Like right now, I can smell that you reek of that big kitty-cat sitting right next to you, which means you two are sharing close quarters. Not judging, just pointing it out.*

I bit my lip, trying not to grin. *We might be.*

So I'm guessing he is the prey that keeps getting away. Yes?

He . . . might be.

Tease!

Okay, he is. And he sucks at tuning in to flirting.

I have experience with that. Again, I heard her giggle over at her computer, and I couldn't resist smiling at mine. *Ramsey wasn't exactly forthcoming when we got together. Okay. Without delving into personal lives too much (because my Huggy Bear would kill me if I shared all our secrets), let me give you a tip. Remember what I said about shifters and sense of smell?*

Yes? I resisted the urge to drum my fingers impatiently.

It's very keen. They can smell everything. Fear, because it brings on a sour kind of sweat. And arousal, because it brings on . . . well, a different kind of wetness. Do you get me?

Oh wow. I had no idea! So if I want him to know I'm turned on . . .

Yeah. Pretty much just walking past him will do it. It's very hard for them to resist. BUT I TOTALLY DID NOT TELL YOU THAT.

My lips are sealed.

I eyed Hugh speculatively, unable to stop smiling as he frowned down at the glossy pages of the magazine, trying to make heads or tails of a picture of a royal wedding.

My chat program pinged again. I glanced back to the computer.

So . . . Sara had typed. *Since we are sharing secrets . . .*

Oh, no. I felt a sick sort of dread in my stomach. Had she figured out what I was? I forced myself to reach for the keyboard. *Yes?*

Exactly what kind of shifter is he? He smells like cat, but . . . different. Earthy. It's kind of hard to describe. Like . . . cat hair times ten. Normally the wolf nose isn't a fan of cougars, and right now, I hate to say it, but your boyfriend there stinks.

I smothered a laugh.

Hugh glanced over at me sharply.

"Just . . . read something funny. That's all." I glanced over at Sara, but she was still typing away at her game, acting as if nothing was going on. "Go back to your magazine."

He frowned at me, then turned another glossy page, his nose wrinkling up with distaste when he ran across a perfume sample. "This book smells foul."

"It's perfume," I said, leaning across the desk toward him. The action pushed my breasts up and the neckline of my shirt down, and I made sure Hugh got an eyeful. "It's supposed to smell nice."

"It does not," he said in a low voice. "It is putrid. My eyes are watering."

"Grumpy," I teased. I slid my wrist under his nose playfully. "Women rub it on their pulse points so they smell good. Like here." I wiggled my wrist at him. "And then here." I reached back and touched under my earlobe. "And . . . here."

I brushed a finger between my breasts and gave him an arch smile.

He stared where I touched my breasts. Stared hard. Then turned back to the magazine and violently flipped to the next page.

The chat program pinged several times in a row. I slid back to my chair, still smiling, and glanced over at it. Sara had typed several lines.

Yeah.

That guy says he's not interested?

TOTAL LIAR.

I saw the way he just looked at your boobs. I'm telling you. Scent. It always works in your favor.

Sara was awesome. I was totally going to use this information to my advantage. *It's good advice. Thanks, Sara.*

You still didn't tell me what kind of shifter he is.

I hesitated. It wasn't exactly a secret, was it? It just raised a lot of questions that had no answers. Questions that I didn't want asked at the moment, in case they pointed back to me. So I typed a vague answer. *He's a rare form of tiger. His family's from some little third world country, and they don't see a lot of outsiders.* And I stared at the monitor, waiting to see if she'd accept that.

Her reply came a few seconds later. *Gotcha. Tigers do have a unique stink to them.*

He doesn't smell, I chided her.

He does to the wolf nose.

I'm glad I'm human, then, I sent back playfully, testing to see how much she knew.

I'm glad you are, too!

I breathed a small sigh of relief at that. Sara hadn't guessed what I was.

Just then, Marie popped on to chat. I immediately sent her a *Hello* and waited for her to respond.

Hey, girl! You're finally talking to me! What happened at the café?

More pinky swear stuff. Can't talk about it.

Merde!

I know. Sorry.

You're lucky that we're friends. So. What are you doing in so early?

Working on projects. The usual. Got a minute?

Of course. I'm between meetings, but I don't have to dash for another fifteen, which is good. Beau's a good boss but I'm not sure I'm a fan of conference calls, and we sure do have a lot of those. She typed in a smiley face sticking its tongue out.

Beats unemployment, you doofus, I sent back.

That it does.

So . . . let me ask you a question. Time to play it smooth; that way, Marie wouldn't guess what was up. *I'm seeing a guy*, I began to type. *Sorta. Except he thinks we're just friends and I want to be more than friends. How can I ease into sexytimes without him freaking-out?*

There was a long pause.

Then, *I am laughing over here*, she wrote back. *You're asking ME for romantic advice? You're the one that flirts with anything with a penis.*

I was starting to get annoyed with the fact that everyone seemed shocked that I wanted romantic help. *Yes. Just answer the question.*

Okay, well. If it was Josh and I was in the mood and he wasn't—which has never, ever happened, for the record—I guess I'd start by making it all about him. Like, oh you poor baby, did you have a hard day? Let me rub your shoulders and get you a beer. And then sexy rubdown turns into more. But for the record? Josh is never not in the mood. He—

Oversharing, I typed back quickly.

—seriously gets turned on by the sight of my oldest, rattiest pajamas. What? Oversharing? You asked!

Yeah, but now I'm picturing you and Josh in bed together. Actually, wait, this is good picturing. Josh is hot. Is he naked?

Back off, woman. He's mine! Picture me raising my hands and pretending to claw your eyes out in jealousy.

I chuckled at my screen. *Funny, funny.*

I know. I crack me up. Now go be a good little office worker and drink your daily quart of Red Bull and get back to work, unless you want to tell me more about this mysterious man.

You can't see it, I typed, *but I have my pinky in the air.*

Curse you and your inevitable pinky.

I grinned and looked over at Hugh thoughtfully. Would that work? Fawning all over him and offering to rub his shoulders? I admired his shoulders from afar. They were really nice ones. I wouldn't mind getting to put my hands on those. And maybe I could lead him into giving me a massage, too.

I thought on this as I opened a work folder and began to type.

In the early, early hours of the morning after work, we stopped by my apartment again and checked things out. Still no signs of other fae or any unusual scents. Hugh seemed to be pleased but suspicious. I raided my apartment for more sexy underwear, a cute baby-doll nightie that had been on sale and I hadn't been able to resist (despite having had no one to wear it for), and a bottle of unscented body oil, since I sometimes had dry skin in the winter and that worked better than lotion, given my scaly other-self.

We checked into a different hotel, and I rubbed at my shoulders and neck meaningfully as we got into the elevator. "Sure has been a long day, hasn't it?"

"It has," Hugh agreed. "Your job is quite dull. You enter a square little room and stare at another square all day."

I blinked at him. Well, that was one way of looking at it. I knew he was bored babysitting me, though. We'd headed out to the local bookstore a few minutes before they'd closed, and I'd bought him some picture books on medieval warfare and *The Pop-Up Battle Book*. He'd been fascinated by them and had paged through them for hours on end without bothering me, which had allowed me to work with customers and get my job done. I'd drawn up the schedules for the upcoming month and created flyers for the scheduled events—even the sock party. It had been a productive night. "I got a lot done," I told him, then rubbed at my neck again. "Though it's hard on the back and shoulders."

He said nothing. Not disagreeing, simply not all that interested in small talk.

"What about you?" I asked as we got off the elevator and onto our floor. "How is your back? You sat in that stool all night, so it has to be aching you."

He turned to frown down at me. "I am a warrior. Minor aches and pains do not bother me."

"Well, it's not a question of your warrior-ness," I said smoothly and inserted the key card in the door. "I mean, you could always take a nice hot bath."

We entered the room, and sure enough, the tub was in the middle of the bedroom again. I'd selected this particular kind of room on purpose.

"I think not," Hugh said in a flat voice, clearly reaching the same conclusion.

"You sure? I won't mind. I want you to be at your peak physical prowess for guarding me, and if you're all stiff, I worry that you won't be able to handle it." I sidled past him into the room and sat down on the foot of the bed, watching as he shut the door and began to run the rune around the edge. When he was done, he turned to look at me, and I smiled brightly. "You know what I think?"

He gave me a wary look, as if not quite trusting my sunny expression. "What?"

"I think I should massage your shoulders for you."

The wary look intensified. "I never said they ached."

"Yes, but mine do, and therefore I'm sure yours do, too." I patted the end of the bed. "Come. It's a human custom to massage each other," I lied. What he didn't know wouldn't hurt him.

"It is?" He said it so flatly that it sounded more like a statement.

I nodded and patted the corner of the bed again. "Come over here and strip that shirt off."

He hesitated a moment longer, then approached and sat on the edge of the bed carefully. It sank down hard at his weight—Hugh was enormous and packed with muscle—and I shifted backward so I didn't fall into his lap.

Not that I would have minded, but he'd probably have bolted.

A moment later, he rolled his shoulders and pulled his shirt over his head, and I sucked in a breath at all that masculine beauty before me. Hugh sure was easy on the eyes. His shoulders were enormously broad and tanned, and as I peered closer, I saw small white lines of scars crisscrossing his skin here and there. For some reason, they only added to his attractiveness, perhaps because they spoke of danger. I admired his back without touching him for a long moment, then I reached for my pink backpack and pulled out the body oil. I warmed it up a bit between my hands and lightly laid them on his shoulders.

He jerked in response, bolting to his feet.

I tumbled forward, barely able to catch myself before I slammed to the floor. My oily hands went to the bedspread and I winced, knowing I'd have a dry cleaning charge on my hotel bill when I checked out.

Hugh had turned and was staring at me with feral, almost wild, eyes, the whites disappearing. "What are you doing, Ryder?"

"I'm trying to rub your shoulders," I said with a grimace. "It's a friendly gesture, nothing more."

He hesitated. "Nothing . . . more?"

"Do I look like I've turned into my monster?" I gave him an impatient look. Truth was . . . I'd felt it shift under my skin the moment I'd laid my hands on him. I'd fought it back like I'd never fought back before, biting the inside of my cheek to concentrate. His subsequent retreat (and my near fall on my face) had shoved my changeling side back into its hiding place. "You're safe with me."

"Very well. I . . . apologize." He thumped back down again, the look on his face a mixture of frustration and pained determination.

It was almost funny . . . except for the fact that I was trying to seduce him. "Are you going to stay put this time?"

"Yes."

At least he sounded contrite. It was probably the sight of me nearly taking a header that had changed his mind. I waited a few moments to see if he was going to get up again. Two oily spots gleamed on his tanned shoulders where I had touched him before, and they called to me. "I'm going to put my hands on you again," I warned him.

"Very well," he said, and I watched his back lock up and tense, anticipating my touch.

I bit back my chuckle at that and leaned forward, lightly putting my hands on his shoulders again. He jerked under my touch but didn't get up again.

"Okay," I told him, feeling my changeling side

flex and begin to beckon under my skin. I fought it back as best I could, concentrating on Hugh before me. "Now I'm going to rub your shoulders. Close your eyes and stay still, all right?"

I watched him for a moment, but he didn't get up or tense, and I experimentally slid my oily hands over his broad shoulders. His skin was hot, like a furnace, and touching it was far more pleasurable than it should have been. Just the heat coming off him filled me with lust, and running my fingers over his skin? Massaging those thick cords of muscle and running my hands along them?

It was surely the best thing I'd ever felt.

My monster had fully arrived, my nails lengthening and my skin becoming scaly. I felt the wings burst out of my back, felt my tail slither forth from the small of my spine, and bit my lip to keep from groaning with pain at the sensation. It was quickly gone, though, and the hands that flexed and rubbed Hugh's neck and shoulders were scaly, but not a muddy green. More of an iridescent green that seemed to shine from within. My fingernails were no longer talons but smooth, pretty claws with dull tips, slightly longer and more curved than normal fingernails. Not grotesque.

He was right; I was changing.

Would Hugh like my new form? I wondered, but I didn't ask. I just continued to massage his neck, rubbing my thumbs against the sides of his spine, then dragging my nails down his skin.

He gave a low groan, the first sound he'd made.

I froze in place, waiting for him to flick me away once more, but he didn't. He simply remained in place. His head bent forward, and he seemed to be asking for . . . more.

Ooooh.

My pulse throbbed heavy in my veins with excitement, and I kneaded his shoulders, my movements soft and sensual. I explored the hard ridges of his neck muscles, fascinated by them, and rubbed my knuckles against the base of his skull, where his hair had been shaved short. The bristle of it was thick and almost wiry, and I loved the striping. It made him unique. Different. I liked that about him. I liked that his lower arms were thickly furred, and that the stripes continued there. I wanted to run my hands all over him, but I worried he'd shy away again.

And I wanted to keep touching him. I loved the feel of his skin. The feel of him. The way his muscles flexed, hard but giving, as I massaged.

I couldn't help it, either—I became aroused. I didn't know when I'd become turned on by touching Hugh; for all I knew, it could have been as soon as I'd laid my oiled hands on him. But right now? My body ached to be touched. My nipples were hard with need, and my pulse had settled somewhere south of my belly button and beat there, steadily. When I shifted on the bed, I felt the slickness between my legs.

In front of me, Hugh stiffened, and I knew he scented my desire.

He sucked in a sharp breath, and then another groan escaped his throat. As I watched, his hands fisted on his legs, and his nails elongated into sharp claws again.

He'd lost control of his own beast. The sight of that made my breathing quicken, made my pulse race even faster. It was the most erotic thing I'd ever seen. "Hugh?"

"What?" The word was more groan than question.

"Now do me," I whispered.

Chapter Twelve

He was silent for so long that I thought he'd protest. Declare that he was done and storm back into the bathroom again. I eyed his wide back with anticipation and dread, waiting.

Then, Hugh turned and gazed at me, his eyes so hot with lust and need that I felt the air suck out of my lungs. "Rub you?"

"Yes," I whispered, nearly choking around the words. "I ache, too."

He got to his feet and towered over the bed, staring down at me. His gaze was so intense that I practically felt it skittering along my skin. "You transformed."

"I couldn't help it." I knew what I looked like—all scales and horns and compressed wings under my nightie. My hand went up to shield my face. "I'm sorry."

Hugh's big hand reached out and caressed my face, brushing aside my shielding hand. "You . . . were aroused by touching me?" His big thumb, tipped with claw, grazed the scales close to my mouth.

I nodded.

That thumb grazed over my lip, sending shivers down my spine. "And yet you hide your face."

"It's because it's awful."

"Never awful," he said, his voice husky and aching with need. "Just . . . forbidden."

And that made me ache with a sweet longing. "Please, please touch me, Hugh. I want so badly to be touched." I leaned into his caressing hand. "I feel like I don't have much time left, and I want to know what it's like. Don't . . . aren't you curious about me? Even a little?"

"More than a little." His voice was hoarse now, his eyes nearly black. He glanced over at the side of the bed. "Where is the oil?"

I fumbled for the bottle with my own slick hands, uncapped it, and offered it up to him.

"You will undress for me?"

A hot blush scorched my cheeks. Weird that I was going to be shy now. I tugged at my dress, but it was tight at the neck, and with my wings in the way, I couldn't pull it over my head. I scratched at it with my claws, only to whimper in frustration when I realized that my now blunted claws were useless. "I can't . . ."

Hugh grinned, displaying enormous fangs that had lengthened recently. I wanted to lick them so badly. The sight of them distracted me, and I nearly missed it when his hand shot out and his claws ripped down the front of my dress. It fell to shreds about my front, my bra going with it.

I gasped, my hand flying to my front in shock. "Th-thank you." I shrugged the clothing off my shoulders, feeling weirdly vulnerable to be topless in front of him. I was feeling like I had lost all control of the situation . . . and didn't mind in the slightest. I did wonder what he thought of my body, though. My belly was covered with paler scales than my hands and arms, my breasts the same milky shade except for the darker nipples. The scales trailed down my arms, and a hard line of points extended down each of my biceps. My wings lay flat against my back, and my tail thumped against the bedspread, flicking like a cat's.

Any human man would run.

Luckily for me, Hugh was pretty unique.

He squeezed some of the oil onto his big palms, and I watched, fascinated, as he rubbed them together, mimicking my own motions from a few minutes ago. Then he looked back to me, his eyes nothing but black in his face. "Turn, Ryder."

I got to my knees and turned on the bed, presenting him with my wings. I clenched my hands at my breasts, anxiety and anticipation tumbling through me. Was he setting me up only to push me away once more?

Two big, warm hands clasped my shoulders.

A soft cry escaped my throat, more from surprise and shock than anything else. That warm, intimate touch was so very startling to my soul . . . yet it filled me with an intense ache. I'd held myself closed off for so very long that even this was overwhelming. A knot formed in my throat, and to my horror, I realized I was about to cry.

Not sexy.

I swallowed hard, but the tears wouldn't go away. And as Hugh began to rub, tears started to slide down my face. A sniffle escaped me.

Hugh paused. "Ryder? Do you cry?"

"I'm okay," I told him, but my voice betrayed me—it was husky and tear-clogged. I swiped the tears away with my fingers. "I'm sorry. I'm just being silly. It's just—"

"—That you ache to be touched." His big hand stroked over my shoulder again, a welcome caress. "I know this feeling."

More tears welled up inside me. "Yeah. It's just a bit overwhelming is all. I don't know why I'm getting all weepy over it, though. It wasn't like you wanted to touch me. I kind of forced you into it."

Hugh's hands turned me, and then he pulled me into his arms. His big, bare chest was warm against my scales, and for the first time in my adult life, I didn't feel like a monster. Inhuman and unlovable. I just felt like . . . Ryder.

And that was what made me so choked up.

He held me, and I wept like a baby for what felt like forever. He simply stroked my back and hair, and his hand reached up and caressed my cheek. He didn't even flinch away when his fingers ran over the hard blades at the tops of my shoulders. He just brushed over them and continued on.

Eventually, I recovered enough to stop crying. I

sat up against him, reluctant to leave the delicious warmth of his chest but feeling like a fool. "I'm sorry. Here I was trying to be sexy and I ended up crying all over you. That wasn't part of the plan."

"So this was a plan?" He raised one thick eyebrow at me.

I gave him a sheepish grin. "You have to give me points for trying."

He didn't smile back at me, and I thought for a moment that he was mad at my manipulative tactics. "Do you tell me that you did not wish to touch me?"

"No, I did," I admitted. "Sometimes I want to touch you so badly that I ache."

His hand went to the small of my back and he jerked me against him, my hands going to his shoulders in surprise. "And do you feign the smell of your desire for me, Ryder?"

"No," I said breathlessly, unable to look away from his intense gaze. "Never."

His fingers went to my chin, and he tilted my face toward his, even as he tugged me closer. My breasts—scaled, but still sensitive—pressed against his chest, and I could feel the hard ridge of his erection against my belly. Excitement thrummed through my body, and I stared up at him, waiting.

And then Hugh kissed me. All on his own. Without me having to ask or persuade. His mouth swept over mine, hesitant at first, as if asking permission.

When I made a sound of pleasure in my throat, he pulled me tighter against him, and the pressure of his mouth became firmer, almost bruising with its intensity. I loved it, though; he couldn't hurt me in my tougher changeling form, and I liked the raw edge of his passion. His fangs scraped against my lip, sending ripples of excitement through me. I moaned, my blunt claws digging into his flesh. The feel of his hot skin against my breasts as he licked into my mouth was incredible. I wanted it to go on forever.

As his mouth moved over mine, I felt his hands stroke my sides, sending ticklish waves through my body. He stopped kissing me for a moment to whisper, "May I touch your body?"

I nodded, excitement pulsing through me. "Touch me anywhere you want."

He leaned back, studying my body, and I cringed slightly, imagining what he saw. "You are lovely, Ryder."

I winced. "No, I'm not."

"Are you calling me a liar?"

Oh, right. I shivered, feeling weird about it. "No. I'm not. I just . . ." I gestured at my body, seeing nothing but scales. "I can't see beauty in this. All I see is . . . a creature."

"Do you know what I see?" Hugh's voice was low and soft, and his stern face above mine was gentle. He put his hand over my shoulder, and his thumb grazed my collarbone.

"What?"

"I see a beautiful body, with delicate bones." He ran his claw down my collarbone. "And yet strong enough that I don't have to worry about hurting you."

That claw dragged against my scales and I shivered, aroused by the sensation.

His hand slid lower, and he cupped my breast, his big hand shocking in its heat. "I see these breasts, lovely and ripe, and just begging for the scrape of my fangs."

I moaned, arching against his hand. He was highlighting all the things that were weird and different about us, and yet . . . it was incredibly erotic. "Tell me more."

His thumb grazed the diamond-hard peak of my nipple. "I see this, and it begs for my mouth. Not only for sweet, gentle kisses but rough, wild biting." His fangs bared, and he grinned down at me. "My kind likes to bite."

"How do you know?" I asked breathlessly. "If you have no women, how do you know?"

"Because I dream of it," Hugh said, his voice low and hoarse. "Every night, I dream of taking you into my arms and biting down on your lovely flesh, and watching you arch with pleasure under me."

I shuddered, feeling liquid heat between my legs. My blunt claws dug into his skin. "God, Hugh, why does the thought of you biting me sound so incredibly sexy?"

"Because you're not afraid of me," he said, and his thumb-claw grazed my nipple. "Because these scales make your body impervious to anything I can do to you. And you find that arousing. That I can be rough and wild with you, and it won't matter."

He was right; I did like that thought. I loved the idea of him losing control, of that big, strong, scary man not holding back as he showed me his desire. When he bared his long, frightening fangs? I didn't get scared. I got aroused.

His hand slipped lower, to the curve of my waist. "I see a slim, beautiful body under my hands, Ryder. I do not see ugliness. I see a woman who tempts me to forget everything." Hugh leaned in and gave me another kiss on my mouth, sucking lightly at my lower lip. "And that is why you are so dangerous to me."

I moaned and brushed my breasts against his chest, wanting more. Wanting more touches. More kissing. More of his mouth—and teeth, and claws—everywhere.

But he only pressed his forehead to mine and gave a heavy sigh. "And that is why we should not go further than this."

Disappointment swept through me, but I nodded, my arms wrapped around his big shoulders. "I can't even be mad," I said softly.

He'd given me the greatest gift that anyone ever had.

He'd seen my natural form . . . and made me feel pretty. I couldn't be upset about that. I nestled against his chest and was pleased when he pulled me closer, into a comforting embrace. My hand slid up his neck, and I played with the thick hair at the edges of his jaw, the sideburns that seemed a natural extension of his feline form.

I was perfect for Hugh. He was perfect for me. Making love to Hugh would solve all of my problems.

And he would disappoint all of the other primordials if he broke his vow. Prevent them from receiving their mates. I felt that old, familiar guilt well up again. Once again, it felt like I was choosing my own happiness over that of two dozen other people. It felt cruel, but at the same time, I was trapped.

Could I be selfish enough to press on? To push for Hugh's seduction even when I knew the costs?

I didn't know what to do. Only that it seemed that someone lost no matter what was chosen.

"I wish I could do more, Ryder," Hugh said, and I felt his strong jaw move under my fingers.

"It's okay," I told him. "Really, it is." I was in a jumble of confusion, my thoughts in turmoil and my guilt raging, but as long as he held me, it all didn't seem to bother me so much. Just feeling warm skin against my own felt like decadent pleasure.

Then someone knocked at the hotel door.

Chapter Thirteen

I looked at Hugh, then glanced at the alarm clock. Almost five in the morning. It was far too early for housekeeping. That meant . . . it had to be the fae stranger I'd seen at the restaurant. He'd tracked me down. Somehow. I began to tremble, hard.

Hugh bounded off the bed and launched himself at the door, putting his hands to the wood and glancing through the peephole. I noticed that his shorts were tented around his arousal, and his claws had grown out again. He was fighting his own beast, as well.

Hugh looked over at me. A mixture of shame and disappointment crossed his face, and before I could ask what was wrong, he put his hand on the doorknob and opened the door, breaking the portal.

Finian strolled in.

At least, I assumed it was Finian. He was wearing a different celebrity's face now, but there was no mistaking the perfectly tailored suit, the gold necklace at his throat, and the big *F* dangling from it. His cool gaze scanned Hugh's half-naked body, stopping for a long moment on his dark, pupil-less eyes. Then his gaze swept over to me, where I was still in changeling form, now clutching a sheet to the front of my scaled breasts.

"I see I arrived just in time," Finian said.

I gasped, holding the sheet tighter to my front. My gaze went from Hugh to Finian. How had the fae known we were here? My wings gave a little flutter of distress, and I felt my tail flick against the pillows of the bed. I looked over at Hugh questioningly, but he avoided my gaze. "We weren't doing anything," I blurted, feeling weirdly guilty at the fae's accusing gaze.

"Nothing?" Finian sneered, and his full mouth pulled into a thin-lipped grimace that looked odd on the sensual, famous face he wore. "I suppose that's why I find my bodyguard half turned, his cock erect, and my changeling naked on the bed, wearing her scales? That is nothing?" He turned to Hugh and spat the words, "I should have you removed from your post."

Oh, God. No! I needed Hugh with me. "I promise," I said quickly. "We didn't do anything. Ask Hugh. You know he can't lie!"

Finian's head swiveled, and he looked at the primordial shifter. "Well?"

"We kissed," Hugh admitted, and I mentally cringed. "I wanted to show her that she was lovely despite her changeling form," he said in a simple, brusque voice. "We kissed, and then I told her we must stop. And we did."

Finian stared at Hugh for so long that I thought he would snap. The tension in the room was palpable.

I felt like a teenager that had been caught making out in the backseat of a car, and just like that, my desire and easy mood withered away to nothing. I felt my wings sliding back against my spine, sinking into my skin as I began to change back to my human form.

"We did stop," Hugh repeated. "I have no intention of breaking my vow to you."

My heart withered in my chest a little at that statement. Hugh couldn't lie.

It seemed to please Finian, too. "Good," the fae said and rubbed his hands. "I'm glad I arrived anyhow. I thought it was time to check up on things. I felt you using the portal rune and thought it appropriate to stop by." He beamed at the two of us as if he hadn't just caught us rolling around in bed together. "How are things going?"

Hugh leaned against the now shut front door of the hotel room. His eyes were back to their normal catlike state, and his brows were low on his face. He looked ready to punch something, but his tone was polite, efficient. "There is another fae. He located her amongst a crowd and confronted her. I was able to get her away, but he is aware of her presence. I have reason to believe that he will attempt to take her."

Finian frowned and crossed one arm over his chest, the other stroking his bare chin thoughtfully.

"Another fae, you say? That is most displeasing." He nodded after a moment. "You're right to take all precautions, then. I don't want you to take her to your home realm again, though. Every time you take her there, it delays her transition and she is in a critical stage right now."

"I will remember," Hugh said.

Sheets pressed tight to my breasts, I watched the two of them talking. Finian was somehow tracking us through Hugh's necklace. Every time we used the runes, he seemed to be aware of it. I didn't like the thought; it felt like an invasion of privacy.

It was nothing compared to what happened next, though.

Finian clapped his hands. "Well, since I'm here and she is in form, I might as well check out how my little treasure is progressing." He looked over at me expectantly.

I remained where I was. "Excuse me?"

He waved a hand at me impatiently.. "Come stand here before me, girl. I want to look at how your transformation is coming along."

"I . . . don't have a top on."

"Even better. I can get a good look at your scales." When I didn't move, he flicked a hand at me again. "Come on. I don't have time for modesty. We've all seen a pair of breasts before." He smirked and turned to Hugh. "Well, most of us, anyhow."

Hugh's face remained impassive and stony.

This man expected me to just prance in front of him and show off my body? Was he crazy? I was back in human form now, my changeling side having deserted me as quickly as my desire had. "What if I say no?"

"Then I switch your bodyguard for someone else." Finian's expression was tight, though he was still smiling. "And Hugh and his men lose their opportunity to have their mates. Are you going to keep stalling, then?"

I slid to the edge of the bed at that, unhappy. More blackmail. I dragged the sheet along with me and moved to stand in front of Finian. Goose bumps prickled my now human arms, and I was on the verge of trembling from a mixture of fear, loathing, and anger.

If the fae prince noticed, he simply didn't care. He reached out, lightly stroked his fingers down my arm, and waited for me to change.

I felt a shudder of revulsion ripple through me and turned my face away.

No change. No scales. After a moment, it became apparent that Finian's touch was a huge turnoff. I wanted to laugh at the irony of the situation, but I was too wigged out.

How ironic that the only man who couldn't turn me into a freak show was the one that wanted me to change. I glanced over at the fae prince to see how he was taking this.

He seemed displeased. He waited a moment longer, then snapped his fingers at Hugh and pointed at me. "You do it. I don't want to have to keep touching her."

Any pride or self-esteem I'd rebuilt after my lovely interlude with Hugh immediately crumbled to the ground at Finian's callous words.

Hugh stepped forward and moved to my back.

"Please don't," I whispered.

Big, warm hands closed over my shoulders. His thumbs stroked my skin.

Just that simple touch was enough to make my changeling side explode into action. A whimper escaped me and I felt my skin ripple, felt the scales emerging as my wings tore out of my skin. My tail slithered forth, and the horns in my forehead grew so quickly that they left a sharp ache, and I felt as if I'd banged my head against a wall. I groaned, the sudden, throbbing pain in my head dulling my desire again.

"Keep touching her, Hugh," Finian said, his voice clinical.

So Hugh kept brushing his fingers over my shoulders, sending skitters of unwanted desire through me. I gritted my teeth, trying to fight it, but it was useless. For days now, I'd been craving Hugh's touch, and now that I was finally getting it, my body was determined to soak up the sheer pleasure of it.

In what seemed to be my quickest transformation ever, I was back in changeling form in a matter of moments. I glared at Finian and clutched the sheet harder against my breast.

He rubbed his chin, looking down at me thoughtfully. "We're coming along, aren't we? I definitely see improvement in your scale quality." Finian reached out and flicked a fingernail against the scales on the backs of my biceps, then pinched one of the hard plates that rose up from the bend at my elbow. "Still a ways to go before these turn lustrous, though. At least two weeks, maybe more." He frowned at that and glanced at my angry face. "You're quite the slow developer, aren't you, little Ryder?"

"Fuck you," I spat at him through my own fangs. I wanted to use them to bite that smirk off his face.

"Temper, temper," Finian said absently. He ran his hand down my arm, then squeezed it, as if testing my muscles. He grabbed my hand and, despite my attempts to jerk it away from him, held on and examined my fingernails. "Nails are coming along," he said, pleased. "They no longer look like uncouth talons. These will be alabaster before we know it." Finian smiled at me. "Won't that be lovely?"

I jerked my hand out of his.

He made a flicking motion with his hands. "Drop your sheet so I can get a look at the rest of you."

I gritted my teeth and held the sheet tighter. "No."

Finian turned to Hugh. "Get it from her."

"Do not ask me—" Hugh rasped, and I felt his hands tighten on my shoulders.

"Need I remind you about the mate that's waiting for you on the other side?" Finian asked in a dulcet voice. "And the mates of all your men?"

I felt Hugh shudder against me. Then, with an angry growl, he shook his head. "You ask too much."

"This is ridiculous." Irritated, Finian ripped the sheet from my hands and tossed it to the ground.

A bleak pain settled over me as my hands rose to cover my breasts.

But Finian wasn't looking at me with desire. The looks he was giving me were efficient and bored. He hummed to himself as he leaned in and scratched at one of the scales on my collarbone. He made a grunt of approval, examining me the way a doctor would—or a butcher would examine a slab of meat. He put his hands on my hips and dug his fingers in, feeling my pelvic bones. "Good, good. Nice and wide." His fingers skimmed along my tail, my wings, my back, all of it with that same sort of bored interest. Then he turned back to me and put his fingers on my chin, turning my face back and forth. "Open your mouth, Ryder. I want to look at your teeth."

My nostrils flared with anger, but I opened my mouth as hot tears ran down my face.

"Good, good," Finian said, lifting my lip to peer at my gums. "Nice and healthy."

I snapped my jaw shut, wishing I could snap my jaws around his hated neck.

"I don't suppose you'd lift your tail—"

"Don't even think about it," I said angrily, jerking away from him so hard that I stumbled.

"Things are progressing rather slow, but overall, Ryder, I'm pleased. Your scales have a good color to them. You should be a lovely specimen, given a few more weeks to bloom. Remember to take your vitamins and brush your teeth, and you'll be gorgeous before long." He smiled at me as if I'd find this praise appealing. "I'll return to check on things in another week or so. For now, I'll leave you two alone." He stepped forward and gave Hugh a pointed look. "Remember what you risk, my friend, when you kiss my little pet."

"I will not forget," Hugh rasped. His jaw was tight with anger.

"See that you do not," Finian said. He opened the hotel room door and stepped out. The runes lit up again, the faint purple lines resealing the door with magic after he stepped through.

Silence fell in the small hotel room. I didn't move for a long moment, and then it hit me that Finian was gone. The agonizing humiliation of what I'd just been put through slammed into my senses a second later, and I collapsed to the ground in a heap, weeping.

Hugh was at my side a moment later, his hands stroking my hair. "I am sorry, Ryder. I am so sorry." I wanted to push him away, even as he gathered me in his arms and held me close again. I wanted him to hurt like I was hurting, to burn with the shame that I felt at the moment.

But most of all? I wanted to be comforted. I wanted Hugh's strong, warm arms around me, his hand stroking my hair and letting me know that everything was going to be okay.

Even if it wasn't going to be okay, I wanted to think that for a little while. So I sobbed and let him hold me in his arms, while he pressed his mouth to my hair and whispered apologies.

My mood was foul when I went in to work that evening. Hugh and I had come to an uncomfortable standstill.

I was doomed. I was doomed because I understood why Hugh was the way he was but I still wanted him. I went to bed dreaming, every night, of his mouth on mine, his hand at my waist. His claws dragging across my scales and the sweet words he'd whispered to me.

For days, I went through the motions, existing in a fog of depression. I'd go in to work, Hugh at my side. I'd work, but the light had gone out of me. I didn't have the heart to flirt with clients or the Russell men who showed up at the agency. I did my job, and that was it. I skipped lunch with Marie and was short in my texts with her.

I was withdrawing into myself, just waiting. Waiting for everything to come to a head so I could get this horrible, horrible *waiting* over with.

Each night we moved to a different hotel room. There'd been no sign of the fae—Finian or otherwise—but I went along with the protective measures, even though my credit card was becoming close to maxed out. I just didn't care anymore. What did it matter?

Hugh cast me tortured looks throughout the day, but I ignored them. When they gave us a room with a double bed the next night, I took it as a sign and didn't complain. Nor did I try to seduce Hugh. I simply fluffed my pillow, lay down, and tried to sleep.

We got double beds for the rest of the nights, too. I was done. Defeated.

Finian had won.

Chapter Fourteen

Are you okay, Ryder? Savannah says you've been superquiet lately, and that's not like you. I'm worried about you! Text me back.

I glanced at the text message, then sighed heavily. Marie was sweet to be worried about me, but there was nothing I could say that would make her feel better. *I'm fine, I promise. I just have a lot going on.*

If you say so. You're still coming to the party tonight, right? My engagement party?

Of course I'll be there! I made myself add an exclamation point to the sentence so I'd sound more like me. *You're my best friend. I wouldn't miss it for the world.*

Awesome. See you tonight!

Will do!

Truth be told, I'd thought about missing it. The whole situation with my changing and Hugh and everything made me want to crawl away and lick my wounds quietly somewhere.

But I couldn't, because it would hurt Marie. She'd think I had an issue with her or Josh, so I had to go to show my support for them and their relationship. And I loved Marie. She'd been quietly supportive of me and my issues ever since I'd met her. I could never hurt her by ditching her party.

This might be the last time I ever saw my friends.

So I resolved to go and have a great time. And if this was the last time they were going to see me?

I was going to look totally fabulous.

Despite Hugh's protests, I insisted on going shopping again. If he was going to the engagement party, his muscle shirts wouldn't do, no matter how delectable he looked in them. We returned to the men's clothing store and picked out a dark blue dress shirt and a pair of slacks. When he came out of the dressing room, adjusting his sleeves, my mouth went dry at the sight of him.

Hugh was stunningly handsome. The collar of his shirt was slightly open, revealing a hint of chest hair and tanned skin. It highlighted the impressive breadth of his shoulders and the slim taper of his hips. His hair, now cut in a modern style, framed his strong features. I couldn't stop staring at him.

"Well?" asked the clerk, a grin on his face. He knew he'd done well in helping Hugh select the clothing.

"Sold," I said breathlessly. It seemed I wasn't the only one who was going to turn heads tonight.

Hugh's mouth quirked in amusement at my reaction. "If you were this awed by uncomfortable clothing, Ryder, I should have worn gear such as this all week."

"Ha-ha," I said, but I couldn't resist running a hand along his sleeve, feeling the strong arm underneath.

Our next stop was a clothing store for me. I picked out a skintight white bandage dress with long sleeves. It covered me from wrist to midthigh and had a high neck with a square cutout over the cleavage. It looked amazing and dangerous and incredibly sexy. I normally went for cute and colorful, but tonight, I wanted something different.

Mostly, I wanted Hugh to regret what he was going to miss out on.

As I paid for my dress, I glanced over at Hugh, hovering at my side. "So are we clear on tonight?"

"I am to be your date."

"That's right. Everyone would think it was weird otherwise. And you know how to act as my date?"

"Take your arm," he recited. "Pull out your chair. Be attentive. Do not flirt with other women." He gave me a patient look. "I am not stupid. I see how other men act to their mates. I will just copy them."

"Just don't hold my hand," I said, though I wished he could. "You know it'll set me off."

"I will remember," he said gravely. "I will protect you, Ryder. Do not worry."

We returned to my apartment. While Hugh sniffed out and examined every inch of the place for whiffs of fae, I changed into my slinky dress and fixed my hair and makeup. I lined my eyes with dark blue liner so it'd make my irises seem almost purple. I slicked my lips with a peachy gloss that made them plumper, curled my hair into big movie-star ringlets, then finger-tousled them until they formed a gorgeous mess of blond waves. My shoes were a pair of pink sparkly heels with peep toes.

I looked amazing. *Suck on that, Hugh.*

When I emerged from the bathroom, Hugh stopped at the sight of me. He stared for so long and so hard at my slinky white dress that my nipples got tight, and I felt my pulse begin to pound between my legs once more.

Silence fell between us.

After a long moment, Hugh swallowed hard and cleared his throat. "Your dress. It is revealing."

"It is," I said proudly, deliberately running my hands down the curves of my ass. "I plan on having fun tonight."

"You should change. You cannot leave this public bed wearing that."

"Do not even start that with me. I can wear what I want." I flicked an imaginary piece of lint off my sleeve. "And tonight, I want to look incredibly sexy."

"Ryder . . ." He swallowed again and shifted on his feet. I noticed his hand went to his thigh, and then he adjusted himself, oh-so-discreetly. "Men will want to touch you."

I gave him an innocent smile. "Well, that is what you're going to be there for, right? You're bodyguarding me. And these people are friends. No one's going to touch me." I patted the slinky fabric of my dress. "And if they do, I'll make sure it's on one of the covered sections, deal?"

I practically heard him grinding his teeth. "I do not approve of this," he told me after a long moment.

"Then call your boss and tell him you can't handle me," I said, grabbing my purse and slinging it over my shoulder. "I'm sure he'll be totally understanding." I ignored Hugh's glare as I pulled out my keys. I had him right where I wanted him. He couldn't call on Finian without risking being removed as my keeper and losing the chance of getting mates for himself and his men.

When he remained silent, I grinned, knowing I'd won that round. "That's what I thought. Now come on. We'll be late."

"A toast," Beau said, raising his glass of champagne and grinning down at the long table full of shifters. "To my brother, Joshua, and the only woman willing to put up with his shit full-time."

"Hear, hear," Everett Russell said with a grin, raising his glass. Two dozen other people raised their glasses into the air, myself included, and we catcalled and hollered our approval as a laughing Josh Russell pulled Marie into his lap and kissed her again.

At my side, Austin Russell put two fingers in his mouth and whistled loudly.

Tiger's Tail was a small family restaurant in Little Paradise. Most people would uncharitably call it a hole-in-the-wall, but since it was shifter owned, people were much more polite and forgiving of scuffed tables and chipped dinnerware. The food was good—barbeque—and perfect for a crowd of shifters. Marie and Josh had rented the place out for the evening, and the room was filled with friends and clients from the Midnight Liaisons service.

At the head of one table, Beau Russell, leader of the Alliance and Marie's new boss, sat with his wife, Bathsheba, at his side. The next table over, Ramsey Bjorn sat with his mate, Sara, in his lap. She was clearly already drunk as a skunk, and it looked like she was doing her best to tickle him. Sara could not hold her alcohol, I thought wryly. Nearby and watching their antics stood Everett Russell and two of the local werewolf alphas, Alice and Jackson, who had recently mated. At another table was a heavily pregnant were-tiger woman I didn't know, seated next to her mate, Vic, the tiger alpha. She was drinking water, of course, and it made me think of Savannah, the other pregnant woman I knew, who'd opted to cover at work tonight so the rest of us could hang out and party.

A weird assortment of people sat at my table. There was an old lady who I was pretty sure wasn't a shifter, and she was seated at the head of our table. Josh came by frequently to dote on her, and she seemed thrilled they were getting married. Also at our table were Marie's dad and his girlfriend, both clearly human. Hugh sat on one side of me, and Austin Russell sat on my other side. The rest of the room was made up of a variety of shifters—from Jeremiah Russell, who'd shown up with his boyfriend and his girlfriend, to a few vampires, who were steering clear of the humans, and the occasional werewolf.

It was an eclectic mix, but a fun one. The room had been decorated in honor of Marie and Josh's engagement. The normal checkered picniclike restaurant tablecloths had been removed for simpler, white tablecloths, and colorful streamers and balloons lined the walls. A CONGRATULATIONS JOSH AND MARIE-PIERRE banner hung from the ceiling, and Marie had groaned at the sight of it, shaking her finger at Josh as if he'd done something naughty. Everyone was laughing and talking, pigging out on barbeque, and drinking like fish. There was a small dance floor and an old-fashioned jukebox, and it played rollicking country song after country song.

Even Hugh seemed to be having a good time. He ate platefuls of barbeque and chatted with Marie's dad. If the man thought there was something odd about Hugh's manners or speech (or general lack of knowledge about most modern things), he was far too polite to bring it up.

I was having a good time, too. The champagne was flowing, and the bar was an open one, so I had a mixed drink in one hand and a glass of champagne in the other. I was getting good and toasty.

Marie was gorgeous tonight. Her black curly hair had been groomed into a fashionable hairstyle. She wasn't as pale as she'd been a few short months ago, and her skin was glowing with health. She'd put on a few pounds, too, and was no longer frighteningly skinny. Her red, strapless, body-hugging dress showed off her new curves, and Josh couldn't take his eyes off her. He'd been a playboy in his past, but now he had eyes only for Marie, and he looked as content as she was.

It made me so, so very happy for my friend. She deserved her joy. I glanced over at Sara and Ramsey, who were still having their mock-tickle fight, though Sara was clearly winning. Ramsey's face was flushed red, but I noticed he wasn't fighting very hard, and Sara was squirming all over him, giddy. My gaze slid to Beau and Bathsheba, who had their heads together and were talking quietly to each other. Beau's eyes gleamed as he looked at his mate, and I felt a swift pang of misery.

Everyone was pairing up. It seemed that I was the only one who couldn't find a happy ever after. Well, me and Savannah, who was about to pursue single motherhood.

At least Austin Russell was at my side and determined to flirt with me.

I'd brought a date to the party, which had put Austin off initially, but when Hugh and I weren't that attentive to each other, the drunker Austin got, the more interested he got. And the drunker *I* got, the more flirty I got. I'd lean in close and flash him my cleavage. I laughed at all his jokes—even the awful ones—and scooted my chair closer to his. When he leaned in to whisper to me, I ignored Hugh's frowns and acted as if Austin's drunk rambling had been the funniest thing ever. Actually, I liked Austin a lot, but mostly as a friend. But when he slid an arm over the back of my chair and pulled me a bit closer, that made Hugh stiffen with anger, his frown turning into a black scowl.

Hugh's pissiness only made me feel better. At least *someone* found me irresistible. So I encouraged Austin. Winked at him, flirted, took every drink that was offered to me, and basically had fun.

Pretty soon, I was in a drunken fog. I normally didn't drink to excess (unless it was coffee), but the party was lively and the waitress kept refilling my cup, so I couldn't resist drinking away my sorrows. Tomorrow might suck, but tonight? Tonight would be fun. "Hey, Ryder," Austin said in my ear. "You wanna dance?"

I peered past him to the dance floor. It was currently empty. "We gonna be the only ones?"

"We might," he said, grinning at me. "That going to bother you?"

"Nope." I got to my feet and wobbled.

Immediately, Austin's hands went to my waist to steady me. At the same time, Hugh got up from his chair, and I heard the low growl in his throat.

"Get your hands off her," Hugh told Austin.

I turned and frowned at Hugh. "Don't tell him what to do."

"I'm here to—" Hugh began, then frowned, as if remembering our pact. "I'm your date," he said flatly.

I shook my head at him, then wondered why it made the room spin. "Austin asked me to dance," I told Hugh. "I'm going to dance with him and you can't stop me."

Hugh just glared at me.

I turned and looked at Austin, who offered me his hand and a smile. My palm itched, and I desperately wanted to slap my hand into his, but I knew that was bad news. So I gestured for Austin to turn around, and when he did, I looped my arms around his neck. "Piggyback ride," I declared.

"You're a weird girl," he said with a chuckle, but he dragged me out onto the dance floor, leaning forward and walking as if I'd just been a heavy sort of backpack.

As soon as we got onto the small wooden dance floor, the music changed to a slow song. Again Austin offered me his hand, but I wrapped my arms around his neck and pushed my body against his so we wouldn't have to touch skin to skin. I tucked my head against his shoulder as we swayed, and I stared out at the audience. Everyone was laughing and drinking and having a great time. Everyone except Hugh, who stared at me with intently burning eyes, his entire posture on alert as I danced with Austin.

Sadness and guilt hit me as I saw Hugh's stiff, unhappy face. I didn't want to be dancing with Austin. I wanted to be in Hugh's arms. I wanted to be his girl. His mate. But he was planning on delivering me to the enemy and ruining my life. I sighed, feeling ridiculously close to crying. Why was life so unfair?

Austin's hands slid down my back and landed on my ass.

I saw Hugh get up, nearly flipping the table over in his haste, and the alarmed looks the other guests shot him. Marie glanced over at me and gave me a worried look, even as I pushed out of Austin's arms.

Hugh stormed over to us, and he looked ready to attack Austin, who was still clinging to me drunkenly. "Get your hands off her," Hugh demanded as he came to my side. The primordial shifter pulled me behind him, baring his teeth, and all I saw in my drink-fogged mind were flashing cat-eyes and enormous fangs.

Neither one seemed to put Austin off. He simply gave Hugh a tipsy smile and raised his hands in the air, backing off. "You wanted to cut in, all you had to do was ask."

"Cut . . . in?"

"He means you wanted to dance with me," I yelled back at Hugh helpfully over the music.

He winced at my loud voice, then looked me over. He nodded. "I will dance with you, Ryder."

Austin gave me a wink and headed back to the bar, leaving me on the dance floor with Hugh. He looked at me expectantly, so I sighed and lifted my arms to put around his neck, pressing my body to his.

Even in my drunken state, I knew that was a mistake. Hugh's big body was warm and familiar against mine, and I had to strain—even in my heels—to keep my joined hands from touching the warm skin of his neck. It also pushed my face close to the juncture of his collar, and I smelled his wonderful, masculine Hugh smell. His hands went to my waist and he held me against him, and then we began to sway, awkwardly, to the music.

I felt small and dainty and feminine in his arms. Normal. And the way he felt against me was something downright heavenly. My body reacted, my senses humming and my monster coming awake, though not quite emerging, since I was careful not to touch Hugh's skin.

His big hand stroked my back, up and down, as we moved to the song in small, shuffling steps. Being in Hugh's arms? It felt like home. Like I belonged here.

He leaned in and I heard the murmur of his voice over the music. "You should not let other men touch you like this, Ryder."

Other men? "Because you want to be the only one?" I asked, whispering.

He hesitated for a long, long moment. Then he said, "No one should touch you like this."

I pushed at his chest, suddenly wanting to be free of his arms. "So it's not that you wanted to be with me, is it? It's not that you wanted to dance with me. You just didn't want anyone else to do it." My words were drunkenly slurred, and the room weaved. God,

I was so drunk. How had I gotten so drunk so fast? I'd never been this plastered.

Hugh frowned at me but said nothing. Instead, he reached for me again.

I shoved his arms away. "No, you know what? You don't get to touch me. Not unless you want to touch me because *you* want to, not because you think you need to guard me. That's crap and you know it."

"That is my job, Ryder." His voice was low, his face pained.

"Fuck you and your job," I said, stumbling past him. There was a bathroom nearby, and I wanted to splash water on my face. That sounded really good to my drunk brain right about now.

When I stumbled past Hugh, he reached for me again, to steady me. I slapped his hands away and stomp-stumbled to the bathroom.

He followed me.

I paused outside the door and pointed at the plaque that said WOMEN. "This means I'm going in here to use the bathroom and you can't follow me in, understand? Now go fuck off." And I stormed in before he could argue.

The door swung shut, and I watched it for a long moment, in a mental fog. Part of me expected Hugh to come charging through, regardless of etiquette, so we could continue our conversation. But he didn't.

And I was stupidly, drunkenly, disappointed.

The bathroom was a small room, nondescript but clean. Two stalls lined up on one side, and two sinks and a mirror were adjacent to them. On one of the walls was a large window covered by a pair of checkered curtains. I headed to the sink and flipped the water on, then splashed my face. Okay, I might have splashed the hell out of the front of my dress, too, but I was drunk and didn't care. I was weirdly overheated and feeling sluggish, too. Maybe it was the long sleeves of my dress?

Another woman entered the bathroom—the waitress. In a daze, I looked in the mirror, and she smiled at me.

"Is it hot in here to you?" I fanned my face.

"Sorry, not to me." She gave me a curious look, watching me through the mirror.

"Huh." I felt dizzy and glanced at the window. It seemed like a good idea to open it. Get a breeze in the room. I struggled to the window, wobbling as the room went hazy around me. Why was I feeling so awful? I tried to open the window, but I felt strangely weak.

"Here, let me get that for you, dearest." The waitress came to my side and helped me open the window.

"Thanks," I mumbled, leaning into the now open window to feel the breeze on my face. "I don't know what's wrong with me."

"Oh, that's easy," she said in a light voice, smiling over at me. "You've been roofied."

"Roofied?" I stared at her dumbly. "Someone roofied me?"

"Not just someone." Then she winked at me.

My fogged brain wasn't piecing things together. "I don't understand."

"It was me."

Why would a waitress roofie me? I squinted at her, then pressed my face to the screen on the window, positively aching for the breeze from outside. "Roofies are bad. Why would you do that?"

"Because I don't want you fighting me while we get out of here." She nudged me aside and began to push at the edges of the screen until it popped out onto the ground.

It was hard to think. I shook my head to clear it, but that didn't work. "Why are we leaving?"

She looked over at me and pinched my cheek. "Aren't you cute? We're leaving, dearest, because once Finian finds out that I've stolen his precious changeling, he's going to wet his pants."

My eyes widened. "I know you, don't I?" I squinted at the woman's face, but she didn't look like anyone famous. "You're the other fae prince, aren't you? Except you're a girl."

"Guilty," she sang out in a cheery voice, then patted the windowsill. "Glamour magic is fun, isn't it? Now come on. Time's a-wasting, and your bodyguard is going to sniff something out if we don't hurry. You're going to be quiet for me, aren't you?" And she pinched my cheek again.

My hand flew to my face. "You touched my cheek and I didn't turn." Was it because he was currently glamoured to be a girl? But he was a guy underneath, wasn't he?

"Roofies. They're a wonder drug," she said. "Can't have you going all changeling on me in the parking lot. That wouldn't do at all. Now, come on. One leg over."

I nodded, unable to resist her encouraging words. I pushed one leg, noticing that it felt about as strong as a wet noodle, onto the windowsill. Roofies sure did mess with you. I yawned as I crawled through the window, lost my balance, then rolled to the grass outside with a giggle.

"Shhh," she cautioned, following me out the window. She closed it carefully and turned to me, grabbing my arm. "Get up. We're going to my car."

Her—his?—fingers dug into my arm and I got to my feet, but it was a struggle. "Oh, man," I breathed. "Hugh is going to be so mad when he finds out you stole me." I gave another dopey giggle, unable to help myself.

"Let's hope he doesn't find out until we're long gone," she said, dragging me behind her. "Come on."

We walked through the parking lot, me stumbling as much as stepping. It occurred to me that I should have fought her. Kicked. Screamed, sounded an alarm, something. But it was like the part of my mind that protested had been shut off and put to sleep. In its place was a hazy, drunken feeling, and I was helpless to object when she opened a car door and gestured that I should get inside the backseat.

I crawled in about halfway, then got tired and lay down.

"Get your legs in," she snapped, and pushed at my limbs. "Come on."

"You're not being nice," I chided sleepily, but I curled up and she slammed the car door. One of my sparkly heels caught in the door, and it bounced back open. She gave a sigh of exasperation, then grabbed my feet and began to undo the buckle across the arch of each pink shoe. I giggled and squirmed, not used to someone touching my feet. I didn't even get pedicures—I'd learned to do my own. "That tickles."

"I'm going to tear your wings out if you don't stop squirming," she said in a deceptively charming voice. "I'm going to clip them so you can't fly away, but if you don't behave, I'll just rip those wrinkled little things out at the root."

I frowned. That didn't sound nice. I pressed my heated face to the seat and sighed, wishing the leather felt cooler against my skin. "Sorry."

"That's better," she said, tossing my shoes into the car and shutting the door.

I yawned, my eyelids heavy. I barely noticed her getting into the front seat of the car and turning the ignition on. The radio blared, but she quickly clicked it off and glanced at me in the rearview mirror. "Just a few minutes more and we'll be at one of the nearby ley-lines. I can open a portal there, and we'll be home free."

"You should just use your rune," I said helpfully. "That's what Hugh does."

"That's different magic, you idiot," she said,

backing the car out of the parking lot. "The fae realm is more guarded than those pitiful pocket realms that the servants live in." She glanced in the rearview mirror again and gave me a shrewd look. "So Hugh has a rune, does he?"

"He does," I said dreamily. "He's got two of them."

"Finian's spent a small fortune on you, then. That kind of magic isn't cheap." The car eased forward, and she shifted gears. Her eyes widened as she looked in the rearview mirror. "Oh, dear."

Something heavy slammed into the back of the car.

I rolled off the seat and slid to the floorboards of the car, wincing. I dragged myself back onto my seat and flopped back down as the fae in the front seat hastily put on her seat belt.

The heavy thing slammed into the back of the car again. I heard the crunch of metal at the same time I heard the feral roar.

"That's Hugh," I said and patted the yawn escaping my mouth. "He's not happy."

A snarl escaped the woman's pretty mouth as she looked back at me. I watched her jerk at the gearshift, then I heard the tires squeal as the car lurched, then shot forward, nearly knocking me off the seat again. My stomach gave a queasy lurch.

We jerked to the side, turning out of the parking lot.

Something slammed into the car again. The crunch of metal was even louder than before, and glass shattered. The world flipped and my body slammed into the roof of the car.

Everything went black.

I woke up a few moments later, blurry. Shattered glass was all around me; and I was lying on the roof of the car, with the street at eye level. Had we flipped over? I could hear a police siren somewhere in the distance, but it seemed so far away. Something wet trickled down the side of my face, and I swiped at it. I glanced at the front of the car, but it was empty.

I was alone.

"Oh, dear," I muttered to myself more than anyone else. I raked aside the broken glass with my hand, then winced when that hurt. Whoops. I examined my arm and watched blood well up through the sleeve of my pretty white dress. *That was stupid, Ryder.* But stupid seemed to be the only brain function I had left. That, and the constant feeling that I needed to take a nap.

I got to my hands and knees and began to crawl onto the street from the back of the car. It took a few moments for me to wiggle out, and by the time I did, both my hands and my knees were cut up from the glass. There was no pain, but it'd hurt in the morning.

Once outside the car, I staggered to my feet and stared, in a daze, at the wreck of the vehicle. There was only one car in the wreck—ours. It had been flipped onto its back, and one side looked as if it had been hit by another car. The door was accordioned and smashed shut.

There was no sign of the fae anywhere. Or Hugh, for that matter.

My eyes closed, and I weaved unsteadily on my feet.

"You okay, miss? Do I need to call nine-one-one?"

I opened my eyes and stared unsteadily at the man who had appeared. On the other side of the street, a car had its flashers on, and the front door was hanging open. The man at my side was older, gray-haired, and wore thick glasses and a sweater-vest.

Was this another one of the fae's tricks? Frowning to myself, I pinched the man's cheek. "Is that you in there?"

He gave me a disgusted look. "You're drunk, aren't you? Give me your keys." He held out his hand. "I'm calling the police. You should be ashamed. You could have hurt someone."

"I wasn't driving," I protested, then yawned heavily. "I just want a nap."

An earsplitting roar came from down the street.

"What the hell was that?" the man whispered.

I turned toward it, my interest pricking. "Is that Hugh? Here, kitty kitty. Nice kitty." I tried to snap my fingers, then became fascinated with the way my fingers didn't seem to work properly. Stupid fingers.

Heavy feet slammed on the pavement, and the man next to me sucked in a breath. "Do you see that?"

"See what?" I peered at the world around me, but everything was fuzzy and black. I couldn't tell what was going on. I weaved unsteadily on my feet.

"I gotta get out of here," the man shouted, and he let me go.

I collapsed on the ground, unable to stand on my own. I was pretty sure I had glass in my butt now, and I whimpered, unable to help myself. I couldn't do anything. What was wrong with me?

Roofies. Oh, right. I decided I hated roofies a second before the world got all black around me again.

The earsplitting roar happened again, dragging me back to consciousness. I cracked one eye open and saw enormous striped paws near my head. I was lying on the concrete, glass glittering all around me and distracting my vision. I whimpered, because everything hurt and I was too weak to get up.

An enormous cat-head appeared in the edges of my vision. I saw stripes, feral green eyes, and enormous, foot-long fangs extending from the barrel-sized head.

Hugh.

"Hey, kitty," I said sleepily.

My head fell back to the pavement, and I was out.

Chapter Fifteen

I came to sometime later, my eyelids heavy as if there had been a brick resting on each one. My mouth tasted like a wad of cotton, and my head felt fuzzy. I could hear crickets chirping, and the grass under my head was wet. My eyes slowly focused, and I looked up at a canopy of leaves overhead.

Huh?

I scrubbed at my mouth, hating the taste of it and wishing I could remember more of how I'd gotten here. Every bone in my body ached, and something hard was digging into my lower back. My head pounded, and I lifted a hand to rub at it . . . and realized that I had horns.

Frowning, I glanced at my hand and realized it was scaled.

Scales . . . trees . . . flashes of last night rolled through my mind. Crawling out the bathroom window. A car wreck. Hugh's animalistic roars. A woman's face slid in and out of memory. Sickness rolled through my gut.

I'd been kidnapped.

I rolled over in the grass, my blunted claws digging into the earth as I assessed the situation. My eyes were having a hard time focusing on my surroundings, but it was warm and humid in the area, and birds chirped somewhere in the distance. Insects buzzed, and the ground underneath me felt wet with dew. The smells of dirt and plants overwhelmed my senses and made my stomach churn sickeningly. I wanted to throw up. Had the disguised fae prince managed to get me to the fae realm after all? Was that why I was in my changeling form?

Something fuzzy touched my back and I jerked upright, flipping over with a shriek to look.

An enormous saber-toothed tiger stared back at me, green eyes gleaming. The long fangs protruded from his mouth, gleaming and dangerous and inches away from my face.

I heaved a sigh of relief. "Hugh." I reached out and grabbed the cat by the ruff to kiss his nose. "Oh, my God, you have no idea how glad I am to see you."

A rough tongue swiped at my cheek, the cat version of nuzzling. I laughed with relief, and it turned into a sob. "I don't know what happened last night. My mind's all messed up. Where are we?"

The cat nosed me again, expectantly.

"I don't speak saber-tooth," I told him. "Nor do I interpret nose-butts."

The cat made a low, grumbling noise in its throat that might have been either a purr, a growl, or a laugh. I couldn't tell. He turned, paced away a few steps, and his shoulders hunched.

I knew what that meant—a shift. I closed my eyes to give him a bit of privacy, waiting patiently for him to finish shifting. A moment later, a big hand brushed my cheek. I opened my eyes and looked into Hugh's human face.

He was stark naked.

I glanced down at my body. So was I, for that matter. "Where did our clothing go?"

"You transformed when I carried you through the portal," Hugh said. His gaze, surprisingly anxious, continued to search my face, and his thumb stroked my chin. "I had to take your clothing off or it would have hurt you. Your dress was very tight against your skin."

Oh. That it was. It made sense, I suppose. I still had trouble focusing. "And your clothing?"

"Tore it when I shifted." He shrugged, as if it wasn't important. "Are you well?"

"I'm not hurt? All my scrapes and bruises are gone." I distinctly remembered broken glass and blood on my hands and knees, but the scabs on my skin were only tender and well on their way to healing.

"Time has passed. You have been asleep for some time."

I pressed two fingers between my brows, wishing my headache would go away. "Last night seems to be a blur." Try as I might, I couldn't recall everything. It flashed in and out of my mind in a vague jumble of images.

"The fae tried to grab you," he said, then angrily bared his fangs. "You went with him. Why?"

I squeezed my eyes shut, trying to think. "I think he drugged me. Roofie. It's something someone can put in your drink that gets rid of your inhibitions. Basically it makes you unable to say no." I shivered. "I can't believe I was roofied."

"And nearly taken." His eyes narrowed, and that hard look crossed his face again. "I nearly lost you."

"I'm sorry," I said, then grimaced. "And I don't know why I'm apologizing. I didn't know I was going to be drugged." I glanced around at our surroundings. "So you took me here? To the primordial realm?"

Hugh gave a short nod. "There was much chaos after your car turned over. People were arriving, and I had lost my clothing because I'd changed. They were going to take you away, so I chased them off and took you. The fae ran and I could not find him." He bared his extended fangs again, Hugh's version of a scowl. "I think he shifted faces once more."

I rubbed my arms, shivering at the thought. "If he can change faces over and over again, I don't know how I'll be safe from him."

"You will be, here in the primordial realm with me," Hugh said fiercely. "You will not leave my side."

"But we can't stay here. Finian won't like my being here, because it messes up his schedule. Time passes differently in this place, so that screws up how much time I have left before I fully turn." I extended my arm and regarded my scales. They were a pale green, softly gleaming. It was . . . pretty. That was strange. I touched my face and wondered how different it looked. I craned my head, trying to glimpse my wings, but they were still wrinkled and lay against my back, not fully developed.

Hugh got to his feet, leaving me eye level with his rather impressive equipment. "At this moment, I do not care what Finian likes or does not like." He extended a hand down to me.

I took it, blushing and trying not to glimpse the cock I had been eye level with just moments ago. My feet were still wobbly, and my legs were feeling weak. I struggled to take a few steps, then sighed at how much it made my head spin. "I think I'm still hungover from the drugs."

"I will carry you," Hugh said. He reached for me, and before I could protest, he swung me into his arms. One strong hand grasped my thigh and supported me behind my knees, and the other crossed my back and pressed me against his chest.

My breast pushed against his bare skin and I gasped, feeling need flood through me. "Sorry."

"Do not apologize for touching me," Hugh gritted as he shifted me against him.

"Yes, but . . . you don't want to be tempted," I said, feeling that same overwhelming sadness. I shifted, trying to get comfortable in his arms without pressing too much of my body against his. "I won't do that to you anymore. It's not fair to you."

"Ryder, do not worry about me." Hugh pulled me closer to his chest, shifting me so I had no choice but to press a hand against one lightly furred pectoral. "Get comfortable. It is a long walk back to the caves."

"The caves?" I looked at him in surprise. "Is that where we're going?"

He gave a short nod and began to walk.

"Are . . . are you sure you want to carry me? I can walk. I just need time to adjust—"

"Let me care for you," he said softly. His arms tightened around me. "Relax. Sleep if you need to."

I wouldn't. I remained tense as Hugh cradled me against his chest and continued to stride forward through the swampy forest. After a few minutes of silence, though, I realized Hugh wasn't breathing hard. He wasn't winded at all. So I relaxed, lulled by the rocking motion of Hugh's steps.

Eventually, I even drifted off to sleep, still exhausted.

I woke up sometime later, my cheek cuddled against Hugh's shoulder, one side of my body warm from lying against him, the other chilly. I glanced around and saw that it had gotten dark while I'd slept. I looked up and saw Hugh's cat-eyes, gleaming in the darkness. "Where are we?"

"Almost to my home," Hugh said in a low voice. "How are you feeling?"

"Better, I guess?" I rubbed my eyes and sighed at the sight of my changeling skin. "Still scaly, though."

"You will be as long as we are here in this realm," Hugh said. "It is part of who you are."

"It sucks." I wrinkled my nose at my scales, though they were now a pale, pretty green. "I hate it."

"You are beautiful," Hugh said, ducking a low-hanging branch. "I could look at you all day and never get tired of gazing at you."

Oh, wow. I felt a wiggle of heat prickle through me at that. "Thank you."

"I speak the truth," he said simply.

He did, because he never lied. I basked in his compliment for a time, still snuggled up against him and feeling too delicious to volunteer to get down and walk. There was something decadent about letting Hugh carry me, and I hated to admit that I enjoyed every moment of it.

"We are almost there," Hugh told me. He shifted, then glanced down at me with concerned eyes. "Can you walk?"

"I can try," I told him and felt a little twinge of disappointment when he shifted and gently placed me on my feet. I wiggled my toes in the grass. I was hungry and tired, but the fuzzy, confused feeling had left me. I took a few steps and nodded at Hugh. "I'm good. Thank you for carrying me."

"It was my pleasure," he told me in a husky voice that sent shivers up my spine and made my folded wings flutter. When he said it like that, it really did sound like it was a pleasure for him.

Was Hugh . . . flirting with me? This wasn't like him. I gave him a surprised look, and another when his hand slid down my back, as if reluctant to release me. "Are you okay?"

He nodded, then put a hand to the small of my back, just north of my flicking tail. "Come. Do not be afraid. I will protect you from everyone."

I frowned at that. "Do I need to be protected from the others?"

"They . . . will not be pleased to see me. Now, come." Hugh nudged me forward.

We dove through low overhanging trees and maneuvered around brushy ferns. The jagged, sheer cliff appeared in the distance, and I felt a pit of dread in my stomach at the sight. Why would the other primordials be unhappy to see Hugh? Had something else happened that I didn't understand? I kept my worries to myself, since Hugh had gone silent, a sure sign that he was troubled.

Timidly, I brushed my hand against his. For some reason, I wanted to be held. To know that someone was going to help me. That I wasn't as alone in this as I felt.

Hugh's hand clasped mine. He laced his fingers through my own, and I felt that weird wiggle of warmth in my belly again. I noticed that his claws were out, though, and glanced up to see his eyes completely dark, entirely animal. He was on high alert.

Then he stopped. He lifted his head and sniffed the air.

I glanced around, seeing nothing. Trees, trees, darkness, and more trees. Just then, a pair of gleaming eyes caught my attention in the nearby bushes. I sucked in a breath and nudged Hugh.

"I know," he told me. "It's all right, Ryder. It's Artur, come to greet us."

The bushes shook, and a moment later, the warrior emerged. He was fully naked as well—strange how I still wasn't used to all the naked beefcake strolling around in this place—and wore a scowl on his brutal, ugly face. His arms were crossed over his chest (which was thicker and broader than Hugh's, which I didn't think was possible). "Brother. You will not receive a warm welcome for this return, I am afraid."

"I had no choice," Hugh said. His hand detangled from mine, and he pressed a kiss to the top of my head before striding forward to confront Artur.

The gesture was so sweet and possessive that I almost missed the flash of longing in Artur's gleaming eyes.

Almost.

Hugh came to his friend's side, and they clasped forearms in greeting, though Artur still didn't look pleased. Hugh talked to him for a long moment, their voices so low that I couldn't pick out what they were saying. The nosy part of me wanted to rush forward and listen in, but I suspected that as soon as I got closer, they'd cease talking. Whatever it was, it was clear I wasn't meant to overhear.

So I shuffled my feet in the wet grass and brushed my hair over my breasts, trying to make it seem like I wasn't wearing only scales.

Artur glanced at me again, then nodded. "While I cannot say my heart is glad, I do understand you, brother."

Hugh nodded. "Let's go tell the others, then. Get this over with."

"Tell them what?" I asked.

No one answered me.

"Tell them what?" I asked again. "Hello? Cute girl standing right here? Likes long walks on the beach and hates being ignored?"

They both just turned and stared at me.

I sighed. "Never mind. Let's go and get it over with. Whatever 'it' is."

The two men flanked me (an act I found unnerving), and we continued forward through the woods until we came to the labyrinth of caves. Each dark cave entrance seemed to have a set of gleaming eyes peering out, watching us.

"Wait here, Ryder," Hugh informed me. He stepped forward and raised a hand to his mouth, letting out a roar that was so loud and tigerlike that it startled me.

"But—"

Artur stepped to my side and shook his head at me, indicating silence.

The other primordial shifters began to emerge from the shadows. I watched, my heart fluttering with something like anxiety as, one by one, they slunk forward, gaze flicking back and forth from me to Hugh.

He glanced around until he seemed satisfied, then said, "You all know of my agreement with Finian. That I sold my services to him, acting as a representative to all of us. I was to complete the vow, and in exchange, we would be given mates so we might end our lonely existence. I am sorry to say that I cannot complete the vow. I have failed all of you."

I gasped. What? How?

With horror, I watched as the other shifters leapt upon Hugh, burying him in a pile of furious bodies determined to attack.

"Hugh," I cried, running forward.

Artur grabbed me by the arm. "Do not. All will be well."

"But they're hurting him!"

"He expected this. He is letting them vent their rage." Artur's hand tightened on my arm. "Do not attempt to intervene."

I looked at the snarl of men, fists and naked bodies flying. It seemed to be a mosh pit of nudity and anger. If I hadn't been so distraught at the thought of poor Hugh being at the center, I probably would have enjoyed all the flexing buttocks and bouncing peen. As it was, it just freaked me out.

One large arm shot through the crowd of angry men and grabbed someone's head, knocking it into another. Two men fell to the ground, only to have another two leap into the fray. Hugh rose for a moment, his nose bloody, a gouge down one cheek. His teeth were bared in a feral snarl, his eyes dark.

Then another man grabbed him by the throat, and down he went into the surging bodies again.

"Hugh," I cried out, then yanked at my arm when Artur grabbed me again, pulling me away from the fight. "Let go of me."

"Let them get it out," Artur told me. "Don't you know he's doing this for you?"

Chapter Sixteen

"Doing this for me?" My voice rose a hysterical note. "How is he doing this for me? It looks like he's being pulverized!"

"He has chosen you over us," Artur said flatly. "He will not give you to the fae. It will negate the vow and leave the rest of us without mates, but you will be safe."

I gasped and turned to Artur. "What?"

"It's true." He gave a quick nod, and only the bleakness in his eyes revealed his feelings. His ugly face was impassive. "He cannot bear to send you to your fate, so he will forsake us to keep you safe."

I looked at the crowd of men, all furiously fighting one another. I saw the helpless rage of the men as they attacked Hugh. One turned and gave me a look of pure longing before leaping back into the fray.

A sob escaped my throat. I wept because I'd been selfish. I'd won, and now I'd destroyed the happiness of so many others. I should have felt good about it, but all I felt was more miserable. So I sobbed.

A cry of rage escaped the pile. It surged forward,

heading toward me. Hugh emerged, a man clinging to his back and another to his leg. He shrugged them off with violent motions and came for me, eyes wild. "Ryder!"

The others fell back, sitting on their haunches in an animalistic way. They licked their wounds and wiped blood from nostrils and mouths. They glared at Hugh, but their gaze didn't have the same anger toward me that they had toward him.

Hugh moved to me and gently cupped my face, scanning it with worry. "Are you hurt? Why do you cry?"

"I don't understand," I told him, shaking my head. I looked up into his face. One of his eyes was swelling shut, and his nostril leaked a thin trail of blood. He'd never looked more gorgeous to me. "You're not going to give me to Finian? But . . . you're ruining it for everyone. I thought that was what you wanted."

"That was before I knew you," he said. His thumb grazed the smooth scales of my cheek, oh-so-sweetly. "And now I cannot imagine doing anything that would cause you such misery."

My breath caught in my throat at his words. I'd wanted to hear that for so long. And yet . . . it was almost too much to believe. It was such a high, brutal cost. "What made you change your mind?"

He glanced around at the others. Filled with sadness, I did, too, and noticed that they were staring at my naked body in a way that could only be described as . . . hungry. "This is not a conversation for any ears but yours, Ryder. Come. We will go to my cave."

"Sounds lovely," I said, dazed. A cave? We were going somewhere private to talk? He wasn't giving me to Finian? I was trying to process all of this, and failing miserably. But when he extended his hand to me, I automatically took it, and he led me through the ominous crowd. I trusted him to keep me safe.

He led me to the rocky cliff, and I stared up at it as we approached. It was easily five or six stories tall, a sheer outcropping that ended abruptly, as if some divine hand had neatly sliced it in half. Up the sides of the cliff were holes riddled through the rock—caves. And each cave, I knew, was the home of one of the primordials. "Which one is yours?"

Hugh released my hand and began to climb, tugging on a few of the vines that had worked their way into the stone. "I am at the top."

"Of course you are," I said faintly. I stared as Hugh climbed the sheer surface as if it had been nothing, his toe-claws digging into the rock and his big hands using the vines to leverage himself up. I moved closer and touched one of the vines. It was stout, all right, but slippery from the clingy mist. I glanced up. I was pretty sure I wasn't going to be able to climb that. At all.

Hugh looked down after a moment. "Do you not come?"

I touched one of the leafy vines. "I don't think I can climb this." I displayed my blunted claws, which now looked more like long, smooth mother-of-pearl chips than deadly killing weapons. "These won't dig into anything, and my wings still don't work."

He leapt down from the ledge, ignoring the fact that he'd just dropped two stories, and landed at my feet in a crouch. Then he straightened, apparently unhurt, and grinned at me, mouth full of sharp teeth. "All you had to do was say so."

With that, he grabbed me and swung me over his arm, my stomach landing on his shoulder. Just like Tarzan. And just like Tarzan, he began to climb once more, moving swiftly up the cliff wall.

I swallowed the scream that erupted in my throat, dug my ineffective claws into his skin as much as I could, and closed my eyes. Hugh wouldn't let me fall. He wouldn't. I trusted him.

After a few moments, the rough swaying stopped, and I heard—and felt—Hugh's body thump to the ground. I squeezed one eye open and glanced around as he set me gently down next to him.

We were inside Hugh's cave. It was dark inside, and I could barely make out my surroundings. There didn't seem to be much to see, though. My toes tickled a pile of furs nearby, but other than that, I could see nothing. "This is your home?"

"Aye."

For some reason, it made me sad that Hugh lived with so little. It was so . . . crude. "You don't have much."

"I do not need much," he admitted. "Most days, I spend my time in my other form. It makes things less . . . lonely. Your other self does not notice things that are lacking nearly as much."

Oh, that was sad. I wondered if that was why the others seemed downright feral at times. Was it because they were all used to spending time in their animal form more than their human one? Because they were so lonely? I wanted to weep for them . . . and for Hugh. I turned toward him in the darkness, his gleaming eyes making him easy to find. My hand reached out to him and landed on smooth, warm skin. "Tell me what's going on. I need to understand."

His eyes closed, the green gleam disappearing for such a long moment that it made my breath catch in my throat. It returned a moment later, and I felt his big, warm hands on my shoulders.

Hugh pulled me against him, dragging me to him in a warm, comforting embrace.

I was startled at first. For me, it was always unusual to feel skin-to-skin contact, much less with a nearly seven-foot-tall man who was totally naked. But Hugh seemed to be a hugger. He seemed to need that comforting touch almost as much as I did, so when his big hand rested on the back of my head and began to stroke my hair, pressing my cheek to his chest, I couldn't really protest. I was enjoying the sensations too much.

But I also wanted answers. So I hesitantly put my hand on his stomach and pushed away a bit, just enough to look up at him. "Tell me what's going on, Hugh. Please."

He sighed heavily, then cleared his throat. "When . . . when I saw you dancing with the small one, it angered me."

"Small one?" I giggled at that. A saber-toothed tiger the size of a grizzly bear probably thought a were-cougar was small, but I doubted Austin Russell would enjoy the description. But then the rest of Hugh's words sank in. "It made you angry?"

"It did." His hands clenched tighter around me, and the hand that began to stroke my hair again was pressing so hard that I was pretty sure I'd be bald if it continued. "You were touching another man and laughing with him, and he was admiring your body. I . . . wanted to hurt him. And . . . I wanted to *be* him."

"You did?"

"I did." His hands tightened around me again. "I was envious of his freedom. He could touch you. He could dance with you and make you laugh. And I am not allowed. I envied him greatly in that moment."

I hugged Hugh, feeling the need to comfort him. My arms wrapped around his waist, and I scratched my nails idly on his back, sensing that he'd enjoy that. "You're jealous over nothing, Hugh. I only like Austin as a friend. And truthfully, you're the only person I trust not to run away screaming at the sight of my real face." I still flinched at the thought of showing Austin my true nature; I imagined his reaction and knew it wouldn't be a good one.

"You are harsh to yourself, Ryder." He shook

his head. "I bring this up only because I am trying to make you understand. I was jealous of the small cat shifter yesterday, and it made me angry. That was why we fought. I deliberately chose to ruin your fun and provoke you. And after you ran off, I felt . . . guilty. Like I was destroying everything for you. And I realized I had to. That it was my job to do this. That feeling did not sit well with me."

His hand paused on my head, then began to stroke my hair again. "When he stole you out from under my nose . . ." I felt his big body shudder against mine. "I cannot describe how it made me feel. How helpless and full of rage. I'd failed in my vow. And I should have thought of my brother primordials, waiting patiently for me to return home with their mates. Waiting for me to fix things. But I was not thinking of them. Instead, the only thing that kept going through my mind was you. That you were lost and scared somewhere. That I had failed you. I only thought of you. Not of the other women waiting for us. Just you."

I pressed my cheek harder against his chest, burrowing against him. I didn't want to interrupt.

"When I found you, my relief was so great that I wanted to scream it to the heavens." He held me tightly again. "I realized that I had no right to feel this way for you. And I also realized I could not give you up. Not to Finian. Not to anyone."

His arms clenched around me even harder, nearly squeezing the breath out of me. I didn't mind. I didn't mind at all. I could scarcely breathe myself, barely daring to hope that what I was hearing was the truth.

"And that is why I must remove your virginity, Ryder."

I giggled at that. "Um, that's a weird way of putting it."

His chest-constricting hug loosened and he glanced down at my face, his hand moving to cup my chin and tilt me into looking in his direction. "How should it be said, then?"

I was glad that it was dark and I had scales, because I was pretty sure that the blush on my face could rival a fire hydrant for its color. "It's not removed, I guess. It's taken."

"But . . . that implies that I am snatching it from you. I do not think I like this wording." He sounded offended.

I couldn't help but laugh again. "How about I give it to you instead?"

"I like the sound of that." His fingers brushed against the scales of my jaw. "Would you . . . do you want to give it to me, Ryder?"

"I do," I breathed. "More than anything. You know this."

"I need to hear it again." His voice was husky, and I wished I could see more than just the gleam of his eyes in the darkness.

"But what about Finian? What about the others? What will happen to all of them?"

"Finian"—he spat the word as if it were foul—"will not be pleased. I do not care what he thinks."

"But you told him you did not want me for yourself. I remember that."

"I did." His expression was grim. "I thought it true at the time. But . . . it is not."

My eyes widened. "Really? What about the others?"

"They will get over their disappointment in time," he said softly. "But I do not think I will be able to stay here, my Ryder. With you at my side, their envy would be too great. The pain would be a daily one, and even I am not that cruel."

"Is this your way of asking to move in with me, big guy? Because I vote yes."

"I would like nothing more than to remain at your side for the rest of my life, Ryder. I care for you as I care for no other."

My heart swelled with excitement and affection. Was Hugh admitting that he loved me? I wanted so desperately to believe this was true. My nails dug into his back, and I pressed myself against him. This was almost too good to be true. "You can come live with me, Hugh," I told him. "But what about Finian? He's coming to collect me."

Hugh pulled me away from him. I immediately felt bereft of his warmth, his heat, his caresses. "Ryder, I must ask you to sacrifice something. If I am gifted with your virginity tonight, you will remain as you are for the rest of your days."

My heart stopped in my chest. "I'm going to be like this forever? Not human?"

"You will be human," he said. "Your glamour

will never leave you. But your changeling form will be frozen at this point in time. Your wings will no longer blossom. Your horns will not spiral and sharpen. Your claws will remain dull, and your scales the color they are now. Once you are no longer a virgin, you will no longer grow more beautiful by the day. And if I take your virginity now, you will not go into heat on your twenty-fifth birthday."

I wanted to laugh with relief. "Is that all? I don't care about that."

"Are you sure? A changeling in full bloom is the most beautiful thing anyone has ever seen. They make the throat ache with their sheer beauty." His thumb grazed along my collarbones ever so gently. "And even though you already *are* the most beautiful thing I have ever seen, I will be robbing you of your potential if I do not at least warn you of the consequences."

"So I can be the most beautiful thing ever, or I can have the man I love?" My voice broke, my heart thrumming at the admission. "That's kind of a no-brainer. All I want is you."

He pulled me gently forward until his head rested against my belly. "I am filled with love for you, Ryder."

I wanted to laugh again at his strange wording, but I didn't. The feel of his head pressing against my belly was setting off every nerve ending in my body. His hair brushed against the curves of my breasts, teasing me. I ran my fingers through his thick, almost wiry hair and was rewarded with his mouth nuzzling against the soft flesh on my belly.

Flesh? Perplexed, I touched my stomach and discovered that my scales had smoothed out from there. Had I missed that transformation somehow? It seemed that I had scales still on my shoulders, back, and buttocks, but my front had gone soft, the skin velvety.

Like an armadillo, I had a soft underbelly. I giggled at the thought, strangely pleased.

My laughter died a moment later when Hugh's mouth dipped and licked at the underside of one breast. A moan escaped my throat, and I dug my fingers into his hair, dragging his mouth toward my breast when he skimmed away. I wanted more of that.

Now that Hugh would touch me wherever? I wanted everything.

He seemed willing, too. His mouth turned and I felt it, hot against my skin, the graze of his teeth against my flesh. Then, he sought the tip of one breast and brushed his teeth against it.

Heat flooded my body, and I gasped. I was incredibly sensitive everywhere, but my nipples seemed to be the most sensitive of all. They ached, hard points of attention, and when his tongue rasped against one, I whimpered all over again. "Hugh. God, Hugh. Your mouth."

"Do I frighten you?"

"Not at all," I said, pressing my breast toward his mouth once more. "I need your mouth all over me."

He groaned as well, digging his hands into my back, and I felt his claws against my scales. Didn't hurt. His mouth sought my nipple, rolling it against his lips, then latching on and sucking hard.

I cried out. It felt so incredibly good that it made me dazed with need.

"Ryder," he said, his voice ragged. He pressed his mouth to the curve of my breast, pushing rapid kisses against my skin. "Ryder, we must be quieter. The others will hear—"

I tore out of his arms, my eyes going wide. Any excitement I felt died in a heartbeat. "Oh, my God. They can hear us, can't they?" I knew Hugh's hearing was supersharp, but I hadn't realized how keen. I glanced at the entrance to the cave, but it was wide open. It wasn't as if anyone could peer in unless they were hiding in a nearby treetop. Which . . . yikes. I pulled away from Hugh.

"What is it?"

"I can't do this here," I told him. "Not with the others close and listening. I . . . it's cruel. And weird. Can't we go someplace where we'd have some privacy?"

"This is my home," he said. "No one will disturb us here."

"Well, that's great and all, but I can't do this with others listening to our every move, Hugh." I reached out and caressed his cheek, feeling the bristly brush of his sideburns. "Don't you have someplace . . . someplace special that we could go, just the two of us? Someplace we could be alone and not have to worry about being quiet? Or disturbing the others?"

He was silent for so long that I thought he'd disagree. Then he pressed another kiss to my flesh. "I know the place. Come."

Hugh got to his feet so abruptly that I felt dizzy, unbalanced by the low light of the cave, where I could see nothing beyond the entrance. Hugh grasped my hand in his and led me out to the ledge again.

"Oh, no," I said, peering over the edge. "Not this again."

"I will have you," he told me.

And before I could protest, he swung me over his shoulder once more.

This time, I knew the deal. I squeezed my eyes shut and waited as he climbed, anchoring my body to him as best I could. It didn't take long before he landed again and that nauseating swaying stopped. I opened one eye tentatively and saw the ground mere feet below my gaze. I lifted my head and saw that the trees were in the distance. We were atop the cliff, and the thick greenery here was interspersed with jagged rock. This was why Hugh was still carrying me. He seemed to know instinctively where to step, bounding between boulders and over stone, dodging ferns and moving rapidly. I settled in for the ride.

Sometime later, I could hear the sound of rushing water. I lifted my head again, looking around. "Are we heading to a waterfall?"

"Yes, but it is not our destination," he told me.

"No?" I wouldn't have minded a nice shower. "But waterfalls are pretty."

"This one also has fish with very big teeth swimming in the pool."

Eeek. "On second thought, let's avoid the waterfall."

He chuckled. "I thought so."

"So where are we going?"

"You will see," he said.

I wanted to grumble at all the mystery, but I couldn't complain. At least this way I wouldn't have to worry about what the others were thinking as Hugh and I figured out how to get the round peg into the, ahem, round hole. It occurred to me that I wasn't the only virgin here. Would Hugh instinctively know what to do? I'd read some romances and watched some movies, and Hugh had watched, well, porn. Our combined experience wasn't exactly setting the world on fire. If it wasn't very good this time, I decided, we could just chalk it up to our newness to things and we'd just have to work on improving. I steeled myself for the reality that I might not get an orgasm the first or second time. I'd be happy just to have sex with a man I loved, really. Demanding an orgasm to boot seemed a bit like luxury. I'd take what I could get and be happy about it, as long as Hugh's skin was pressed against mine and we both enjoyed ourselves.

And it saved me from Finian.

I wanted to weep with joy. It seemed like everything was suddenly in my favor and the other primordials were the ones getting the short end of the stick. I felt incredibly guilty, but if it meant I got my happy ever after and Hugh to boot? I couldn't feel too bad for them. It was either them or me, and I was going to be selfish and pick me.

A mist began to sprinkle my backside, interrupting my thoughts, and I noticed we'd gotten closer than ever to the waterfall. It was a heavy spray of water coming down from the rocky cliff above. No Niagara Falls, of course, but it was enough that the water at the bottom could fill a decent-sized lake. It was pretty, though. I tried not to think of the big-toothed fish at the bottom that Hugh had mentioned.

To my surprise, Hugh took to the rocks at the side of the falls and began to climb up.

"Where are we going?" I asked again.

"You'll see," he told me and continued to climb.

"Okay, well, I'm just going to close my eyes," I told him as the ground began to drop away and my stomach dropped queasily. For a girl with wings, I wasn't a big fan of heights. "Yell when we're there."

"You'll know," he said, a chuckle in his voice.

A few moments later, he paused in his rock climbing, and I felt him shuffle to the side. That was the only warning I got before I was drenched with icy-cold water. A startled yelp escaped me, and I sputtered, shivering. "What the heck! Hugh! A little warning, please?"

"I told you that you would know," he said, and I could hear the laughter in his voice.

I pushed sopping wet hair off my face and peered out from under it. We'd gone through part of the waterfall and, judging from the liquid cascade just beyond my one shoulder, were now under it. It was dark behind here, the only light coming from the blue of the waterfall. I raised a hand in front of my face and could barely make out the outline. "Where are we?"

"It is a cave I come to when I need to be alone and think," Hugh said. He gently shrugged, setting me down on the floor.

I wiggled my feet, the rocks wet underneath them. My hair was dripping on my back, so I pulled it into a ponytail and wrung it out as I glanced around in the darkness. I could see nothing, and that unnerved me. I raised a hand up, trying to feel for the ceiling of the cave, but nothing hit my fingers but air. "Please tell me that this isn't the home of the local prehistoric bear?"

"The water keeps out most. Just not me. I have been known to be more curious than is sensible from time to time."

I smiled into the darkness at that and crossed my arms over my damp skin. "As long as you say this place is safe."

"It is," he said, and I felt his hand brush against mine. "Come with me."

I raised a hand in front of me and gave him my other, and we walked deeper into the cave. I nearly screamed when my foot encountered something furry a moment later.

Hugh must have heard my intake of breath. "It is a sleeping fur, I promise."

"Boy, am I glad to hear you say that," I told him and knelt down to pat my hand on it. Sure enough, a sleeping fur. "I hope it's not covered in mutant bugs."

"No mutant bugs. You forget I can see as well in the dark as I can in the daytime," Hugh said, clearly amused at my antics.

"And you forget I'm totally blind," I said cheerfully. "But I'm glad one of us can see." I pushed wet, dripping hair off my face. "Though you might prefer not to see me if we're going to do this."

"I see you. I see all of you. And you are so beautiful that you make my body ache with want," he said softly.

A thrill of delight shot through me at his words. I put a hand out. "I'd like to know where you are right about now, because I really want to kiss you, Hugh."

He laughed. "The feeling is mutual, Ryder. Do you want to see, or do you prefer the dark?"

Oh. "I want to see." I wanted to see everything. Hugh was gorgeously attractive, and I couldn't wait to look my fill at him.

I heard a whistle of air, and light bloomed. I watched, entranced, as Hugh blew on a bit of moss hanging from the ceiling and it lit up like fire.

"Pretty," I breathed. "What is that?"

"I do not know what it is called, only what it does." He looked over at me, all grinning fangs, and blew on the moss a bit more until the cave was full of light.

"How long will that last?"

"Long enough," he said and turned back toward me, easing down into the furs at my feet. The cave was no longer dark, the moss providing a glow for me to see him by. It was almost like having a romantic, candlelit evening.

He patted the furs. "Come and sit with me."

I sat down across from him, feeling a little nervous about what we were going to do. I'd have to get over it fast, though, if we were going to get rid of my virginity. And then I paused. "I just thought about something. Do we need condoms?" It had never even occurred to me that I'd soon be having sex. I was totally unprepared.

"I do not understand this word."

"Condoms are, um, sheaths that a man wears over his penis to catch his semen and prevent him from getting her pregnant."

"Are you in heat, Ryder?"

"I don't know?"

"I think you would know. Also, you will not go into heat as long as I take your virginity prior to your twenty-fifth birthday. If you are not in heat, I cannot get you pregnant."

"That's good, at least. We'll go bareback, then."

"Bare . . . back?"

"Never mind," I told him and waved a hand in the air. "I'm just spouting things because I'm nervous. I've never had sex before and it's making me anxious. I love you, and I want you, but it doesn't mean I'm not freaking out a little about it. I have no idea what to do, after all."

"Ryder . . . remember, I have never had sex, either." He shifted on the furs, his face solemn. He looked rather unhappy about the fact. "I do not wish to disappoint you."

"I know," I breathed, gazing at him shyly. "You can't disappoint me. Somehow, I kind of like that we're both new to this. We're not going to judge the other's performance, because neither of us has had sex before. We can just figure things out as we go. Explore."

"I like the thought of exploring you," he said, his voice low and practically humming with tension. His eyes gleamed in the low light.

And oh, mercy, I liked that thought, too. "Well, then," I said. "Can I start first?"

"I am yours, Ryder." He sounded so breathless that it made me breathless, too. My pulse began to speed up as I scooted closer and reached for him.

My hands landed on warm chest. I peeked up at his face, even as my hands slid over his pectorals. His eyes were closed with ecstasy, and his fangs had grown so long that they distended from his upper lip. Oh. I glanced down, admiring his body where I touched him. His chest was lightly furred with hair, his skin slightly damp. I grazed nails over his skin, seeking his nipples. I heard his sharp intake of breath, and it excited me. I ran my blunted claws over the hard tips, feeling and enjoying his groan of reaction. "Tell me what you like."

"I like everything so far." His voice was full of tension and anticipation, his face tense.

"Good." I wanted to do more to him, too. Licking my lips, I ran my fingers higher and felt along the lines of his neck muscles. I could feel the strain in them, the tension in his body. I smoothed my fingers down his arms, enjoying the light furring on his forearms. Hugh had a bit more body hair than most men, but I didn't mind it. He had a bit more everything than most men.

Which led me to the next place I wanted to explore. Feeling daring, I moved my hands back to his chest and trailed them down his stomach.

He sucked in, his stomach flexing.

Mmm, fun. I scratched my pale little claws down the length of his stomach, enjoying the feel of his flat abdomen. It was all hard muscle, and I could trace the ridgelines with my fingers. I did, feeling each breath that he pulled in, noticing that his breathing was becoming rapid . . . as was mine.

He jerked as I touched his belly button, and his cock brushed against my hand, leaving a slightly damp trail against my scales.

I drew back hesitantly. "Are you okay?"

"I am sorry," Hugh said immediately, leaning backward. His eyes were open, and they were entirely cat at this point, a transformation I found fascinating. "I . . . your fingers felt . . ."

"Ticklish?" I suggested.

"Perhaps that is the word." He looked embarrassed.

"No, it's okay," I told him. "Don't be shy. It's just me."

"What do you think makes me shy?" Hugh panted.

"Oh." I giggled a little at that, feeling giddy with excitement and desire. "Do you mind if I keep touching you?" I wanted to explore him some more, especially in that particular area.

"I do not mind," he said, voice strained. His face had shifted toward his saber-tooth form, the bones in his face more pronounced, more feral, more wild. "But I . . . I am . . ."

"You are . . . what?"

"When I get . . . aroused . . ." He exhaled sharply, and I could practically hear the struggle in his mind to say the words. "The tip of my cock . . ."

He trailed off again.

I decided to find out for myself. I reached for him, ignoring the sharp inhalation of his breath, and my fingers brushed against the head of his cock again. I glanced at his face, but his jaw was clenched, as if he'd been in agony—or feeling something intense. He wasn't brushing me away, though, so I returned to exploring. The head of his cock was slightly damp with a slick, almost sticky liquid. Pre-cum, I told myself. I'd read about that. I brushed my fingers through it, then lifted one to my mouth to taste it.

Salty. It had a bite that wasn't altogether pleasant, but not bad, either. Hugh's reaction was even better. He gave a groan, as if in pain, his head tilting back.

Oooh. I licked my fingers again, the taste growing on me, especially since it got that type of response. Hugh's panting became rapid, and he gave another low groan when I reached for him again. He looked for all the world as if he wanted to hiss at me.

"Do you mind if I put my hands on you here?" I asked permission even as I curved all of my fingers around his thick length.

Hugh was big. Thick. Girthy. I'd expected this, since he was a large man, but staring at it and feeling it between my fingers were two different things. This hot, long rod of flesh was going to go inside my body.

I was pretty sure that was going to be an awkwardly tight fit.

And for the first time since we'd come to the cave, I pulled back a little. I released Hugh.

"Is something wrong?"

There was concern in his voice, along with disappointment. His green eyes shone at me, pupils dilated, and I felt like a jerk. He was worried that his body was displeasing or that I'd drawn away because he'd done something wrong.

And that was selfish of me. Of course he was just as nervous as I was. Maybe more so.

So I put my hands back on his cock and stroked the fine, velvety skin. "Nothing's wrong. You're just bigger than I thought."

"Is . . . that is bad, is it not? You are small, Ryder."

"You're fine," I told him, keeping the sultry purr in my voice. When he tried to pull backward, I tightened my fingers around his length. "I'm still exploring, Hugh. Don't go anywhere."

His choked gasp and wide eyes told me that he liked my hands squeezing around him. Encouraged, I did it again, one hand atop the other, like holding a baseball bat. The analogy was an apt one, I thought wryly.

Hugh's big hand suddenly covered mine. "Not too tight, Ryder."

"Oh. Oops, I'm sorry." I released him again, chagrined.

"No, it's all right. I liked it. I just . . ." He let his words trail off.

Hugh was . . . shy about discussing sex? That was charmingly endearing and made me love him all the more. Maybe we were going about this all wrong. I moved my hands to a safer place—his broad, taut thighs—and rested them there, then looked up at him. "Hugh, baby, can I ask you a question?"

"You may ask me anything, of course." He gazed down at me, his hand brushing my bony, scaled cheek in affection. "I am yours to command."

"Do you ever touch yourself? Like when you get . . . too lonely?" My claws idly scratched at his thighs in what was hopefully a soothing, yet enticing, motion. "Or when you watched the movies I gave you?"

He was silent for so long that I wondered if he didn't understand the question. Then he gave a ragged sigh. "It is . . . not something discussed."

"Not even with me?"

He held his breath for a long moment, as if debating, then quietly admitted, "Yes, I have touched myself before."

Now we were getting somewhere. I dug my claws

in, loving the way his muscles clenched in reaction. "Ever thought about me while doing it?"

His ragged groan was the only answer I needed.

"What did you imagine me doing?"

Hugh's breath was coming in swift, ragged pants, his eyes squeezed shut with concentration. I felt him shudder a little under my hands. Just seeing his reactions to my touch was driving me wild. I felt slick between my thighs, and my own pulse was pounding like I'd just had a hard workout.

And yet Hugh still wasn't telling me about his fantasies. I needed to prod him a little. My hands slid to the interior of his thighs and I leaned in, gazing into his face. "Was I holding you in my hands?" I scratched his skin lightly. "Or were you thinking about my mouth on you?"

He growled, then bit out, "Mouth. I saw it in one of the moving stories."

"That sounds like fun," I told him, my voice sultry. "Do you mind if I practice and put my mouth on you, then?"

He gave me a grunt of approval, not opening an eye.

I shivered a little in anticipation. Part of me was excited to be doing this to Hugh, and part of me was wildly nervous. My teeth were long and fanged in my changeling form. What if I did something wrong? I knelt forward, then paused. "Um, Hugh? Did you dream about my human mouth or my changeling one?"

"Changeling," he rasped.

I never got enough of hearing that. "Because I'm fiercer that way?"

His eyes opened and he reached out and brushed the back of one clawed finger down my cheek. "Because I know that when you are changeling, it's because you want to be touched. It is . . . exciting to me."

I'd never thought of it that way. Just hearing him say it made me ache between my legs, and I pressed my thighs together, hard. "Oh. But what if I scrape you with my teeth?"

"Then you do. It will not lessen my excitement. I do not think anything could at this point," he said, and there was a bemused, wry note in his voice that made me want to smile and kiss him all at once.

"All right, then." I smiled at him, so happy. My fingertips fluttered back to his cock, and I traced the outline of it with them, establishing his size and shape. Then I leaned in, preparing to put my mouth on him. This close to his skin, I could smell his musky scent and feel the warm heat radiating from him. It made the ache between my legs intensify, and I wrapped one hand around his length and leaned in, giving him a tentative lick with my tongue.

His entire body jerked in response.

I flinched backward, releasing him. "I'm sorry!"

"No," he said quickly. "No, it's okay, Ryder. I was just . . . surprised. It felt good."

Oh. Duh. Of course it did. I was being way too skittish about this. Where was flirty, devil-may-care Ryder when I needed her? I needed to be more confident. My shyness was freaking Hugh out, too. "Just making sure," I told him and slid back down until my face was between his thighs once more. "I'm going to put my mouth on you again."

"Do it."

His commanding tone made me grin, mostly because I knew he'd probably flinch again as soon as I came close. I put my hand on him once more, gave him a little squeeze to prepare him, and leaned in. I heard his sucked-in breath, but this time I didn't pull back. The heat coming off his body and the scent of him were making me crazy with lust. I put my lips on the head of his cock, closed my mouth, and felt the slickness of his pre-cum wet my mouth. I licked my lips in response, my tongue flicking against his cock as I did so.

Hugh groaned. His hand covered the one I had resting on his thigh. He clenched against my hand, and I hesitated for a moment, then realized that he just wanted to touch me. He didn't want to interrupt me, though. Pleased, I opened my mouth and tongued the head of his cock. His gasp was encouraging, so I continued, licking off the pre-cum and sliding my tongue against the divot at the center of his cock head. I wanted to take all of him into my mouth, so I opened wide and slid him along the length of my tongue.

He was bigger than I'd pictured, and the head of his cock rubbed along the top of my tongue, tickling my mouth. I made a small noise of frustration and ended up sucking him deeper. His groan of response was encouraging, and I closed my lips around him and sucked harder, mindful of my fangs.

Hugh groaned again, the sound so deep and delicious that I felt it vibrate in my mouth as I pulled on his cock. His hand clenched over mine rhythmically, and I wondered if he wanted me to follow that motion. My other hand was still wrapped around the girth of his cock, so I tugged at the shaft as I sucked him deeper, experimenting.

The breath hissed out of him, and I felt Hugh's hand go to my shoulder, dragging me away. "No, Ryder."

I pulled back, releasing his cock from my mouth, and sat back on my haunches, searching his face for emotion. "What did I do wrong?"

"Nothing. Mercy upon me, nothing at all." His fangs bared again, and instead of scaring me, they turned me on. He reached forward and dragged me against him, pulling me into his lap. His hands slid underneath my crumpled wings, and he held me tight. "I just . . . you cannot continue to do that and expect me to have control."

My body was pressed against his now, and I felt the heat of his cock against my lower hips. I gave a pleased little wiggle, wrapping my arms around his neck and leaning in toward him, studying his face. "So what I was doing felt good?"

"Incredible," he assured me. His eyes were glowing like beacons. "But now I wish to kiss you for a time."

"I can handle that," I said and leaned forward. His hand knotted in my hair, and Hugh dragged my mouth to his. His teeth clashed with mine for a moment, then we adjusted. His lips nibbled at my own, and I decided to let him take the lead for a bit. My hands went to his neck and I played with the back of his hair, even as his mouth devoured mine. I loved kissing Hugh. It didn't matter that they weren't soft, gentle kisses. He kissed me like he wanted to consume me, like the world would end if he didn't kiss me hard enough. And his kisses drugged my senses and made my knees weak. I could kiss him for hours and it wouldn't be enough.

As we kissed, I rubbed my body against him. The tickle of his chest hair felt good against my nipples.

His mouth pulled away from mine and I mewed a protest, opening my eyes.

He chuckled. "If you're going to move on top of me, Ryder, I want you to feel it as I do." His hands on my waist settled me against him, and then I was sitting atop the long length of his cock, straddling him.

I gasped at the sensation of his thick, hot length between my legs. He wasn't pressing into me—I was simply hovering over his length. And when I moved against Hugh again, it rubbed against my sex, an ever-present reminder. I moaned in response and rocked my hips against the length of him, loving the feeling. "More."

The look on his face was intense as he watched

me, like a predator, and it made me shiver even as it made my nipples hard. There was something so erotic about knowing Hugh was so dangerous and yet . . . he couldn't hurt me. As a changeling, I was stronger, tougher. His claws couldn't hurt my skin, nor could his fangs.

For the first time in my life, I was wildly, absurdly glad that I was a changeling and not just a human. I rolled my hips wickedly against him, rubbing up and down his length like the naughty tease I was.

Hugh groaned and shifted his hips. This time, it was him rubbing against me and not the opposite. "Do you like the feel of my body against yours, Ryder?"

I whimpered and nodded, moving my mouth toward his blindly. I wanted more kisses. More deep, tongue-stroking kisses to go with the constant rubbing of his cock against the slick heat of my sex.

I licked and lightly bit at the lines of Hugh's jaw, even as I rolled my hips against his length. It was driving me crazy, that feel of him brushing between my legs. I wanted so much more; I wanted to keep going like this forever.

"Ryder," he chanted, his voice a breathless singsong. "Ryder. My Ryder." With each uttering of my name, his hands moved on me. They slid along my back, smoothed the place where my wings joined my shoulder blades. Slid further down and danced along the small of my back, where my tail met my behind. Slid to my ass and cupped it, hard.

Mmm. And that felt incredibly good. I rocked against his hands and bit at his earlobe, my movements becoming frantic. I needed him and I needed all of this. "Yes, Hugh. Oh, yes."

He growled low in his throat again, the feral sound driving me wild. It was the sound of a man who was having trouble holding on to his control, and I loved that. He leaned in, lips brushing against my ear. "You're so wet, Ryder. I can feel how wet you are along my cock. Are you excited?"

I moaned at his words. Had I thought Hugh's growls were sexy? They were nothing compared to a little bit of dirty talk. "Do you like how wet I am?"

"I do," he said thickly. I felt his claws dig into my buttocks, brushing my tail, and I was suddenly grateful again for my scales. "It reminds me that I haven't had my turn to explore you yet."

"Oh," I breathed. "I want my turn." Now that he'd mentioned it, I practically quivered with excitement at the thought.

"Then I want you to lie back so I can get my fill of your body."

"You don't have to tell me twice." I gave one last rock of my hips against his cock, then squirmed off his lap. Sliding backward onto the furs, I twisted my legs under me and waited. "How do you want me?"

To my surprise, Hugh grabbed my ankle and jerked me forward.

I yelped, flopping onto my back, my fall cushioned by furs and my wings. My tail was trapped under my hips, which was good, because it was thrashing with surprise. I hadn't expected to be dumped unceremoniously backward.

All irritation disappeared when I realized Hugh's plan. He'd dragged me forward until my spread thighs were wide open on his lap and I was flat on my back, my breasts pointing into the air. And he was grinning down at me wickedly.

"This is a beautiful sight," Hugh said.

I sighed with pleasure at his words, closing my eyes and stretching languidly. The action pushed my breasts high, and in that moment, I felt as beautiful as any woman, despite my changeling form.

"I'm going to touch you now." Hugh's hand brushed over my waist.

"Only on my stomach?" That was disappointing.

He chuckled. "Impatient one. I am just getting started." But his caresses remained where they were, and he had a look of intense concentration on his face.

I squirmed, wanting him to touch me in all the places where I ached. This was so unfair. "Didn't you like it when I had my hands on your cock, Hugh?"

He growled in response, his hand stroking my side just a little bit more forcefully.

"How about when I put my mouth on you?" I cajoled. "Didn't you like that? Or when I sucked you into my throat—"

One big hand pressed over my mound. "Is this what you want?"

I moaned, lifting my hips. "Oh, yes."

The heel of his palm rested just above the lips of my sex. "Here?"

I nodded, biting my lip.

"But what about your breasts? What if I wanted to tease your nipples and watch them stand up?"

Ooh, bold words. My hands went to my own breasts and I cupped them, since he wasn't doing it for me. His hiss of breath and the gleam of his catlike eyes told me that he liked that move. "Like this?" I asked him.

"Just like that," Hugh growled. "Touch your breasts for me." And his thumb slid down the wet seam of my sex.

I moaned, throwing my head back, as if that would somehow make his touch hit me in all the right places. My fingers went to my nipples, and I plucked at them obediently.

He groaned low in his throat and his thumb stroked deeper, moving between the lips of my sex.

I held my breath as his fingers brushed between my thighs, exploring me. He caressed my sensitive folds, tracing them with gentle claws. I shivered as he touched me, my body quivering with each tender stroke.

Then he discovered my clit.

A sharp spike of desire blasted through me. I stiffened, gasping, and forgot all about teasing him with my breasts. My entire being suddenly centered on that small spot of pleasure.

Hugh had noticed my reaction. "I remember seeing this on the moving stories you showed me," he murmured. "The man would touch the woman here, on this tiny little bit of flesh, and she would go mad with need. I thought it fascinating, as I do not have such a thing on my own body." Mindful of his claws, he carefully rubbed at my clit, green eyes gleaming as he watched me.

A sob escaped my throat. My hips arched and my hands tightened on my breasts, clenching at my own skin. My entire body felt tight, taut like a bow, vibrating with need. I rocked my hips against his fingers, needing more. "Please, Hugh," I begged. "More."

"Ryder, you are so very wet against my fingers. I touch you and my skin glides over yours." His thumb circled my clit, careful of his claws, and driving me even wilder. "And your scent is driving me to distraction."

His hand lifted away from my sex. I whimpered a protest, only to watch as he lifted his hand to his mouth and inhaled.

"I must taste you," he breathed. And then he licked them and groaned with need. "Sweeter than nectar, love. You taste incredible."

I dragged my blunted nails over my nipples, panting at his words. The thought of him licking the taste of me off his fingers was driving me crazy, almost as much as the fingers teasing my clit were.

"More," he breathed. "I need more of this."

He shifted, my spread legs moving into the air as he slid his legs out from under mine. Then he pushed me up the furs. Opening my eyes, I made a wordless sound of protest.

I opened them just in time to see him lean over me. His hands pushed between my thighs, spreading them wider, and he pushed his face between my legs. I moaned in surprise as I felt his breath on my sex. A moment later, he was spreading the lips of my sex with gentle fingers. His groan of pleasure made me even wetter. "Never have I smelled anything so good, Ryder. I am going to put my mouth on you now."

I shuddered, loving that he was telegraphing his moves to me. My hands slid away from my breasts and down to his head, searching for his hair. I found it a moment later and dug my fingers in just as he put his mouth on my flesh.

His tongue was hesitant at first, as if he was making sure I wouldn't protest the intimate caress. He didn't have to worry about that part. As soon as his mouth touched my clit, I sucked in a breath, waiting for stars to rain from the heavens.

I didn't get that, though. It felt odd at first and I shifted my hips, wondering if I was missing out on something. He lapped at my flesh, a groan of pleasure rising in his throat, and his pleasure escalated mine. Then his tongue stroked against my clit again, and I realized that his tongue was . . . rough, like a cat's. It dragged against my skin, and all of a sudden, I felt like every inch of his tongue was pushing right on my nerves.

I gasped, shocked at how good it felt.

Hugh made a pleased noise in his throat, and he continued to lick and suck at my clit with his mouth. I moaned again, my hips lifting with every drag of his tongue across the nub of my flesh. "Oh, God, that feels amazing," I blurted, then realized that I'd said it aloud. I didn't have time to be embarrassed, because he was encouraged by that and began to lick me harder, and faster.

It didn't matter that I was a changeling. Not to Hugh. He loved me and wanted me wildly, no matter what I looked like. That thought was as intoxicating as his tongue on my body. I moaned and writhed under him, my fingers tight in his hair, my heels digging into the furs as he pinned my thighs against his shoulders, holding me in place so he could continue to lick at me to his heart's content.

He lifted his head between licks, pressing kisses to my mound. "Do you like my mouth on you, Ryder?"

"Yes," I sobbed, twisting his thick hair between my fingers and pulling on it, trying to drag him back toward that aching, wet flesh that wanted more attention from his tongue.

"I want to keep touching you," he murmured, then he raked his teeth against the inside of one thigh. That savage—yet delicate—gesture sent shivers up and down my spine. "Don't be frightened."

"I'm not," I breathed. "Never frightened. Keep touching me, Hugh."

"I will be careful," he told me, and I wondered what he was talking about. A moment later, he distracted me by placing his mouth on my clit again and sucking hard. It almost distracted me from the finger he pressed into my core.

Almost.

I jerked, keening at the feeling of his finger invading me. I realized a moment later that it wasn't his finger he'd pushed into me but a knuckle, ever mindful of his claws. It felt thick and urgent, and my flesh was tight around it. I whimpered against him again. It felt good, but I knew it wasn't nearly the size of his cock, and it already seemed like too much.

"My Ryder," he breathed against my wet flesh and tongued me hard all over again. "My love. Your body is wondrous. I could not ask for more in a mate."

Mate? So we were going to be mates after all? He'd never said the words, even though he'd confessed love to me and I'd confessed it back. I wanted to ask him about it—

—But then he rapidly flicked his tongue against my clit and all of a sudden I was coming, the orgasm blasting through me like a shock wave. I dug my fingernails roughly into his scalp, pinning him against my sex as my entire body locked with the force of my release, my core clenching around his knuckle. It seemed to go on forever. Hugh continued to lick me, growling, that rough tongue working at my flesh, and I continued to come and come and come until my thighs were twitching with aftershocks and my cries turned to soft mews of exhausted release.

Panting hard, I released Hugh, and he gave another dragging rasp of his teeth against my thigh. When he pulled me upright, I wrapped my arms around his neck and tilted my head back, accepting the fierce kisses that he pressed against my mouth. His lips tasted wet and salty with my own flavor, and I languidly stroked my tongue against his. I felt incredible. Delicious.

Hugh's teeth sank into my lip. He then grazed his tongue along my lower lip, licking away any pinch.

That gave me an odd thrill. His bites and nips—despite his enormous teeth—didn't hurt me. I could thank my changeling hide for that. He continued to shower nipping kisses on my face, moving up my ridged cheekbones and even up to the horns on my forehead. When he licked the base of each one, I was surprised at the moan of pleasure that escaped me. Who knew that horns were such pleasure centers? There were so many things left to explore, and we didn't have to worry about hurting each other. Hugh didn't have to be gentle with me. I loved that.

His hand dragged at my ass, and he thrust against me. I felt his cock push at my stomach, felt the slick trail he left against my skin. "Ryder," he groaned. "Can you take me?"

I quivered at that, opening my eyes and looking up into his tight, concerned face. My thighs ached from my recent release, and I felt drenched between my legs. I felt good, so good.

But Hugh looked worried. He was big, and we'd

just proven that I was small. This would work, of course—everyone had sex—but it was going to hurt like the dickens.

Even as I hesitated, he continued to kiss and caress me, his mouth moving to my throat. He licked at my skin, then raked his long fangs against it, dragging new shivers of pleasure from my throat. His hand moved to cup and caress my breast. "I'll be gentle," he whispered.

I felt a bit selfish in that moment. "Of course you will," I told him, breathless when his thumb rubbed against my nipple. If he was determined to get me all worked up again, he was doing a good job of it. His frantic, insistent touches were making my own desire rise again, his need a palpable thing in the air. I clung to him, loving his touch. "How do you want me?"

I could see the gleam of his eyes as he considered my words. "Turn around for me."

Oooh. I felt a surge of excitement at that. He was going to take me from behind? I slid out of his arms—not without a little protest, a little kissing, and a lot of rubbing my body against his. Then I obediently presented my back to him, and he gave my shoulders a little nudge, urging me forward. I leaned forward until I was propped up on my elbows, my hips in the air behind me. It was a good thing I was facing forward, because I was blushing furiously. I felt exposed, open, and excited at the pose he had me in.

His hand brushed over my hip and I jerked, anticipation making me tense. I was aching and wet all over again, and the empty feeling had returned between my legs. Suddenly I didn't care that Hugh was going to be too big. I just wanted that gnawing ache filled. I leaned forward a little more and spread my thighs, then rolled my hips encouragingly at him.

Hugh groaned behind me. "Ryder, you drive me wild."

"Good," I said breathlessly. "Now come drive into me."

He growled low in his throat, pleased by my words. I felt him shift on the furs behind me, and then his big, warm body was pressing against the backs of my thighs. I felt his cock slide against my sex once more and I arched, trying to rub up against him.

His fingers sought my wetness, and he rubbed through my folds. I cried out in surprise at the touch, then moaned when he guided his cock against my sex and began to stroke through my wetness, back and forth. He was lubricating his cock with my own juices. Smart Hugh. Delicious Hugh. Teasing, maddening Hugh. The whimpers in my throat rising, I began to push against him, needing more.

Then one big hand went to my hip and pinned me in place. "Be still, Ryder, so I do not hurt you." And I felt him shift his weight again.

I nodded. My hips were spread wide, and I felt his cock drag against my flesh one more time, then settle at my entrance. I moaned even more loudly at that sensation. God, he felt so good, and he wasn't even inside me yet.

The head of his cock fit right at my core, and then he pushed in, just a little. I winced, feeling a tight pinch, even as Hugh's growls increased. He was clearly enjoying this, so I just needed to be patient. Unfortunately, the pinch increased as Hugh continued to press forward, and I dug my nails into my palms, no longer enjoying this. It hurt. I'd known it would hurt, but knowing and experiencing were two different things. I tensed, bracing myself for more of the pain.

"Ryder," he rasped after a long, painful moment. "How do you feel?"

"I'm . . . hanging in there," I said, though the pinching had led to burning and my entire insides felt as if something way too large had been shoved into something way too small. Which, I supposed, it had. "Are you in all the way?"

His breath exploded from him and he pulled back. "I am not in hardly at all. This will not work."

All that pain and he hadn't made any progress? I felt a twinge of worry. This was what came of two virgins trying to de-virgin each other, I supposed. We were both really bad at this. "Did you push hard?"

"I know how to push, Ryder." He sounded exasperated and frustrated.

"Do you think it's because I'm a changeling?" I was suddenly worried that my parts wouldn't mesh with his parts. "What if changelings are too small?"

"I think I am just too big." He made an irritated growling noise in his throat. "I do not want to hurt you."

"Hugh. I'm a virgin. It's going to hurt anyhow." I sat up and reached backward to caress him, and my hand brushed over his erect, straining cock. His breath hissed out at my touch, and I felt guilty. "You're hurting, too."

For a moment, I hated that we were both virgins, dammit. One of us should have known more about what we were doing. The hesitation on both sides was probably making things worse than they were.

"I do not want to hurt you, Ryder," he said raggedly, and I felt his hand reach for me. He caressed my belly, then slid lower, brushing over my mound again.

I moaned, leaning back against him as he touched me. "It's going to hurt me a lot more if we don't get rid of my virginity, Hugh. Please. Let's just go, all right? I promise I'll be fine."

He kissed me fiercely atop my head, just above my horns. Then he released me. "Go back down again, Ryder."

I did obediently, trying not to tense as I got into position once more. Resting on elbows, hindquarters in the air. Ready to get this over with.

His hand stroked over my hips and thighs, and then I felt him seek between my legs. I sucked in a breath as his fingers brushed over my clit, teasing it.

"Hugh," I cried out, rocking my hips. Instant desire raced through me, and I moaned, spreading my hips wider and rocking them as he continued to rub at my clitoris. Already sensitized, it was sending skitters of pleasure racing through me.

I felt him brace behind me, felt his cock press at my entrance again. I stiffened, but he continued to rub at my clit, and it distracted me. Now the press of Hugh's cock against my entrance made me ache for more, and I rolled my hips, butting back against him.

He hissed out a breath. "Ryder . . ."

"Just go," I moaned. "Sink deep. Get it over with. Please, Hugh."

He surged forward, burying himself to the hilt.

I cried out in surprise at the sensation. That earlier flash of pain was quickly gone, followed by an indescribable feeling of being . . . filled. So gloriously filled.

"Ah," he sighed, and I could hear a wealth of emotion in his tone.

I felt stunned. The feel of Hugh deep inside me was fascinating and deeply satisfying. I remained utterly still, trying to make sense of the feelings rushing through my body. How could it be so intensely pleasing to have another person stick a body part inside you? And yet . . . damn.

I'd been missing out.

Hugh's fingers remained on my clit, continuing to coax my body, and my surprise just as quickly turned back to pleasure. The feeling of Hugh buried deep inside me added an entirely new layer to the sensations, and after a moment of his teasing fingers, I moaned again.

"Ryder?"

His words were a soft question. Was I okay? Was I in pain?

"Keep going, Hugh," I breathed. "I'm fine."

He drew backward, and I felt him push forward again. Again, my pelvis twinged with an ache, but it was less than before. When he stroked in the third time, I felt nothing but the curious sensation of being utterly filled.

"Okay?" he asked, his voice full of tension.

"Better than okay," I agreed, lifting my hips when he stroked again, letting my actions speak more than my words.

He brushed his fingers over my clit again, and I cried out, feeling pleasure racing through me. My toes curled, and I was close to another orgasm. Oh, God, the feeling of Hugh buried inside me while he played with my body was driving me crazy. I sucked in a breath and it exploded out of me in the next moment, when the orgasm peaked once more. I felt my entire body tighten around him, the pleasure rippling through me again.

With my orgasm, Hugh became unleashed.

His fingers left my flesh, and suddenly both hands were on my hips. He rocked into me, his hands anchoring me in place. Then, as if he couldn't stop himself, he continued to push into me faster with each stroke. My body was shaking with the recoil from each thrust. And I wanted to protest, but the slam of his body against mine was making an entirely different and new sort of pleasurable ache between my thighs. In moments, I was screaming his name, needing another orgasm—this one fierce and wild—as my primordial lover made wild love to me.

My orgasm exploded through me like a supernova, and I gasped for air, the scream lodging in my throat even as my forehead pressed to the furs. I felt Hugh shout and tremble as he gave another enormous thrust inside me, then he collapsed on top of me as he came. I felt the wash of his release inside my body and heard his long, extended exhalation.

And then he rolled onto the furs next to me.

Which was good, because I didn't think I could move at the moment. To think that I'd been worried the sex wouldn't be any good? If it had been any better, it would have killed me.

I laughed into the furs.

Hugh exhaled deeply and pulled me close to him, cuddling my smaller body against him. "Any regrets?"

I pressed my face against his hard pectorals, breathing in his wonderful scent and loving the feel of his skin pressed to mine. "None whatsoever. You?"

"That I did not take you for myself sooner."

Sweet man. I snuggled closer and sighed with contentment.

Chapter Seventeen

I awoke sometime later to the sound of a large body snoring and a clawed hand protectively placed on my breast. I smiled even with my eyes closed, cuddling closer to Hugh. It was nice to wake up next to a man, to have his big body pressed against my back. I didn't even mind that I was a little stiff and cold from the damp.

Unfortunately for me, my bladder and my stomach both protested being ignored, and I knew I'd have to get up soon. I slid a bit closer to Hugh and found that he had morning wood. Maybe I could help him take care of that. Sneakily, I tried to turn over.

And a groan of pain escaped my lips.

Everything below my waist was stiff and aching. I knew some people got sore after vigorous sex, and I'd figured I would be, too, but this was more than I'd expected. Guess we'd been rough with each other.

Hugh immediately woke up at the sound of my voice, and his hand reached for my cheek. "Mmm, Ryder? What is it?"

"Just stiff," I told him with a wince. "Nothing too surprising."

He sat up next to me, and I realized I could make him out a bit easier in the low light of the cave. The sun had to be up outside. "Did I hurt you?"

"I'm a little tender. I think we were overly enthusiastic. It shouldn't be a problem in the future, though, and I wouldn't change a thing about last night."

Hugh kissed me fiercely. "I love you, Ryder."

"I love you, too," I told him, feeling warm and delicious at his words. "But can we go find a bush or something? I hate to ruin the moment, but I really need to pee."

Hugh chuckled. "As you wish."

A short time later, we had climbed down from our waterfall cave and discreetly taken care of our bladders behind separate bushes. I was eyeing the water of the pool with longing; I was thirsty and felt achy and dirty, and a soak in a pool of water sounded great. Then I remembered Hugh's words about fish with teeth, and I decided that cleaning off could wait until I got home.

A big arm wrapped around my waist from behind, squishing my wings and trapping my tail. Hugh nuzzled my ear, making me squirm at the ticklish sensation.

"You should be walking around. Stretch out your legs."

I gestured at a nice, leafy plant near the water. "I was just wondering if that was edible."

"Not unless you want to be violently ill."

"It's not high on my list of things to do," I said cheerfully. My stomach growled under his hand, and I patted his arm. "I don't suppose there's a drive-thru around here?"

"No. The only food here is either foraged, caught, or hunted."

"Sounds delicious," I said, wrinkling my nose. "I think I just might wait until we get home to eat."

His face was unreadable. "Do you want me to come home with you? Do you regret this?"

"Of course I want you with me. I don't want to go home without you." I reached up and caressed his cheek. His face was hard and unyielding, but I sensed the vulnerability underneath. It made me want to give him a hug. "I don't have anything if you're not with me."

He tilted his mouth and kissed my palm. "You are my world, Ryder. Wherever you wish me to be, I will be there."

"I'm glad," I told him softly. "The thought of staying here scares me. I don't know how time passes here compared to home. And it's dangerous here. You're cut off from everyone but the fae. But if you cannot leave . . . I will stay. As long as we're together."

Hugh pulled me close to him again, dragging my body against his in a tight embrace. I went willingly—this man loved to hug and cuddle more than anyone else I'd ever met, and I was a sucker for it. He pressed another kiss to my hair. "The other primordials are my brothers. My friends and companions. But I have chosen you over them. I do not know how it will affect their hearts. I would not want them to try and take you from me."

I clung to him, a bit worried by that statement. "I don't want them to try that either, big guy."

"I must come with you, then. Back to your world." He seemed disappointed.

I felt a twinge of dismay at his lack of enthusiasm. "Do you hate my world?"

"Not at all." He seemed pensive. "I do not like the cold is all."

The cold? "I live in Texas." I poked his abdomen. "We don't get much of a winter at all. Barely any snow."

He looked down at me in surprise. "What about the ice glaciers?"

Ice glaciers? "In Texas?"

He nods. "Everywhere. Great amounts of ice. It is hard on our kind. The herds fled south, so we followed the herds, and so did humans. But they fear our kind."

I blinked at him, then gave him a little shake. "Hugh, sweetie . . . exactly how long have you been in this world that the fae created for you?"

He shrugged. "I told you. Time passes differently here."

"Didn't you notice that we've sort of moved beyond a hunter-gatherer society? Shapeshifters are living amongst humans. The humans just don't know it." My hand smoothed along his stomach. "And the Ice Age ended about ten thousand years ago, Hugh. Your kind is long extinct. No one worries about ice ages anymore. We're actually handling a little problem called 'global warming.'"

He stiffened against me. "Extinct?"

"No more saber-toothed tigers, I'm afraid. You'd be the biggest, baddest shifter on the block."

He grunted. "We came here under promises from the fae, you know. They would make this realm for us to keep us safe and let us hunt undisturbed in a warm, peaceful climate. They made the offer to us one by one, and we did not realize that the paradise they had created had left us more vulnerable than ever. There are no women here, and we did not realize until too late that they intended to keep them separate from us."

"More bad deals from the fae," I agreed. Shifty bastards.

"And time passes here as if in a dream. The only time we interact with the fae is if they demand favors in exchange for a boon."

"Have they demanded favors before?"

He nodded. "In the past."

"What kinds of things?"

Hugh frowned. "I . . . do not recall. It is possible there is something in this place that tampers with our memories."

I believed it. The fae liked to tamper with everything. "And did those who worked with the fae come back?"

"I . . . do not recall that, either." He didn't look happy.

I didn't blame him. It was disturbing to think about. I imagined the jobs the fae must have come up with over time. Who knew how many millennia Hugh and his primordials had been here? How many had disappeared while performing another fae task, never to be seen again? It sounded ominous. The fae liked to play games. Now it seemed that their games had an even more sinister edge than we'd imagined.

I gave Hugh's arm an encouraging little squeeze. "This doesn't sound like a safe place after all. So why don't you *all* come with me?"

He looked down at me, the worry smoothing into surprise. "All of us?"

I nodded, gaining enthusiasm for my idea. "You don't have to stay here. You can come with me. You, Artur, all of your friends. The world now is very different from the world you remember. There are a lot of shifters in the Fort Worth area, so you'd have a support network. I'm positive they'd help you all acclimate to modern society. And if the others leave this place, you will no longer be beholden to the fae. More than that . . . the others can find mates. There are shifter women. Not tons of them, but they are there."

His eyes gleamed with excitement, but then he shook his head. "The fae will not like it, and they are holding our females. What if they punish them for our disobedience?"

I hadn't considered that. I thought for a moment, then snapped my fingers. "You can all still come with me. We'll just play hardball."

"Hard . . . ball?"

"Yes. Basically you come with me and tell the fae you'll only return to this realm—and to being their errand boys—if they give you the mates they are holding. They will have no choice but to release them if they want to keep you."

"Do you think that will work?"

"If it doesn't, Finian's going to have to explain to all his buddies that he's lost all of the primordials. I bet that's a conversation that won't go over well."

Hugh looked down at me, eyes dark. "Do you truly think it will work, Ryder?"

"They will want you back, so they'll have to give in. And what do your men have to lose?"

"Nothing," he admitted. "If what you think is true, this place is as deadly a prison as any. We will ask my men what they wish to do."

I beamed up at him. "This will work. I know it."

Hugh grinned down at me, all fangs showing in his delight. "You have a good heart, my Ryder."

"I hear a lot of things are pretty good about me," I teased back. My flirty ways had returned.

His hand slid to my ass and cupped it. "I could not agree more. There are many things about you that are more than merely good. They are mouthwatering."

Oooh. *Mouthwatering* was a rather descriptive word. It sent a shiver of excitement down my spine. "Such as?"

He squeezed one buttock. "The way your lower back curves in just before your tail. The smooth lines of your spine nestled between your wings. The way that your nipples perk when I say your name. The way I catch your scent when you are aroused, and it makes me hard."

I sucked in a breath at his words. Just like that, I wanted him again.

"Like now," he murmured huskily. "I can smell your desire, and it's making me crazed." He leaned in and nipped at my lower lip with those big teeth.

My knees went weak. "Hugh," I breathed. I glanced around at the wilderness surrounding us. "Are we safe here?"

He kissed along my jaw. "You are always safe with me."

"Good. Then let's have sex again." Who cared if I was sore? I was going to be sore anyhow. And right now? I wanted Hugh. My hand moved to his cock, and I grasped it. Already hard and ready.

He groaned at my touch and his tongue swiped at my open mouth, licking me.

I gasped at how good that felt and squeezed his cock again. "Point me to where we can lie down."

"We don't need to lie down," Hugh said. He pulled me against him and scanned the area.

"We don't?"

He hauled me over his shoulder again, my stomach thumping against his skin. "I know just the place. Over here."

"Okay," I agreed breathlessly. His hand was

pressing down on my behind, and I wanted to push back against him, to have those fingers seek out my flesh. I was already wet and aching with need. Who knew that sex was like an itch that needed scratching once you started?

He paced across the brushy forest floor, and I squirmed with anticipation. A moment later, he put me down again, his hand caressing me as he released me to the ground. As soon as he did, he pressed another fierce kiss to me, distracting me before I had a chance to look around. His hand hitched to my leg and he pulled me up against him.

I pulled away from him in surprise when he dragged my other leg against him and pressed me backward. My back was against a smooth tree, and I clung to his shoulders. "What—"

"I saw this in one of the moving stories you gave me to watch," he said, mouth pressing against my neck urgently. His hands clung to my hips, keeping me balanced against him.

"You . . . you did?"

"I did." His voice was a low growl of pleasure as he nipped at my collarbones, then slid down to take the peak of one breast in his mouth.

I moaned, clinging to him. "You're a fast learner."

He licked at my nipple, teasing the sensitive point. "Do you hurt?"

"Mmm. I ache. Deep inside."

He suddenly stopped, looking at me with concern. "Did I hurt you?"

I dug my pearly nails into his shoulders. "I hurt a little, but I'm fine. I want you. Please." I rocked my hips, feeling them press against his cock. He was so close, yet so far away. "Don't tease me like this and then pull back."

He moved to my mouth and kissed me again. "If you're sure."

"More than sure."

His hands shifted my hips, then I felt the head of his cock pressing against my sensitive opening. I sucked in a breath, and a tiny whimper escaped me when he sank deep.

Hugh groaned as he seated himself inside me. Then he stilled, and his gaze searched mine. "Ryder?"

The fullness felt different sitting upright, pressed between him and a tree. It ached a little, but it was also being rapidly taken over by the sensations that pricked at my nerve endings. It hurt to have him buried in me, but it also felt really, really good. That itching, needy ache had suddenly been filled . . . and had left another craving in its wake. "I'm good," I reassured him and lifted my mouth for another kiss.

He groaned again and pressed his mouth to mine, his tongue slicking against my own. The kiss deepened even as he thrust inside me, and there was no thought of pain in that moment. Instead, every bit of my body sang to life, and I tightened my legs against his hips. The way he'd thrust against me had pressed my clit against him, so when he'd stroked forward, it had felt incredible.

And the rotten man had stopped again. I dug my claws into his shoulders, silently begging for more.

Hugh didn't need encouraging after that. His mouth forcefully ravaging mine (someday we'd have a conversation about sweet, gentle kisses, but I was enjoying the rough ones too much), he began to pump into me with slow, sure strokes that left me writhing against him.

I came moments later, in a hard, shattering burst, clenching around him and shuddering with delight even as I dug my nails in harder. "Hugh," I cried out as the orgasm took over me. "Oh, God, Hugh!"

"Ryder," he growled against my mouth. "My Ryder. Mine." And his thrusts became hard and jerky. A moment later, he came, too, pushing hard between my legs and shoving me so fiercely against the tree that I heard the limbs creak.

Once again, I found myself thankful that I was a changeling, because I could take all that Hugh had to offer, and more. I dug my fingers into his shoulders, utterly pleased with myself. That had been a short, rough round of sex, and it had left me totally sated. "You're pretty good at that, Hugh," I told him breathlessly.

He chuckled against my neck and nipped lightly at the scales on my throat, sending skitters of pleasure through me all over again. "I am pleased you think so."

"Oh, yeah," I said dreamily. "If you were any

better, they'd have to scrape me off the floor of the forest here."

He laughed again. "I do not know what that means, but I think it was a compliment."

I gave his chest an affectionate pat. "It was."

Hugh looked as if he wanted to comment on something, but a distracted look crossed his face. He tilted his head and lifted his nose into the air, sniffing.

"What?" I asked, worried. I clung to his shoulders. "What is it?"

He looked down at me and grinned. "Are you hungry?"

"Well, I could eat, but I don't know . . . why?"

He pressed a finger to my lips, indicating silence. I fell quiet, and he let me down from where he had me pressed against the tree. He crept forward a step, hunched behind a nearby bush, and indicated that I should do the same.

Curious, I followed and squatted next to him. My fingers curled around one of his big biceps. Any excuse to touch this big, delicious man. "What are we looking at?" I whispered.

"Our next meal," he murmured in a low voice. "Just wait."

We waited. A few moments later, a creature stepped out of the brush and headed toward the stream.

It was white, with four long, slim legs, a gleaming mane, and a single, spiraling horn on its forehead.

A friggin' unicorn.

"Delicious," Hugh murmured.

"Oh, my God, no!" I said, and I began to laugh. I'd thought Hugh had been messing with me when he'd said his favorite meal was unicorn. This was unreal. "We can't eat that!"

The unicorn had bent its head to drink, but at the sound of my laughter, it went on alert. It remained still for a moment, then bolted back into the woods.

Hugh grunted. "You are not much of a hunter, my Ryder."

I didn't care. I couldn't stop giggling.

A unicorn. A real, live unicorn. Unbelievable.

Hugh led me to a stream that, he assured me, was quite safe. We drank our fill as I tried not to think about waterborne parasites, then we washed up. Heading back to the primordial camp and stinking of sex? Not the politest gesture, so I was glad it was no longer a worry. I wished we could find some clothing, but I supposed one couldn't have everything.

My muscles ached and my legs were completely stiff. In addition, certain parts of my anatomy felt a bit bruised. This made walking agonizingly slow. Hugh was patient, though. He held my hand—since I insisted on not being carried like some sort of caveman's captive bride. I gladly held his hand, since I wouldn't have this luxury when we returned to the human world. That made me a little sad, though, but it was what it was.

The caves came into view sooner than I wanted, and I instinctively moved a little closer to Hugh. "Do you think they'll like our suggestion to come to the human world?"

"I do not know." His voice was surprisingly grim.

"Well," I said cheerfully. "All we can do is ask." And I gave his hand a reassuring squeeze.

The greeting we received from the others was downright frosty. Two dozen eyes watched us emerge from the brush, but no one acknowledged us. All were silent, even as Hugh strode through the midst of the camp with me at his side.

I began to doubt our plan just a teensy bit. What if we were making all these grand schemes to save guys who didn't want saving?

Artur strode forward, his ugly face a welcome sight. "So you have returned." He moved to Hugh's side and clasped forearms with him in greeting.

"To gloat?" another called. A man stepped toward us, his wild, dark hair and savage expression almost as alarming as his large, muscular build.

Artur glanced backward, seemingly dismissing the man's anger. "That is not well done, Cahal. Would you not have made the same choice if presented with such a lovely woman?"

Cahal went silent, though he crossed his arms over his chest and glowered at Hugh.

"We do not all resent you, brother," Artur told

Hugh. His craggy face held a note of concern. "But I do not know if it is best that you remain here."

"My mate has a suggestion," Hugh said, and he turned to look at me with such fondness and affection that I knew we'd both made the right choice.

"So she is your mate now?" Artur asked.

"Of course she is," Cahal said, striding forward to confront Hugh. His lip curled as he looked at me. "Did you not see the way she waddled into camp? She has been well used by our brother."

Oh, wow. If the earth could have swallowed me up into a sinkhole at that moment, I wouldn't have objected. Embarrassed, I took a tiny step behind Hugh again, wishing my hair was long enough to cover my breasts . . . or other areas that were totally naked. Waddled? *Waddled*? How humiliating.

"That is my mate you insult, Cahal," Hugh growled, stepping forward. "My mate who even now thinks of ways to retrieve our mates from the fae. You would do well to be kind to her."

Artur's heavy brows drew together, and his attention turned to me. "You know of a way?"

"I have an idea," I told him. I stepped forward, doing my best to pretend that I wasn't totally naked and in changeling form. These men had never seen me otherwise, so it wouldn't be as awkward to them as it was to me. "The fae need you guys. From what Hugh has told me, they have you do their dirty work and make you think you're beholden to them because of this realm they created for you. But the human world is different now. You primordials have been gone for a long time. A long, *long* time. Humans aren't living and hunting in packs any longer. They're domesticated. They hold jobs and farm. And shifters mingle with them and live in safety right under their noses. You don't have to stay here. Hugh has a necklace that can make a portal. Like it or not, Finian's given you a way out of this place. You can leave and come to my world with me."

"And what of the women promised to us? What of those mates?" Cahal demanded.

Clearly Cahal spoke for others. I could see several angry nods in the background.

"That's the beauty of it," I told him. "You come with me for a few days. The fae figure out that you're gone, and now they need to offer you something to make you come back. You can then bargain for your mates in exchange for returning here." I gave a tiny shrug. "Or you can stay in my world. There are lots of women there."

All eyes riveted on me with an intensity I found a bit unnerving.

"Your world is full of women?" Artur asked.

"Primordial women?" Cahal wanted to know.

Well, that had gotten their attention. "No primordial women. There aren't any primordials other than you guys. There *are* shifter women, though they tend to be rarer than shifter men. But yes, there are single shifter women. I work at a place where our job is to make matches between single men and single women who are shifters or other supernaturals. There are also lots of human women."

"A lot of them," Hugh agreed. "Enough that they will tackle a man and give him sex simply for delivering food to her door."

All eyes widened.

Oh, dear. I suspected that the porn Hugh had watched had given him a skewed concept of courting rituals. "Not exactly, but—"

"We wish to go to this place," Cahal demanded.

"Aye," Artur agreed, glancing back at the others. A chorus of nods followed. "Either way, it does not sound like we can lose."

"There's just one problem," Cahal said. "How do we get the fae to realize that we have gone?"

"Finian will be coming back to look for me," I told them. "We'll just use me as bait. Right, Hugh?"

Silence.

I turned to look at Hugh and noticed he was frowning fiercely at me.

"You are not safe around Finian," he said. "I do not like this aspect of your plan."

"Perhaps she should stay here while we venture to her world. Then, once things are established, we can return her to her home."

"Whoa, whoa," I said, holding up my hands. "I'm not staying here. Not without Hugh."

"We need Hugh to lead us through the portal," Cahal explained. "It is keyed to him. No one can enter or exit without him going through first."

"She cannot stay here alone," Hugh said. "Ryder is helpless in this place. She has no defenses."

I put my hands on my hips, not exactly liking

Hugh's words, even if they supported my stance. "No one is staying behind. We'll just have to lay a trap for Finian or something."

"It's dishonest," Hugh said, frowning.

"It's genius." Cahal rubbed his hands together. "Bring us to this land of eager women. I will feed them."

Chapter Eighteen

There was nothing like having two dozen naked men in your bedroom to put a new perspective on things.

Hugh and I had been the first ones to go through the portal back to my world. The rune was keyed to Hugh and only Hugh, so he'd had to go through the portal first. He hadn't allowed me to enter until he'd gone to the other side and determined that everything had seemed normal. Then I'd been permitted to join him.

After that, the rest of the primordials followed. Cahal was the third one through, followed by two blond men, then another so tall he made Hugh look normal-sized. Then shifter after shifter continued to push through the portal Hugh had made (in my closet once again) and into my pink, girly bedroom.

I tried to count heads, but the room was rapidly filling up with big, naked bodies, and everyone was insisting on picking up and handling my things. As I watched, one jerked my alarm clock off the table, hauling it to his face so he could look at the bright red numbers, ripping the cord out of the wall in the process. Another, I was pretty sure, was drinking from the toilet. I followed as many as I could, slapping hands that went into my underwear drawer out of curiosity, keeping others from wandering outside, and generally trying to corral the chaos until all of the primordials arrived through.

It had been less than two minutes, and it was already a nightmare.

The primordials were like kids on Christmas morning. My apartment was a wonderland, and they were determined to get into everything. I pulled one of my pink ruffled pillows away from a man who was trying to bite through it, clearly thinking it was some sort of treat.

I was going to need help with this. Pulling dozens of men through to my world to save them had seemed like a great idea until I'd realized they were all suddenly my responsibility and they knew absolutely nothing about this world. I began to feel overwhelmed as I wrestled my favorite pink lipstick out of another man's hands. "Hugh?" I called.

An arm snaked around my waist.

I panicked, momentarily, until a kiss was pressed to the side of my face and I smelled Hugh's warm scent.

"I am here," he murmured in my ear. "You sound troubled."

"I'm just freaking out a little," I told him, leaning into his embrace. "Everywhere I look, there are naked buns."

"They are not the only ones unclothed," Hugh said even as he pressed a kiss to my hair. "You are changing back."

So I was. I groaned in dismay as my protective scales retreated and left me more naked than ever. It had felt like I'd been wearing something even when I'd been naked. Now they were going to see my very human, very naked, flesh.

Unless Hugh kept touching me, of course. And there was so much going on that it would be near impossible to ensure that.

I grabbed clothes, shooed the men out of my bathroom, and dressed. By the time I emerged, I was fully human again and Hugh had most of the men in the living room of my small apartment. I could hear him describing the "wondrous cave" that produced cold food. While he kept them busy, I needed to get organized.

First thing on the agenda—clothing. Hugh had half a dozen pairs of casual workout clothing, but it wouldn't be enough for all the men currently filling my living room. I still grabbed all of his clothes and some of mine. Maybe they wouldn't realize that my pink bathrobe or my yoga pants weren't exactly "guy" clothes. I just needed something to cover their parts so I wouldn't spend the next few hours blushing wildly.

Next, I pulled out my gear bag that I brought to every dating event. It had a clipboard that I could glance at easily, which I used for recording names. I also had name stickers. Both would come in handy.

Then I emerged from my room and set to work.

A few hours later, we'd ordered so many pizzas and sodas that we'd finally maxed out my last credit card. Everyone was dressed in either underwear, shorts, a bathrobe, or a towel. Everyone also wore a name sticker (some stuck on bare chests), which allowed me to carefully record them on my clipboard, along with their shifter type, just so I knew what I was dealing with.

Twenty-three men, not including Hugh. There was Artur, who, along with Hugh, seemed to take on a leadership role. He told me his shifter type, but I didn't know what "horned armored beast" was, so I just wrote *rhino.* A lot of them seemed to be cats, bears, and wolves, based on their descriptions, though most didn't match up with cats, wolves, and bears that I was familiar with. But if Hugh was a saber-toothed tiger, then it was possible that they were all some sort of Ice Age breeds.

They all politely ate the pizza, though it was clear that none of them were enjoying it particularly. Of course, pizza also led to different questions. Was this the food that made women so crazed with lust? What was it about this particular food that made them so wild? I tried to explain that it was simply a story line in an admittedly bad movie, but the mention of movies brought entirely new questions to the foray, so I gave Hugh the remote and let him explain to the rapt men crowding my small living room.

"Ryder," he told me a moment later, frowning at the sitcom on TV. "Give me a kissing story, female. I wish to educate my men on how to please their mates."

Oh, jeez. Blushing, I helped him pull up a pay-per-view and ran out of the room.

While the primordials were busy, I decided to call work. Bath would be there, and if there was anyone that was good at organizing unruly people, it was my boss. I pulled out my cell phone, intending to call her, only to find it was dead. A sinking feeling hit the pit of my stomach. How long had we been gone for? I plugged my phone into the charger and fired up my laptop, waiting for the date to pop up.

I gasped when the calendar popped up. Two weeks. We'd been gone two weeks. My birthday was tomorrow.

My boss was going to think I was dead.

I drummed my fingers as the men exclaimed in the next room over something on the TV, then checked my phone again. A sliver of a red bar. Close enough. I dialed work.

"Midnight Liaisons," Bath answered.

"It's me, Ryder," I said. "I need to explain."

"Ryder! Oh, my God. You're all right!" Bath sounded like she was about to burst into tears. "We've all been so worried about you. No one's been able to find you since the night of Marie's party. You just vanished with that big bruiser guy. We wanted to call missing persons, but you know that's a last resort, considering our business." She bit her lip, clearly feeling awful about that. I knew what she meant, though. Supernaturals tried to stay out of the sight of the law, since the last thing they wanted was the police investigating a group of people who tended to make their own societal rules and grew furry from time to time. And since I worked with them, I was included in the "No police unless absolutely necessary" category. "I was going to call tomorrow if you didn't show up, though."

"I'm fine," I soothed her. "Really. There's just a lot going on that needs explaining. A *lot*."

"I'd say there is." She sounded a mite annoyed now that the initial relief was out of the way.

"And I totally want to explain everything," I told her. "But I need your help."

"Are you coming in to work?"

"Not unless you know where I can find a school bus," I said, only half joking. "Can you come to my apartment and bring two dozen pairs of extremely large men's clothing?"

Bathsheba was silent on the other end of the phone for so long that I wondered if she'd hung up.

"Hello?" I ventured.

"I'm here," she said. "I'm just . . . trying to imagine why you'd need a school bus and two dozen pairs of men's clothing."

"You wouldn't believe me if I told you," I said.

"Try me."

"I have two dozen overgrown Ice Age shifters sitting in my apartment because they're trying to blackmail the fae into giving them women."

She was silent for a moment. "You're right. I don't believe you."

"Figured."

"I'll be over there in an hour," she said, sounding mystified.

"I'll be here."

There was a knock at my door precisely one hour later. With relief, I bounded for the door and got the attention of every single pair of eyes in the room.

Bathsheba Ward-Russell stood at the door, smiling, a big laundry basket in her arms full of neatly folded clothing. Behind her stood Beau and Savannah, curious looks on their faces. "We're here," Bath said, stepping forward as I opened the door wider. "Though you're going to have to tell me what's going . . . on . . ."

Her voice died as four men, clad only in Hugh's borrowed tighty-whities, sprinted for the door.

"I saw her first," one bellowed.

"I claim her for myself," yelled another, pushing people aside to get to the door.

"Mine," growled a third at the same time.

Bath's eyes widened and her jaw dropped, just a little.

I stepped in front of Bathsheba, protecting her from the overzealous primordials. "No one is claiming anyone right now," I said, my voice so shrill it was almost unrecognizable. "Go sit down!"

"I have pizza," Cahal said, joining the crew of men surging toward poor Bathsheba.

There was an audible groan of dismay as the others realized they had been trumped. "Now she will go wild and offer him sex," one muttered. "He has pizza to give her."

"What . . ." Bathsheba said, baffled. She shrank back a step or two.

"Don't ask," I said. "And whatever you do, do *not* accept the pizza."

"What's going on?" Beau pushed forward, edging around Bath and her laundry basket and giving my widespread arms a curious look. "Someone's trying to claim my mate?"

"They don't know any better," I said, even as more mutterings began.

"Already claimed," one said behind me. The name sticker on his bare chest said HI, MY NAME IS BEVAN. Bevan sounded incredibly disappointed.

Cahal lowered the slice of pizza in his hand. "Someone has already fed her pizza?"

"Back off," I said. "She's mated, and this is her mate." I pulled Beau forward with an apologetic smile. "I am so, so sorry about all of this."

"It's okay," Bath said, sidling a little closer to Beau. Her eyes were wide. "That stuff you said on the phone—"

"Not a joke," I told her. "I have twenty-three primordial shifters who are staying here for a time. They will be going back to their world, or dimension, or whatever it is, once we force the fae to give back their women. Until then, they're staying with me." I took the basket from Bathsheba with a wry smile. "And we need clothes and food. And help."

"You look incredibly stressed, Ryder," Bath said sympathetically. "Is this where you've been for the last two weeks? Not that I'm not still furious about that, but I'm starting to understand."

"Actually," I said with a heavy sigh, "that is just the tip of the iceberg. I have a lot to tell you. Come in and we'll see if we can find you a seat."

I led Bath and Beau into my tiny, overcrowded apartment.

"Did you see the mark on her neck?" one primordial muttered to another. "He claimed her with a bite."

"Barbaric," agreed the other.

We managed to squeeze our way to my tiny kitchen. From there, we sat down with a pot of coffee—coffee, how I'd missed it!—and talked. Hugh sat at my side, his chair pulled close to mine and his big hand resting on my jeans-clad thigh, as if he was afraid they might somehow snatch me away from him.

I understood that worry. For some reason, I had the same dread in the back of my mind—that Finian would show up and somehow steal Hugh away from me as punishment. I didn't know how the fae prince would react to what we'd done, but considering he gave no thought to destroying my life? It was a pretty safe bet that he wouldn't just shrug his shoulders and walk away.

I wanted to hold Hugh's hand, but I knew I couldn't. Not right now. Not in front of the others.

Savannah, to my surprise, had quickly taken charge of the primordials. They sat in the living room, talking, and I could hear her laughingly, but politely, declining pizza. It was interesting, the way that the primordials treated Savannah in comparison to Bathsheba. Bath, they'd tried to claim.

Savannah, they were in awe of.

Her rounded belly and something in her scent told them that she was carrying a child, and they treated her with the utmost respect—to the point that Beau hadn't felt alarmed at the thought of leaving his cousin in the other room with them as we talked. They fawned over her, insisting that she sit down in the best seat in my living room, and they hung on her every word as she softly chatted with them and passed out the clothing that they'd brought.

Thank goodness they were listening to *someone*. Even now, I heard Savannah's amused voice gently explaining about why she was pregnant and yet had no mate mark.

"So you're a changeling?" Bathsheba asked, interrupting my thoughts. "You're sure?"

I frowned. "Pretty darn sure. Two thieving fae princes can't be wrong."

Hugh's hand tightened on my thigh. "Do you accuse my mate of lying?"

"Hugh, sweetie," I said. "It's okay. Really."

A flush rounded Bath's pale cheeks. "I'm sorry. I wasn't trying to insult. It's just that we don't have anything like a changeling in our database, and I thought we'd run across everything at this point."

"Can you . . . show us?" Beau asked, and I knew he'd phrased it as delicately as he could. He wanted to see for himself, though.

"I can." I sucked in a breath, hating the anxious knot that formed in the pit of my stomach. Why was I so nervous? Beau and Bath were here, listening to me. They weren't running away screaming. They weren't even mad. They just wanted to understand. So why did it freak me out so much?

"I am here, Ryder," Hugh said in a soft voice. "Do not be frightened. I will not let anything happen to you."

I knew that, but hearing the words come out of his mouth made me feel better. I clasped his hand in mine, lacing our fingers tightly, making my decision.

He lifted our intertwined hands to his mouth and gave the back of my hand a kiss, and I felt the prickle of my transformation begin. Fangs popped out of my gums, and I felt my horns push through my forehead. Scales climbed up my arms, and I felt the press of my wings and tail as they struggled to get out of my restrictive clothing. I didn't turn to look at Bath and Beau; my fingers woven with Hugh's, I just waited for the transformation to finish. My nails grew, and the decorative spikes that lined the length of my arms made my sleeves tighten.

And then it was all done. I carefully pulled my hand from Hugh's and rolled up my sleeve so they could see more of my scaled skin. "Here we go," I said thickly, studying my scales. They were the same pale, pearly green as before, my nails the same mother-of-pearl shade.

"Wow," breathed Bathsheba, her eyes wide.

"Yeah," I said quietly, feeling sick with anxiousness. "I have wings and a tail, too, but you'll forgive me if I don't feel like undressing to show you everything."

"It's all right," Beau said easily.

"I don't know why you're so negative," Bath said after a long moment of studying me. "You're beautiful. I can see why the fae value changelings so highly."

I looked up in surprise, feeling the tight, constricting bands of anxiety ease from my chest. "Thanks," I mumbled around my fangs. I glanced down at my scales and guessed they were attractive. I was just used to seeing the hideous creature I'd been before I'd started changing. "I'm supposed to be prettier than this, actually, but, well . . ." I felt an embarrassed flush creep up my cheeks.

"She and I have mated," Hugh said bluntly. "This halts her transformation. Finian will be most upset."

"You should have said something earlier," Bath told me. "We would have understood. We could have helped."

I shook my head. "The fae have magic. If they

can create a world for Hugh's people to live in simply because they feel like it, who knows what they can do to shifters? Just because we can start a war doesn't mean we should."

"But—" Bath protested.

"She's right," Beau said, laying a hand on his wife's arm to ease the sting of his disagreement. "We don't know what kind of hornet's nest this will stir up as is. Better to keep the Alliance out of it."

Bath huffed and tossed her long, pale ponytail. "What happened to Mr. We're All In This Together?"

A wry smile tugged at the corner of Beau's mouth. "He just realized the fae have magic, and that changes the playing field."

"It's fine, really," I said before they could continue arguing. "I don't want anyone solving my battles and getting into danger for me. Hugh's done enough, and we've now placed the lives of all of his men—and the women they want to save—in jeopardy. That's enough for now."

"Well," Bath said briskly. "You can't keep all of these men here. There's not enough room, and I doubt you can keep enough food in the house. Plus, your neighbors are bound to complain about the noise. They'll simply have to come with us."

"Really?" I tried not to sound too excited about that, but I'd hoped for Bath to intervene and rescue us from the plague of shifters that had descended upon my condo. I looked at Beau, but he was only giving his wife a fond smile of approval. He didn't mind that she'd just volunteered them for babysitting duty.

"Really. We'll call Beau's brothers and cousins and get them to swing by with their vehicles, since no one has a school bus. The Russell house has plenty of room. And they seem to like Savannah, so she can help settle them in. Between the boys, myself, and enlisting Sara and Ramsey, I'm sure we can hold down the fort until things are decided."

"Shouldn't you ask them all first, love?" Beau said to Bath, amused. "You know Ellis is still busy trying to acclimate Lily, so he's out of the question."

She waved off his concerns. "Ellis and Lily can stay hidden. I know she's sensitive around strangers. As for the others? They'll pitch in to help. I think they'll be more intrigued than anything. Most probably will be. And then if the primordials decide to stay, we can see about setting up permanent conditions to house them. They shouldn't be forced to return to the fae. That's no kind of life at all."

"I agree," Hugh said. His hand caressed my scaled one, and he gave me a look that melted my heart. "I want my brothers to have a chance to know the happiness that I know with Ryder."

"Oh, Lord, you two are too cute." Bathsheba brightened. "Can we say that you met through the dating agency? I can always use another success story."

"I don't see why not," I told her. "That *was* where I first met Hugh."

"The best day of my life was the day I agreed to ruin yours," Hugh said.

I laughed, but I couldn't shake off the vague feeling of unease. Finian was not going to take this turn of events well.

Hours later, my living room had been vacated of primordials. Every room in my tiny condo was a mess—I found pizza crusts in the bathroom, my fridge had been ransacked, and every towel I owned was dirty. They'd eaten all of my toothpaste and drunk my mouthwash and taken bites out of the lipsticks I'd tried to protect. I hoped they wouldn't have to make a trip to the Alliance doc for some upset stomachs. I texted a note to Savannah, suggesting a conversation about which household goods were edible and which were not.

It was deathly quiet without the noise and press of so many other bodies. I felt a little uneasy as I picked up discarded wrappers in the kitchen, garbage bag in hand. They'd eaten everything in my pantry, even the flour. Not that picking up noodles and empty cartons from my floor mattered right now. I just needed a distraction.

My mind kept spinning to tomorrow. My birthday.

Finian would be coming to retrieve me.

All of this would be at an end, for better or for worse.

The primordials would retrieve their women and

return home. Or they'd stay after all. Either way, everything would be solved in one way or another.

But what about Hugh? What if Finian somehow took Hugh from me? I shivered, not liking that line of thought. Hugh was his own person. He couldn't be forced to return to the primordial realm if he didn't want to go . . .

. . . Could he?

I wished I'd had more answers. I wished I'd been more confident. Instead, I was full of worries and concerns.

"Ryder?" I heard Hugh moving through the condo, heading for the kitchen. "What are you doing?"

"I'm just cleaning up," I said, but I straightened and tossed the half-full bag aside. Garbage could wait. "Did you see them off?"

Hugh entered my small kitchen a moment later and I immediately felt better, just soaking in the chance to look at him. Big, solid, tanned body. Strong arms and thick neck. His short, reddish-brown hair with the odd striping through it. The square jaw with the tufted sideburns. Warm eyes that lit up at the sight of me.

I'd never get tired of looking at him. Never.

Even now, I wanted to put my hands all over him. I washed them quickly, then toweled off as he moved toward me.

"They are gone," Hugh said. "Bevan and Cahal were the last ones to leave, and they were very interested in someone named Gracie."

I groaned. Redneck Gracie was one of the local Anderson wolf pack females. She had a loud mouth, skimpy wardrobe, and liked to go barefoot. She also had very questionable morals, so I suspected she'd like the primordials indeed. "Why am I not surprised."

He chuckled and pulled me into his arms. "You do not sound pleased."

"She's a little rowdy. But the last thing I care about right now is her." I slid my hands under his shirt so I could feel the warmth of his skin. For once, I didn't care that a touch would bring on a transformation. It didn't matter with Hugh. I could be the beast 24/7 and he'd still find me as sexy as he ever did.

Hugh's hands went to my waist, and he pulled my body against him. "And what is it you *do* care about, my Ryder?"

"You and me, in my bed together."

His hand went to my jaw and lightly stroked it, making my scales emerge even more. "I did not like the thought of leaving you unguarded, even for a brief moment."

"The guarding thing is kind of moot at this point, isn't it?" I asked him, leaning in to the caress. "I'm not going to turn more changeling-ish than I am now, so they won't want me anymore, right?"

"I still wish to keep you safe above all things, Ryder," Hugh said, and he leaned in to kiss my mouth with a soft, gentle kiss so unlike our normal devouring ones. "You will humor me if it takes some time for me to break of this habit."

I wasn't sure I *wanted* him to break from that habit. I kind of liked Hugh hovering around me constantly. "You're the boss."

"Am I? Your friend Bathsheba said that you had me wrapped about little fingers. I cannot say I disagree with this assessment."

I grinned at his mangling of the saying. "So you want my little fingers on you? Is that what I'm hearing?"

He groaned. "Your fingers are not that little, but I will take them wherever you wish to place them." He ran his tongue along one of my small, spiraling forehead horns. "But first, I must lock down your door."

I reluctantly released Hugh as he went to the front door, pulling off the chain of runes he wore around his neck. As he ran one glowing rune along the edges of the door frame, I touched the horn that he'd licked. The horn didn't have much feeling, but just the idea of Hugh licking me there sent skitters of heat all through me. Like there was no part of my body that was ugly to him.

I loved that. Almost as much as I loved Hugh.

My gaze went back to him, and I couldn't help but stare at his tight ass as he raised the rune over his head, slowly running it along the door frame, busy at work. When his arm was lifted, his ass seemed clenched, and it made me want to dig my claws into it.

I couldn't resist any longer. I moved to his side and ran my hands down his backside, my nails scratching through the fabric of his clothing. "You almost done?"

He groaned. "You are a terrible distraction."

"I am," I admitted shamelessly. "But I couldn't resist this muscular ass of yours." I circled my hands on his buttocks. "I . . . kind of want to bite it. What do you think?"

Hugh's breathing was ragged, and the hand holding the rune shook a little. "I think you are trying to distract me."

"I think you could be right." It could be my last night with Hugh. I wanted it, and I wanted it now. "Hurry up and finish, or I'm going to start ripping your clothing off your body."

"You are a demanding female," he said, bending over to continue running the rune along the door. "But I suppose that is what I agreed to when I agreed to be your mate, is it not?"

"Less talking, more working," I told him. And I might have nipped at his ass anyhow. No sane woman could resist.

I heard Hugh's sucked-in breath, and then the low growl in his throat. "Lucky for you, I am now finished." A moment later, Hugh had lifted me into his arms and was carrying me to my bedroom. Heat was blazing from his catlike eyes. "And now you shall get exactly what you want."

He was right about that, for sure.

Chapter Nineteen

The last twenty-four hours had gone by in a whirl, and I was twitchy and nervous. Today was my twenty-fifth birthday.

That meant I was locked into my prime. It meant that Finian would come to collect me today. It meant that everything, for better or for worse, was going to happen tonight.

I was crossing my fingers for "better."

The office was empty. To clear it out, Bathsheba and Sara were throwing a party for the clients at Konstantine's. Savannah, my nighttime coworker, was keeping the primordials busy at the Russell house. Only Hugh was in the office with me.

"You're pacing," he observed from his perch on the stool.

"Sorry," I said breathlessly. "I can't stop thinking about—"

The cowbell on the front door clanged and I froze, then turned to the door.

Two men walked in. One looked mild and unassuming, and he was wearing a dorky short-sleeved shirt with a hideous pattern. The other was . . . Batman. Or rather, the actor who'd played him in the last movie.

My stomach dropped at the sight of him. "Finian," I greeted, moving back to my desk. I'd feel better with something between us.

"Happy birthday, darling one," Finian crooned at me as he swanned in, his light, airy footsteps at odds with the rugged, masculine face of the actor he wore. "Today's a very special day, isn't it?"

I picked up my glittery ruler and began to flip it back and forth, trying not to look at him. Or at Hugh. If I looked at Hugh, I'd have my heart in my eyes. Hugh hadn't moved since Finian had entered, but there was a weird, simmering tension in the room that I knew didn't belong entirely to me. I ignored Finian's cheerful mood. "So what brings you here?"

"You know what, dearest. And I brought you a birthday treat." Batman put his hand on the back of the frumpy man at his side. "Guess who this is?"

"I couldn't possibly guess," I told him and risked a glance over at Hugh. He'd gone completely rigid on his stool, big arms crossed over his chest. His face was impossible to read. He was deliberately not looking at me, and that made me feel weird. Like he was trying to forget I existed. I suddenly needed reassurance. "Hugh," I said in my cheeriest voice, "can you guess?"

"Another changeling," Hugh said.

That brought me up short, and I dropped my

ruler. "Another changeling? Really?" This boring-looking guy?

But Finian looked excited. He gave the man another nudge forward. "That's right! You'll be a breeding pair, so I thought I'd bring my charming Walter with me and let you two meet. Say hello, Walter."

Walter waved a limp hand at me. "Hello." His voice was accented strangely, and I wondered if Walter was from this time or just another one of Finian's time-misplaced toys, like Hugh was.

I gave him a halfhearted wave. "Um, Finian, I think we need to talk."

"Not before you get a good look at each other." He gestured me forward. "Come on and touch Walter so you can see what a mature changeling is like. It's quite something to see."

I didn't want to touch Walter. I didn't want to touch any man other than Hugh. But a tiny part of me was incredibly curious about what a fully formed changeling would look like. Were they truly as beautiful as everyone went on and on about? Uncertain, I hesitated.

Then I glanced back at Hugh.

He nodded at me, as if understanding my voiceless question. He was telling me it was okay.

Fingers snapped in front of my face.

"Hello," Finian said, trying to get my attention. When I turned to him, his expression was sour. "Your master's right here, girl. Don't look to Hugh for permission. He's just the hired help."

Well, he was about to be in for a rude surprise, wasn't he? I gave Finian a coy smile. "All right. Have it your way." I stepped forward and approached Walter, keeping my expression wary.

Truth was, I was curious about Walter's form. But now? Finian's pissy move of snapping his fingers in my face proved to me that he was a little unsettled. He kept giving Hugh irritated looks, and I realized that even when we were silent, the bond between us was strong. And suddenly, I was no longer scared of Finian. He thought he could control us as long as he could manipulate us and keep us rattled.

Now he had nothing on us. He didn't know it yet, but the power had shifted.

So when Walter approached me, I gave him a friendly smile and extended my hand for him to shake.

Walter leaned in to kiss me.

I ducked him, sideswiping his slobbery mouth. I heard Hugh give a barely audible growl in response. I straightened, then shook a finger at Walter. "I didn't say you could kiss me."

"He's going to do more than that. Quit dancing around the subject," Finian said, his voice extra-irritated.

I refused to be bullied by him. I shook my head and extended my hand to Walter again. "This or nothing."

Walter glanced at Finian, who rolled his eyes. Then Walter grasped my hand.

The first thing I noticed was that Walter's hand

was clammy and moist. Ick. I forced myself to keep holding on to it, waiting for the transition to happen. Mine felt sluggish, struggling to the forefront, as if it didn't want to. I didn't blame it—Walter wasn't exactly hitting my hot buttons. Not with my delicious Hugh seated so nearby.

Walter, however, bloomed immediately.

He was beautiful. More beautiful than anything else I'd ever seen, for that matter. I watched, fascinated, as the scales emerged from his pasty white skin. His scales were a pearly, opalescent shade, something between sunrise and sunset, and seemed to gleam with an inner light. It was the most gorgeous color I could imagine. The horns that spiked out of his forehead were long and twisted and ivory, like dual unicorn horns, and glints of gold traced up the curls, making them seem more like works of art than mere horns. Walter's dippy shirt split apart, and a pair of powerful, gorgeous wings unfurled behind him. They were like butterfly wings, all color and beauty. I gasped at the sight of them.

Walter smiled at me, and he was truly gorgeous in that moment, no hint of the bland human left behind. This was what I could have been if I hadn't halted my transformation, I realized. My own transformation was no longer hideous, but it was not even close to this glorious creature.

"Wow," I breathed, impressed. I looked over at Hugh and Finian, as if needing to somehow share how wonderstruck I was at the sight of Walter's transformation.

Hugh didn't look happy, though. If anything, he looked . . . jealous? He kept glancing at my hand clasped in Walter's and twitching in his seat.

Finian didn't look happy, either. He was rubbing his chin, a frown on his face as he regarded me. "You're not transforming," he pointed out after a moment.

I glanced down at my hand locked with Walter's beautiful, claw-tipped one. Sure enough, my hand was still human. I could feel my changeling side doing its best to try and wake up, but it felt sluggish, as if it couldn't be bothered. "Huh," I said. "That's odd."

"Yes," Finian said, and his voice was flat. "Quite odd." He snapped his fingers again, gesturing at Hugh. "Touch her."

Hugh stood, uncurling to his full height. His gaze was on me. "Only if she wishes it."

As if I wouldn't want Hugh to touch me? I smiled at Hugh, and then I was embarrassed when my change began to trigger. Between Walter's hand in mine and simply looking at Hugh, I'd become aroused.

Embarrassing. But at the same time, I was elated. Walter's touch wasn't doing it for me. It was just Hugh, I realized. Only Hugh. No one else mattered.

I kept my gaze on the primordial as I felt my own transformation slowly move through my body. Wings pushed out of my back and pressed against my dress, and I felt my tail slither out, even as my claws extended and my mouth filled with fangs.

Once my transformation was complete, I glanced over at Finian, waiting for his reaction.

He was frowning. Hard.

Walter pulled his hand from mine, making a noise of displeasure at the sight of me. I glanced down as his hand left mine. The pearly green of my scales didn't match the luminescence of Walter's, and I couldn't blame him for drawing back from me.

As changeling babes went, I guessed I was pretty disappointing-looking. And that delighted me.

"What is this?" Finian strode forward, glaring at me. He scowled at Hugh, then back at me. "She is still weeks away from her final beautiful form. Look at this color." He made a face at my scales. "Her wings haven't even unfurled. Did you drag her back into your primordial realm? Are we delayed by several more weeks?" The fae's hands went to his hips in annoyance, and his fingers drummed there. "I'm removing you from this assignment, Hugh. It's clear you're incompetent."

"You can't fire him," I told Finian. "He already quit."

"He quit? When?"

I moved to Hugh's side and was pleased when his big arm went over my shoulders. I curled up against him, locking my hand at his waist. "The night he took my virginity."

"What?" Finian's voice was almost a shriek. "He what?"

"We slept together," I said proudly. "I'm his mate, and he's mine."

The fae's wide, angry eyes met mine, then flicked to Hugh. "That was not part of the deal! We had a vow! You swore to me that you were not interested in her—"

"I changed my mind." Hugh's calm words made me smile. His arm tightened around me.

"You've ruined her," Finian said. "Ruined! She was priceless, and now she is worthless! Look at how ugly she is!"

Hugh's big hand curled around my jaw, tipping my face up to his. I saw nothing but love in his eyes. "She is the most beautiful creature in this world."

I smiled up at him.

Finian's snarl of rage broke through our happiness. "You know what this means, then?"

"I do," Hugh said, and his arms tightened around me. His voice was sad. "No primordial mate for me, nor primordial mates for my men."

"That is right," Finian said as he stabbed a finger at Hugh. I supposed he was trying his best to look furious and full of wrath, but he mostly looked comical. All he was doing was shouting. That wasn't frightening at all. It was like . . . he couldn't do anything to us.

And I couldn't stop smiling.

"No mates for anyone," Finian said, hands clenched into fists. "Are you truly so selfish, so foul a creature?"

"You asked me to ruin one life in exchange for twenty-four," Hugh said. "At the time, it seemed like a smart bargain. However, as I said, I changed my mind."

"And he's not the only one," I added, then patted Hugh's flat stomach. "Tell him about the other primordials, sweetie."

Hugh's expression turned to one of menacing pleasure. "My brothers are no longer in the primordial lands."

It was clear Finian didn't understand. His gaze rapidly flicked back and forth between my face and Hugh's. The fingers on his hip drummed at a wild, furious pace. After a moment, he snapped, "What do you mean?"

"They left. They are here in this world," Hugh said simply. He reached for the chain around his neck, snapped it in an easy gesture, and offered it to Finian. "The primordial lands are a haven for our kind, but no one is happy there because they are lonely. There are no mates for them. They have left and arrived here, in the human realm."

The look of dawning horror on Finian's face was priceless. I almost felt sorry for the guy.

"But," Hugh said, "they will return to the primordial realm in exchange for their mates."

The fae's lip curled. "So you think to force my hand? Is that it?"

"More or less," I chimed in. *How's it feel?*

Hugh was the voice of reason. "My brothers would be more than happy to return to the primordial realm and await any tasks that the fae might request. However, they will only do so with their mates at their side. They will not go otherwise."

Finian was silent.

I found the fae's silence a bit unsettling. Didn't they want to keep the primordials happy? From what Hugh had told me, the primordials did all kinds of dirty errands for the fae, and did them willingly. Why wouldn't the fae want them back?

But Finian was saying nothing. He was simply glaring at Hugh, his fists clenched.

"Think of it as a consolidation of forces," I blurted out, trying to help the situation along. "You get the men and the women together, and everyone's happy. Don't the women want to be with men of their own kind? Aren't they lonely?"

Finian's glare turned to me. "I am sure they are."

"So let us talk to them," I said. "Pick a representative and bring her here, and we'll discuss it with her. I'm sure the women want families, too."

Still Finian said nothing.

"You cannot keep us trapped without mates forever," Hugh said, his voice hoarse with anger. I felt the hand on my waist tighten, as if he was barely controlling himself. "It is unfair to both my men and to the women you deprive of companionship."

"Let us just talk to one of the women," I cajoled. "How hard can that be? What's the leader's name?"

Finian glared at me, angry panic in his eyes, and hesitated.

And an awful realization hit me. "There *are* no women, are there? You've been lying to them."

Two bright red streaks of color flared on Finian's famous borrowed face. "Of course there are," he said quickly.

I stepped out of Hugh's embrace and approached Finian, crossing my arms over my chest. "Oh, really? What are their names, and what are their shifter animals?"

"Please," Finian blustered. "As if I would remember their names? I'm much too important."

"Yes, but you've worked with them for centuries, right? I'm sure you know a few names. Just give me one."

"I don't have to tell you anything, you changeling mongrel," he said furiously. "Nor am I required to rattle off the names of useless shifters just to appease you."

"Where do they stay?" Hugh asked abruptly, surprising me.

"Excuse me?"

"The female primordials. Where do they stay?"

"Why, in their own realm, of course."

I turned to look at Hugh. His body seemed relaxed, but I could sense the tension in his face. His eyes were narrow slits of anger and loathing. "You told me once," Hugh said, his voice deadly soft, "that maintaining a separate, private realm for the primordials cost the fae a great deal of time and energy. That we should be grateful that you cared so much for our well-being that you would do this for us. That we owed you."

"Yes, that's right."

"And now you tell me that you hold not just our realm but a realm for females entirely separate from our own." Hugh's eyes looked as cold as ice. "And you will not combine them?"

Finian said nothing.

"My mate is right," Hugh growled, and the sound was so deadly that I shivered. "You have been lying to me. All this time. There are no females in a separate realm, are there? There are only the fools kept locked in our own private realm, called out when the fae need a favor. Yet we cannot remember these things with clarity. How many times have you called upon us?"

Still Finian remained silent. Behind him, Walter twitched, his wings folding back. His gaze was entirely on Finian with something akin to devotion.

"I suspect you do something to make us forget our memories. That is why we believed you when you told us you would bring us females." Furious, Hugh strode forward until he was looming over Finian. "Do you deny it?"

Finian straightened, smoothing a hand down his jacket. It looked as if the man was fighting not to take a step backward. "I have nothing to explain to you."

Hugh grabbed Finian by the front of his jacket. His long canines were bared in a feral snarl. "You have lied to us and manipulated us all this time. I should kill you."

I gave a squeak of alarm and surged forward to pull Hugh off Finian. "Hugh! No!"

Walter made a distressed sound, moving behind Finian and trying to pull him backward, as if he could somehow safely drag him away from Hugh's anger.

As I watched, Hugh's fangs distended, and his eyes became more catlike. He was losing control of his humanity with his rage. He leaned in closer to Finian, threat evident on his face.

"Don't kill him," I said, placing a calming hand on Hugh's arm. I didn't know what might happen if he harmed a fae prince. "Finian's going to bargain with us," I said, thinking fast. "It's in his best interests."

"Oh?" Finian still managed to sneer despite the long fangs inches from his face. Sweat had broken out on his forehead.

"Yes," I said. "You're going to release all claims on me and the primordials. And in return, we're going to keep our mouths shut about how you managed to lose everyone in one fell swoop. I'm sure the other fae will be wondering just what happened to all their little playthings. And I'm sure they're going to be curious—and unhappy—if they find out that you lost everyone." I gave him my most winning smile. "So in return for our silence, you'll leave us alone for the rest of our lives. And Hugh lets you keep your face." I fluttered my eyelashes at him. "Because he really, really wants to remove it right about now."

Hugh let out a growl so menacing that even I shivered.

I watched Finian's Adam's apple bob nervously. After a long moment, he said, "You'll stay silent about who was responsible for the primordials' release?"

I made a locking gesture over my mouth and pantomimed tossing away the key.

Finian's gaze flicked from Hugh, to me, then back to Hugh. He swallowed again. "I suppose that all this is only costing me an ugly changeling."

I gave him a fake smile. "I don't know if you noticed how big Hugh's claws are? I don't think he'll take it well if you keep insulting me."

Hugh clicked his teeth menacingly at Finian.

The fae nodded quickly, his eyes wide. "I accept your deal."

"I thought you might."

Finian's rune necklace was returned to him. In return, a new vow was placed on Hugh, tattooed across his wide shoulders so it could not be broken at any cost. The primordials were free. In exchange, they would be silent to all fae parties about the terms of their release.

My "mark of ownership" was removed from my thigh with a touch of Finian's hand.

After everything was established, Finian couldn't leave fast enough. He grabbed Walter and hastily exited, the car peeling out of the parking lot moments later.

I sighed with relief. An enormous weight had been lifted from my shoulders.

Next to me, Hugh collapsed on his stool.

I looked over at him in alarm. "You okay, Hugh?" My hands moved to his hair, and I stroked it off his forehead, worried. "Not regretting things, are you?"

He pulled me against him and pressed his face to my chest. He said nothing for long, long moments. I began to get worried. After what seemed like an eternity, he said thickly, "To think I almost gave you to him in exchange for mates that did not exist."

I gently ran my fingers through his hair. "You didn't know. Finian and the others clearly did something to make you forget whatever tasks you did for them. Who knows how many times they've offered you mates, only to wipe your memories afterward?"

"I should have killed him," Hugh growled. His hands tightened around me. "He didn't deserve to live."

"That's not our choice to make," I told him and kissed the top of his head. "But the bad news is that you're stuck here with me. He took his rune back, and the primordials are trapped here, too."

"Mmm. So we are." He nuzzled at my breasts, distracting me and making my changeling side flare to life all over again. "I can say that I am not displeased with the situation. Not in the slightest."

"Will the others be disappointed?" I pulled Hugh's head away from my breasts and forced his attention up to my face.

"Only if they are fools," he said and pulled me down for a long kiss.

Chapter Twenty

"And so it was all a lie," I told the stone-faced primordials filling the Russells' huge kitchen. Savannah, Bath, and Beau stood in the back of the room, making piles of sandwiches. I sat at the head of the table on Hugh's lap, straddling one of his enormous thighs.

The room was silent as they digested my words.

"So there were no females?" Artur asked, his ugly face pulled down in a frown. "It was all a ploy?"

Hugh nodded, expression grave. "He lied to get me to do what he wanted. There was never any intention of following through. It was all for nothing."

"You made the right choice after all," I told Hugh, patting him on the arm wrapped around my waist. I was transformed back to my changeling form, but I didn't care. The primordials had seen me like this before. And if one or two of the Russells were staring really, really hard at me, well, they were bound to figure out my secret somehow.

"So we are to remain here," Hugh said. "My place is at Ryder's side."

Just hearing him say that aloud gave me the warm fuzzies. "But you guys don't have to stay here," I added quickly before anyone could speak up. "I am sure that if you wished to go back to the primordial realm, you could. You just know what you are getting into now."

Silence fell. There was no sound except the scrape of sandwich cutting in the background. What were they thinking?

"The women here," Cahal began. "We can mate them?"

"Provided the women say yes," I told him. "And, if they are human, provided you get the permission of your clan leader." I was told that Beau and the other alphas were still working through the kinks of allowing human women to date shifters, considering the fact that the whole shifter thing was supposed to be a secret.

"But women are not a rarity here," Cahal said, face serious. "We can take mates and not worry that our brothers will be without?"

I nodded. "There are just as many females here on earth as there are males. There are fewer shifter females, but you can always go human, I suppose."

"Are all the females like Gracie?" one wanted to know.

"No, not many," Bath said tartly. "And that's something you should be thankful for."

Bevan banged a flat hand on the table. "We wish to stay here and find women."

"Are you *all* sure?" I asked.

"This world is full of opportunity," Cahal said, rubbing his hands together.

"And pizza," chimed in another.

Many of the primordials chortled, as if sharing an inside joke.

I groaned.